PICTURE HOUSE GIRLS
LARGE PRINT VERSION

PATRICIA A MCBRIDE

Copyright © 2020 by Patricia A McBride

All rights reserved.

No part of this book may be reproduced in any form or by any electronic or mechanical means, including information storage and retrieval systems, without written permission from the author, except for the use of brief quotations in a book review.

This book uses British English spelling.

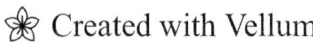 Created with Vellum

1. REVENGE

TO EXACT PUNISHMENT FOR A WRONG

SPRING 1939

You get used to men flirting with you at the pictures. I reckon it's the uniform that does it. It's a smart, bright red suit with gold buttons and gold braid epaulettes. But it's the saucy pillbox hat we wear at an angle that me and Jean love. We feel as glamorous as Imperial Airways air hostesses. Now that's a job I'd really like to do. Imagine all the places you could see - places that are just names in an atlas to me. And handsome fly-boys to work with, too.

Sometimes the blokes do more than flirt. They wait 'til the interval is over and we're walking back in the semi-darkness, our hands full, balancing our trays of ciggies and sweets. Then, if we stray from the exact middle of the aisle, they can reach us from their seats - and they get daring. A pat on the bum here; a stroke on the calf there; a low wolf whistle occasionally. I hate it. What do they think we are – dolls to be pawed at whenever they feel frisky?

But this day was different.

I've got to admit I must have wandered to one side. I didn't mean to; I'm not stupid. I was three-quarters of the way back when the main feature started: *Goodbye, Mr Chips*. I turned round to get a glimpse of that lovely Robert Donat. That's when it happened. I felt something brush my ankle and I jumped, scattering half the *Craven As* and chocolate bars off my tray and onto the floor. When I bent to pick them up my tray caught on a lady's hat, knocking it sideways. She was a good egg about it, thank goodness. Anyway, that's when it happened. I bent over to pick up the ciggies and Aeros, and quick as a flash, someone put his hand up my skirt and pinched my thigh hard, just above my stocking. I yelped and spun round. There were two blokes on rows either side of the lady, but both had their eyes glued to the screen, innocent as cathedral choir boys. But I worked out only one of them could have reached me. The blood pounding in my ears, I decided to take revenge. I pretended to stumble, and when I straightened myself I caught the corner of my tray against his forehead with a thud. He gave a grunted *Ouch!* and put his hand to his head. Before he could do anything more, I walked smartly away.

Rubbing my leg, I walked back through the foyer - past the posters advertising films coming up; past the red velvet throne-like chair in the corner; the tiny box office; and the plush red carpet and walls. I headed for the office. The contrast to the foyer couldn't have been sharper. The walls were pale yellow, bits of left-over carpet from the foyer covered the wooden plank floor and the cheap furniture was older than my granddad. I felt a bit shaky, so I dumped my tray any old how and sat down to gather myself together. I knew I'd have to put everything away neat, but it could wait a little while.

A minute later, Jean came in. She looked at my tray, then at me, and sat down without taking her own tray off. It wobbled dangerously on her lap.

'What's 'appened, Sweetheart?' she asked.

Well, it wasn't much of a story and the telling took longer than the pinch.

''e did *what?*' she asked, her eyes popping like they always do when she's outraged. And that's pretty often; she likes a good outrage, does Jean.

I checked no-one was about to come in, and then showed her my leg. You could still see where he'd pinched me, though the finger marks were fading fast.

'Pig!' she said. 'That'll bruise something terrible,

that will. Would ya recognise 'im again, Lil? We can trip 'im up accidentally-on-purpose when 'e leaves.'

'No need, I caught the side of his forehead with my tray good-and-proper. He'll have a bigger bruise than me!'

We made a cup of tea in the kitchen corner of the office. It was a bit of a joke to call it a kitchen. It was just a rickety old table that teetered every time we put anything on it. We had to use the washbasin in the Ladies for water and washing up, then walk back through the foyer with a tray with kettle and stuff when no-one was looking. Still, we were glad of the sit down, a hot drink and chance to catch up.

'So why's the boss gone 'ome early?' Jean asked.

'His wife's not well. He's asked me to lock up tonight,' I said.

She gave a little whistle, 'Well, 'e must trust you. Never asked me. You're going to learn 'ow to sell tickets too, aren't you? Turning into a right teacher's pet.'

'You know that's not true. He asked everyone if they wanted to learn.'

'Yeah, but you're the only one who said yes. You'll be after 'is job next,' she said with a grin.

When we'd finished we got ready for the end of the film. Jean said, ''Ere Lil, notice how many 'unks there are in uniform?'

I smiled. You can count on Jean to notice the blokes. 'Yes - but don't you ever watch Pathe news?'

She waved my words away. 'Nah, I'm always too busy 'aving a cuppa to watch the news. Too depressing.'

'Well - them young men - conscription started last month for them. Six months training they have to do.'

Jean pulled a face. 'Poor sods. You don't really think there'll be another war, do you?'

'The government seem sure there won't.'

'They why are they calling men up?' She looked at the clock, 'Oy, we'd better get cracking. Film finishes in five minutes.'

As soon as we heard the last notes of *God Save the King* we opened the doors for people to leave. It always seemed to take ages; people dawdled getting their stuff together, they chatted on their way out and never gave a thought to us usherettes who want to get off home to bed.

When they'd finally gone, Jean and I did a quick check of the auditorium to make sure nothing was left behind. Sometimes we'd find a tramp hiding out, hoping for a warm place to sleep for the night. Politicians said the Depression was over, but it wasn't over for everyone. I hated forcing the poor things to leave - especially in rough weather.

But on that night all the seats were empty. I was

staying behind to lock up as Jean was off to meet her latest beau and wanted to leave pretty smartish. I hadn't known her long, we lived in different places before we moved to Sunbury. She seemed to have a new man every week, and she was getting a bit of a reputation - I hoped she knew what she was doing.

I was straightening the leaflets for the next week's show when Frank the projectionist, the only other person in the building, waved goodbye and blew me a cheeky kiss. Everything looked okay so I fetched my coat and bag from the office and turned off the main foyer lights; there was just enough light from the street to see my way. It looks so glamorous when it's all lit up, but now, in the semi-darkness it looked almost spooky. The posters were the worst, it seemed as if the film stars were watching my every move.

I headed for the front doors, keys in hand, noticing I had five minutes until my bus went. I could just make it. My dad always gave me hell if I was late, as if I was a child rather than a twenty-year-old woman with two jobs. My other job, the day job, working at Johnson's factory sewing sleeves into shirts was so boring, but at least I didn't have to wait late at night for a bus, like I did after the pictures.

I locked the door and was just putting the keys in my handbag when, without any warning, it was snatched out of my hand. I was so surprised it took me a minute to take in what had happened. I looked around and there was the man running down the road at a fair crack. I took a deep breath and shouted, 'STOP! THIEF!'

I hadn't noticed another man across the street until he started to run after the thief - and boy could he run. He must have been very fit. They didn't get very far before the man rugby tackled the thief and grabbed the bag off him. He went to drag him up, but the thief slid under his arm and ran away like all the demons from hell were after him.

The man dusted himself off and walked back towards me. He was dressed head to toe in black leather - his helmet now knocked a bit crooked. His riding goggles gave him the look of a gigantic insect - like something out of one of the cheap B rate horror films we show sometimes.

He looked down at me and took off his helmet; I could see he was human after all. He handed me the bag and said, 'Your bag, Madam,' with a lovely smile.

I was so relieved I could have cried. 'Oh, thank you so much. That's the night's takings from the Dream Palace in there.'

'I can see you're wobbly,' he said, 'let's sit on this step until you feel calm. Is that okay? I promise you I'm safe to be with.'

I gave a shaky laugh, 'Well, you would say that, I suppose.'

His educated accent told me he was a cut above me. But his voice sounded warm and he was my rescuer, so I sat down next to him. I could feel my shakes beginning to calm.

'I've never been so glad to see anyone in my life,' I said, my voice trembling. I was mortified to find big tears dropping down my cheeks.

He handed me a big white hanky and put his arm around my shoulders, 'Go on - it's okay to cry. You've had a dreadful experience. I'm here now. You're safe.'

I howled for what seemed like ages. Me - sobbing! I've always thought of myself as a steady person, but here I was blubbing like a baby. My mind replayed the incident like a film that was stuck, showing the same scene over and over again.

My knight in shining leather sat, not saying a word, just being with me until my wails reduced to snivels. Then he shook hands and spoke again.

'We haven't been introduced. My name's Edward,' he said, 'Edward Halpern.'

I used his hanky to wipe my eyes and blow my nose. 'I am really grateful to you, Mr Halpern. My name's Lily Baker.'

'Hello, Lily,' he said, with mock formality, 'pleasure to meet you. Please, call me Edward. Do you come here often?'

I laughed at the corny old line I'd heard so many times before and for the first time took a good look at my saviour. *He's hunky, a real he-man*, I thought. His thick blond hair was all over the place from taking off his helmet, but as he pushed it back out of his eyes I noticed they were a clear blue with some flecks of hazel. Mostly though, I noticed they were warm, and kind. Eyes you could trust.

We sat there, with me talking nineteen to the dozen. Maybe it was nerves or maybe 'cos most men don't listen. The ones I meet are usually too busy talking about themselves or trying to get fresh.

After a while I came to my senses and managed to stop gabbling, although I felt a bit stupid. But at least he hadn't laughed at me, and the daft things I must've said.

Finally, far later than it should have been, I remembered my manners and asked him about himself.

'Not much to tell, really,' he said, 'my life's been pretty predictable. I grew up around here - went to university after school.'

Oh, how I wished I'd had a chance to do that. No-one in my school went to university; we barely knew they existed. If we'd even thought about it, people would say we were getting ideas above our station.

'It sounds really exciting,' I said.

He smiled, 'It was a lot of hard work.'

'But you must have had fun, too.'

'Yes, got drunk more times than I want to remember. Went to a thousand boring lectures, as well as some great ones. Joined the University Drama group and had parts in a couple of plays. Went out with a few girls, but nothing serious …'

I had to swallow down a small smile when he said that.

As he spoke something struck me more than any anything else, he didn't talk about anyone in a way that put them down, or make himself up to be the big I-am. He had this sort of quiet confidence in himself.

I looked at my watch, horrified to find twenty minutes had whizzed by faster than my dad downs a pint.

'Oh, heavens. I've missed my bus and the next one isn't for half an hour. I'll be late. My dad will give me real what-for.' I could feel tears welling up again.

'Just explain what happened. I'm sure he'll understand,' Edward said.

I gave a bitter laugh. 'No, he won't. He'll tell me I've got to give up this job. His word is law in our house and he never, ever listens to reason. Anything he doesn't agree with, he says we're stupid or we're not respecting him.'

'That's hard on you.' Edward said, frowning, 'But look, I can give you a lift home on my motorbike.'

My heart lifted. 'On the level? You're not kidding me?'

I could just imagine my dad's face if we turned up on that. Me, with a man, and a motorbike. Three things to make him explode, not that he needed much of an excuse.

By now I'd stopped shaking, thank goodness, and I'd never been on a motorbike. I could feel a tingle of excitement at the thought of it.

I smiled as if nothing awful had happened. After all, even if I never saw this Edward again, something good had come of it.

I looked at my watch. 'That sounds wonderful and if we leave soon I won't be late. The bus goes all round the houses and takes ages. But you'll have to drop me at the end of the street or if my dad sees me he'll flay me alive.'

Edward helped me on to the bike, showed me where to put my feet and how to hold on to him. I put my scarf on my head tight to try to keep my hair in some sort of shape.

Hugging him round the waist all the way home was something else. I could feel his muscles moving as the bike took the curves and they felt, well, sexy. Everything seemed different whizzing past so fast in the dark. The shops became a multi-coloured blur and the street lights seemed so close together they could have been touching. I wanted to reach out my hands to run them along, the way kids run their hands along railings. It was exciting and disturbing, and I wanted the journey to go on forever. But it was over all too soon. When Edward stopped the Royal Enfield at the end of the road, gossipy Mrs Evans in the corner house twitched her curtains as always. A woman her age should've been in bed. I pretended I couldn't see her, but knew the story'd be up and down the street by the next day.

Edward and I stood and looked at each other. I got crazy tongue-tied and couldn't think what to say.

'It's been lovely meeting you, Lily,' Edward said, 'I'm glad you're okay now. I'd better get off, I'm going to Officers' Training Camp tomorrow so I've got an early start.'

I couldn't help but feel disappointed.

'How long will you be gone?'

'I'm not sure. It's usually three months, but with things as they are who knows if that will change.'

'Oh.'

'Tell you what,' he said with a smile that showed perfect white teeth, 'I'll call by the Dream Palace when I get back and see if you're around. And, I hope to get a few days leave after six weeks.'

I hurried down the road past all the new houses, wiping the silly tears from my eyes, glad all the lights were out at home. When I realised Dad was in bed, I could feel the tension evaporate like steam from a kettle. On my way through the hall, shoes in hand, I pulled a face up towards his bedroom just like a naughty five-year-old. My Dad is such a misery, all he does is moan, moan, moan, I don't know how my Mum stands it. He never has a good word to say about anyone. He's always telling me I'm good for nothing. But I'm proving him wrong, I'm learning to type and I go to evening classes.

I crept into the kitchen - the lino cold on my feet. Wet sheets covered the mangle in the corner, ready to be hung out before Mum went to work next morning. Mum'd been working hard as always, but bless her heart, she'd left me a cheese sandwich, safe from flies between two tea plates. I put it on a tray with a glass of water, went into the living room and sat down on the new three-piece. It was a lovely brown pretend-velvet with wide arms. Mum had made some matching cushions and it looked good enough to be in a magazine.

What a row there'd been about that three-piece suite!

'How'd you get the money for this, then?' Dad shouted, his face an inch from Mum's, eyes bulging like they'd pop out of his head and fall on the floor any minute. 'They don't give women tick. You bin saving behind my back? Ha*ve you? Answer me.*'

She tried to back away, her arms in front of her face to protect herself. He lifted his fist and pulled back his arm, but stopped when he spotted the card from the tally man behind the clock. He reached over and grabbed it, almost knocking the clock off the mantlepiece in his haste. He read it quickly.

'Forged my name, did ya, you bitch. Now we'll 'ave the tally man chasing us for money every week. You'd better 'ave it, you stupid woman, I'm not paying.'

He made to thump her as he'd done so many times before, but without thinking I grabbed his arm and he lost his balance, staggering backwards before he righted himself. He turned round, a look of shock and rage on his face. Neither of us had ever stood up to him before. After a second, he raised his arm to me, then dropped it again. Then he walked out of the house, slamming the door so hard it rattled the whole house. He didn't speak to either of us for a week, but he still took the best seat near the fire every single night.

I finished my cheese sandwich and just as I was washing my plate and glass I heard Mum's slippers pattering down the stairs. I hadn't seen her at all since the day before.

She went off to her cleaning job before I even got up in the morning, so we didn't always see a lot of each other. I decided not to tell her about the attack or

Edward. The attack would worry her and I'd never see Edward again, so there was no point.

'Can't sleep, Mum?'

'No. Got a bit of backache, but nothing a cuppa won't fix.'

As I put the kettle on, I thought how tired she looked. She was far too thin. I could see how her bones barely seemed to be covered by any flesh and she had dark rings round her eyes. Her hair looked a bit thinner than I remembered too. She had had me young so she was far from an old woman, but living with Dad and working long hours year in year out was wearing her out. I resolved to be a better daughter and help out more around the house.

I warmed the pot and put in fresh tea leaves, while she got the cups and saucers ready. I stirred the leaves and got the tea strainer out. We put everything on a tray and went into the living room. Mum stroked the arms of the sofa. 'I love this, it's so much better than that moth-eaten thing we had in the old place. Horrid to have old tat in a new house. Remember how hard it was living there?'

How could I forget? 'Yes, lavvy in the yard, cold enough to freeze your bum and enough spiders to give you the heeby-jeebies no matter how often you took them down.'

She laughed. 'And that tin bath in the kitchen. Filling it up with water from the kettle and geyser.'

'You telling us to hurry up so you could make a cuppa.'

I poured the tea and passed her a cup.

'Sharing bath water.' She pulled a face. 'That was so horrible. No wonder the public baths were so popular.'

'Mould in the bedrooms so bad you could grow mushrooms in it.'

'Small wonder we always had colds. Thank goodness we got this place.'

'Yes, thank goodness. But this three-piece suite, Mum. You all right paying for it? You know how quick the tallyman takes things back, if you miss a week they'll be round here to collect it before you can say Bob's your uncle.'

'I'll be okay as long as I keep well and keep working.'

I wondered how any of us would manage if she didn't. 'Do you want some more rent?' I asked.

She rested her head on her hand and smiled. 'No, love, you keep the extra bit. You know the last thing I want you to do is live the life I've led, and your granny led, and her granny. You save your pennies so you can get yourself an education and get ahead. I'll let you know if I really can't meet the payments and you can lend me a bob or two.'

'As long as you promise.'

The next day was Sunday and I was relieved I

was going to have a day without work for a change. I fell straight into a deep sleep, but it was as if the horrible event at the Dream Palace was waiting to haunt me. I woke up struggling with the sheets, imagining I was fighting off my attacker.

All day I felt low as if I couldn't clear my head of fog that had taken root there. I spent a lot of time lying on the bed trying to read, or mooching about downstairs. Luckily Dad was out doing who knew what, or he'd have had me doing something for him just to be awkward. Mum had a one-off job helping one of her ladies, so I cleaned out the kitchen cupboards thinking it'd take my mind off what happened and help her out.

The only thing that cheered me up a bit was remembering my rescuer. What a lovely man that Edward was. I kept thinking about his kindness and how you could fall into his arms and feel safe. But I shook myself, *you've been watching too many romantic films*, I told myself over and over again. And a high-class bloke like him might be kind, but he wouldn't be interested in someone like me.

Somehow the long, dreary day came to an end and I resolved as I went to bed that I would put the attack behind me. If I didn't, that rotter would have won, and I wasn't going to let that happen.

2. THE WALL

Incandescent
Full of heat and light

The rain had just stopped and the wet road reflected the fast moving clouds over my home. Sparrows hopped in a puddle nearby, enjoying an impromptu bath. I smiled at their lack of fear, distracted for a moment from Jean's lateness. Patience has never been my strong point and as I waited for her, I had no idea that within a few minutes I would come face to face with something that would change my life forever. Funny, the turns life takes.

Our road was fairly quiet, just a couple of pensioners doing some gardening and a mum pushing her pram towards the shops. Jean arrived breathless and red in the face, apologising as usual. We worked at the same shirt factory during the day and some evenings at Dream Palace Pictures in town. What with both jobs we were often so tired we had little spare energy, although she always found enough to go out with her lad of the moment.

As we hurried round the corner to catch our bus I waved to old Mr. Robinson. He was busy doing something in his garden. He'd lived near us before we moved to Sunbury and was enjoying having a bigger space to grow things.

'Make the most of it girls!' he shouted.

'What?' I called back.

'Freedom, there's a war coming as sure as eggs is eggs.'

I wasn't really listening so just gave him a smile and a wave as I walked on.

I turned back to join Jean and almost fell over her as I looked over her shoulder.

'That can't really be there...' I thought, *'... it's not possible.'*

We stood as still as if a magician had shouted *Abracadabra,* put a spell on us and conjured up a mirage.

There, right across the road, was a gigantic great wall. It must've been eight foot high like the walls of the factory where we worked. We couldn't even see the sides; they were tucked between houses.

We stood rooted to the spot for what seemed like an eternity then, released from our spell, we joined a small crowd looking up at the wall. A workman was busy hammering barbed wire to the top.

'What the frickin 'ell … ' Jean gasped, hands on hips.

At least she could speak, even if some would say she was being blasphemous. I just stood there like an idiot with my mouth flapping.

Then the penny dropped and my mind went into overdrive. The bus stop was the other side of that … that … monstrosity. It had to be at least a ten minute walk to go the other way and that's if we hurried. We'd be late for work. They'd dock our pay. I needed that money. We might even get the push, with so many people after every job. The boss would be incandescent with rage. (I learn a new word every week and that was the current one). I love 'incandescent', it sounds as if he would have fire flaring from his nostrils. It seemed that way sometimes too, we don't call him The Dragon for nothing.

I grabbed Jean by the arm, 'How're we going to get to work on time?'

We looked at each other, linked arms and marched up to the wall as if we could blow it down with a huff and a puff. It was so high I felt totally dwarfed. Mind you, that's not hard because I'm only 5'2". As we got closer we could see the joints between the bricks were badly done, like whoever did it couldn't be bothered to make it look good. There was cement splattered all over the place as if kids had been let loose with it.

'What the 'eck's this all about?' Jean shouted, craning her neck so she could see the workman.

He ignored her and kept hammering in the pins for the barbed wire. His cloth cap hid his face from view.

'Oy! You!' she shouted so loud the whole town could've heard her, *'I said, what the 'eck's this all about?'*

He leaned over a section where he hadn't put the wire yet.

'Don't blow yer wig, Judy,' he said. ''S'not my fault. Just following orders. It's to stop you lot from the Sunbury estate using these roads. That's what them nobs said. They reckon you lot from them Welsh valleys…'

'I'm not from the valleys,' a man near us shouted.

'Watch your mouth, Boyo,' someone shouted back. 'What's wrong with being from the valleys? The valleys are fantastic, mon.'

The workman leaned further over, his elbows on the wall, his hammer in his hand, '… you lot from the valleys, *and other places*, will give 'em germs an' scabies an' that. They think you lot're all slum clearance, poxy vermin carriers.'

'Bastards!' shouted the man who wasn't from the valleys. 'We're as good as any of them.' He looked ready to punch anyone who disagreed.

'Well, Mate, they don't think so. They don't wanna sully their eyes looking at you corporation 'ouse lot.'

And with that, his head disappeared back behind the wall.

I stood with my hands on my hips, fury snatching my breath.

'If they think they're getting away with this, they've got another think coming,' I said, my voice shaking with frustration.

Jean clutched my arm, 'You're right, it's a blinkin' disgrace. But never mind that now, we've got to find a way to the bus stop or we'll be even later.'

We hurried round the roads to get to our stop. We passed loads of other people doing the same thing, all worried about being late and losing their jobs.

Jean was quiet for a minute, unusual for her. 'I reckon they started work on that wall on a Sunday so we wouldn't put up a fuss, cos we wouldn't know about it.'

3. THE PROTEST MEETING

PROTEST

Dissent, objection

The following day I had to leave early again because of that blinking Wall. It was a lovely sunny day and I noticed the new bushes and trees people had planted were beginning to grow nicely. The tulips and daffodils hadn't been planted in time because we didn't move in until too late, but salvias, Spanish daisies, polyanthus and pansies all jostled for space in some gardens while others were still bare. Almost everyone had planted a privet hedge, probably getting cuttings from here, there and everywhere. They were tiny, but in time they'd make the gardens feel more personal.

Mum was enjoying turning our mud patch at the front into something beautiful. She'd found a fair size Buddleia bush on a bit of waste ground. It didn't belong to anyone so she went back next day with a bag and a garden fork and rescued it. It was soon alive with butterflies. It's strange living somewhere where everything is new. New houses, new roads, new neighbours, new shops, everything. It all looked like toy town when we moved in a few weeks ago, but it was beginning to look real by now. Or perhaps I was just getting used to it.

There was no sign of any workmen at the Wall, but the mess was still there. Bits of broken brick and lumps of dried cement were everywhere. It made me wonder if the toffs on the other side had paid for the Wall, and thought us lot of 'vermin' wouldn't worry if it looked horrible. People had already started writing rude things on the wall and there was a big poster slap bang in the middle. It said:

This wall must fall!
The wall is a violation of our rights. Join the fight to get it demolished.
Meet Thursday night 7pm at St Matthews Church Hall

Don't let Bardman's Construction get their own way!
We can win the battle!

I'd heard about protest meetings on the radio, but I'd never met anyone who'd been to one. They always sounded a bit scary.

'Load of stupid commies, shoot the bloody lot of 'em.' Dad always said.

But as I walked on I got thinking. Whoever had written that had it spot on - our rights were being stamped on like the lice we were supposed to carry. We'd been talking about that sort of thing at last week's WEA class. We had the right to walk through those streets as much as anyone. Why should we have to walk further to get to the bus stop and the shops? It's not as if many people in Sunbury had cars, there was only one in our road and it looked like it would fall apart any minute. No, it was feet, bikes or buses for us. Not too bad this time of year but in the winter it was another matter; all the old folk and Mums with kiddies freezing and slipping on the ice.

I looked again at the details. *It's tomorrow,* I thought, *I'll go. Not my night at the Dream Palace. I just hope no-one Dad knows is there. He'd say I should know my place and not rock the boat.* For the first time I thought hard about that - *don't rock the boat*. It was like it was my family's motto. Keep your head down. Never challenge rich people or people you work for. Never question what the doctor tells you; he's always right. But boats that don't rock don't go anywhere; they stay exactly where they are and they never get anywhere different. That wasn't what I wanted for my life, and not what Mum wanted for me.

Jean and I half ran, half walked all the way to the bus stop, cursing the wall with every step.

Naturally we'd missed our bus and we stood with about half a dozen other people who'd had the same problem as us.

'We gotta do something about that bleeding wall,' said Dai Evans struggling to slow his breathing. He was the man who said the valleys were great and who lived two houses from us. He grinned at me. 'Don't tell anyone I said so, but the valleys were rubbish. Everything was grey. Grey houses, grey coal, grey earth and grey clouds almost touching yer 'ead. And rain! It never stopped. We 'ad sun about a week a year. Coming 'ere was like opening to my eyes to colour, like I'd never seen it before. Beautiful, it is. Mind you, I'll still fight anyone who says anything against the valleys.'

As usual the bus was full and Jean and I had to stand and hold on to the roof straps. Each time the bus went round a corner we swayed in unison like leaves in a breeze. I'd already told Jean about the attack and Edward. She'd been horrified and excited in equal measure. Horrified about the attack, and excited I'd met a swish bloke. 'Maybe you'll marry 'im and be rich,' she said with a silly dreamy look on her face, daft thing.

'I'll never see him again, and let's forget all about it.' I gave her a look that said I meant it.

'Are you going to that meeting about the wall tomorrow?' I asked.

'What meeting?'

'Jean, you're such a twit. You were giving the workman what for about it yesterday. It's a meeting to get that wall knocked down. You coming or you seeing that bloke?'

She pulled a face. 'Nuh, 'e's got to work late tomorrow. Will your Dad try to stop you going?'

I thought for a minute. 'Tell you what, I'm not going to tell him. If he even asks, I'll say we're going for a walk by the river. He can't moan about that. Now, what about this meeting?'

'Ah, come on Lil,' she said, 'I've never been to a meeting in my life. Wouldn't know what to do.'

I pursed my lips. 'You don't have to do a thing, just being there shows you want something done and the bloke who called the meeting will work something out. It's to help us so we don't have to walk all that extra way. Let's do something about it.'

She pulled a face again and I thought she was

going to say no. She finally gave an exaggerated groan.

'Okay, might as well, I've got nothing else to do. Who knows, we might meet some tasty lads there, then you can really forget Edward.'

'What about the bloke you're seeing?'

'Plenty more fish in the sea,' she said, shaking her head so her beautiful blond curls shone in the light.

St Matthew's Church Hall was like a big wooden shed. It had windows on two sides, a wooden crucifix at one end and a big clock at the other. The walls were a dreary beige, but colourful red, white and blue bunting was strung like washing lines in diagonal lines across the whole room giving a festive feel. I could just imagine a wedding party dancing under those cloth triangles. Dust motes drifted lazily around, spotlighted by the evening sun. Near the door were Parish notices advertising a jumble sale, a baby clinic and a bring and buy sale. I made a note of the last one - my Mum was always after a bargain. She had to be, we could rarely afford to buy new clothes.

I'd never been to St Matthew's before. In our old house we went to St Martin's. Well, Mum did, she went every week, but I'd lapsed a bit so didn't go very often, just Christmas and Easter. Mum was doing the rounds to check out all the churches near our new house to see which she liked the look of. I knew she'd probably go to the one with the best choir, she enjoyed a good sing-song.

Jean and I got to the meeting a bit late deliberately. We didn't want to sit near the front in case we got roped into anything, but we needn't have worried. The place was fairly full, probably about sixty people there. Not surprising I suppose when so many houses were affected by the wall; at least three times that number. We managed to get some seats about half way down over to one side. I looked around and saw a fair mix of people, some old women in their best hats, and old men smoking their pipes. I spotted a couple of Mums with babies in their prams and several sulky looking kids complaining because they'd been told to sit still. The hubbub grew as old friends greeted each other and people introduced themselves to people they didn't know.

Jean nudged me. 'Look at 'im,' she said indicating the front of the room, 'is 'e weird or what?'

A tall, very thin man stood up from the front row and walked down the hall chatting to people and shaking hands. He looked like a puff of wind could bend him over like those trees on a clifftop at the seaside. His bushy moustache was like an awning shading his mouth from daylight, and his bald head looked like he'd just polished it. You could almost see it sparkle under the lights. What caught my eye most though was the brightly patterned waistcoat he was wearing. I'd never seen anything like it.

At seven o'clock on the dot he walked back to the front of the hall and took two steps up to the stage. He stood there not saying a thing, just waiting for the chatter to subside. Then, like a tin toy solder that had just been wound up, he sprung into life.

'Greetings, my fellow oppressed residents of Sunbury. I'm delighted to see so many of you here ready to fight Bardman's, the capitalist construction company on the other side of that wretched wall.'

A few people wriggled in their seats and looked at each other. 'Bet they didn't think they were part of a fight,' whispered Jean. 'Got your boxing gloves with you?'

'Shhh, let's listen.'

'Do we want to see our old people walking all that extra way to get to the Post Office? Do we want to see our young mothers walking all that extra way to take their babies to get weighed at the clinic? Do we want to see workers, already busy people, walking that extra way to the bus stop to earn their daily bread?'

His voice rose with every question.

'DO WE?' he bellowed.

He paused and looked expectantly at the crowd.

'No, we don't,' shouted someone over the other side.

'CAN'T HEAR YOU. DO WE?' boomed the thin man, his hands cupping his ears.

'NO, WE DON'T!' came the shout from at least half the people there.

Jean leaned over and whispered in my ear, 'It's like a pantomime. I feel like shouting *Oh, yes, we do!*'

I couldn't help but giggle, but the mood in the room soon distracted me from what she was saying.

The thin man had to wave his arms around and shout for quiet several times until he made himself heard.

'Some of you already know me, but if you don't you'll soon know my name. I'm Bob Burton and I'm the man who got Simmons Biscuit factory to pay a decent living wage.'

'Yes, but half of them lost their jobs,' I heard someone behind me say quietly.

Mr Burton gestured to the man sitting in the front row, 'I'm delighted we have with us tonight our City Councillor, Mr John Tallis.'

The councillor stood up and faced us all. His brown suit was a bit worn, but his shirt was such a dazzling white I thought it must be new. He shook hands with Bob before speaking.

'I'm delighted to have been invited tonight. I'm

not here to make any political speeches, I just want to hear how I can help.'

And with that, he sat down again and never said another word.

Bob patted his shoulder so hard, he rocked in his chair.

'We all know why we're here tonight. Bardman's Construction have built that wall without any consultation with the people it will inconvenience the most – us, the people of Sunbury.'

There was a round of applause.

'So, here's my question. What are we going to do about it?'

'*Bulldoze it,*' shouted someone from the back.

'If only we could, but sadly we have to act within the law,' Mr Burton replied, his mouth downturned. 'But before we go any further, let me tell you what I've already done.'

There was a stirring that made it clear people were impressed he'd already done something.

'First off, I've spoken to the Head of Bardman's Construction. We had quite a, shall we say, frank and honest exchange of views. Let me cut it short. He doesn't care about Sunbury, only about the rich people who bought his houses.'

A ripple of muttering went round the room.

'All right for some,' someone shouted.

'Yeah, let him walk the extra distance in the bad weather,' shouted someone else from the back.

Mr. Burton waited until the chatter stopped. 'He went on to say he had received a representation, a petition really, from twenty five of those rich house-holders. They all wanted to stop the people of Sunbury having access to their end of the road. He still has ten houses to sell and he doesn't want rumours to stop his sales.'

'What rumours?' an old lady in a green felt hat asked.

Mr Burton held up his hand as if to apologise. 'I'll tell you, but you won't like it any more than I did. In fact what they said is an absolute disgrace. Those rich people are saying the slum clearance people from South Wales have all sorts of dirt and diseases and they don't want to catch them.'

'But there are only twenty families from South Wales,' I thought.

There was a murmuring of outrage.

'We... Don't... Have... Nits,' someone said loudly.

'I clean my house every day, I do,' said the green hatted lady.

Mr Burton held up his hand. 'You don't need to convince me, any of you. It's a load of nonsense. But the wall is there and we need to get it demolished. There are a number of steps we can take. A petition;

speaking to the council; demonstrating. And that's just a start.'

Someone near the front stood up and faced us all. 'Yeah, let's have a demo,' he demanded raising his fist in the air.

People applauded.

'Yes, let's march, it worked during the great depression.' I heard someone near me say.

'No it didn't, a lot of people still starved,' came the reply.

The chatter went on for another minute or two.

Mr. Burton clapped his hands for attention. He addressed the man who had spoken, 'Let's not get hasty, Comrade.'

The word was explosive. Comrade! I heard several people mutter, 'Commie. He's a Commie.' And with that three people gathered all their things and walked out.

Jean nudged me, 'What's a commie? I've never really understood, except people don't like them.'

'Tell you later. I couldn't care less about his politics. What's important is getting that wall knocked down, and he looks like he's got the gumption to do something about it.'

Mr. Burton had to bang his hands on the table to get attention this time.

'Yes, it's true, I'm a Communist. But this is not a political issue. I live in Sunbury just like you. Just like you, I am inconvenienced by the wall. We are all victims here, but we don't have to sit down and take it. We are not helpless pawns in their game. How many of you have sung that hymn All Things Bright and Beautiful?'

Everyone nodded.

Bob nodded too. 'I have as well, but I wonder if you ever really thought about the words of one verse.'

'What's that then?' someone shouted.

'It's telling you to know your place,' Bob said, and I thought again about being becalmed.

'The words are *The rich man in his castle, The poor man at his gate, God made them high and lowly, And ordered their estate.* Just listen. It's telling you God says you should stay poor and keep the rich man rich. Every time you sing that hymn, your brains hear that you should know your place. And that's just what we're not going to do. Are we? Are we?'

He put his hand to his ear again. A good few people shouted 'No!'

Bob held up his hands, 'Right. No. We're going to take action. We're going to fight the rich man in his castle. And this particular rich man is Mr Bardman.'

I could see people looking at each other. The atmosphere changed like a pond calming after a pebble dropped into it has sunk.

'What we need is a steering party. A group of people who will help me to plan our action to get this wall demolished. Will anyone join me?'

There was absolute silence. Not a twitch, not a cough, nothing.

'Come on,' he said, 'we won't win if we're not in the fight. Now, who's going to help me? I can't do it all myself.'

He looked around expectantly, then looked over towards my bit of the room and said, 'Thank you, my first volunteer.' He gave a burst of applause that was picked up by others.

I turned around to see who it was, and to my amazement found my arm was in the air.

'Lily,' Jean said, her mouth forming a big O, 'what've you gone and done now?'

'I don't know. I didn't even know I'd moved my arm. Oh, crikey.'

I put my treacherous hand down and looked at my lap wishing the floor would open and swallow me whole. My mind whirled. How was I going to find time to get involved in this? I had two jobs and an evening class already, and I tried to find time to practice my typing on an old typewriter I found at the market. I must have been mad to volunteer. And I didn't know anything about getting involved in a protest. What about all the people from Sunbury who weren't at the meeting? Did that mean they didn't care about the wall? Would my name be mud for getting involved? What would Dad say?

After a few seconds Jean nudged me, 'Lil, look, a couple of other daft sods have put their 'ands up, too. It's not just you and 'im after all.'

I looked to see who the others were. I didn't recognise them, but I guessed I'd soon be getting to know them.

Mr. Burton gave a big grin, 'Thank you my brave volunteers; my army of change; my fighters for right. Can you stay behind after the meeting for a few minutes so I can get your details please?'

The meeting dragged on for another twenty minutes. It seemed like everyone wanted to moan about the wall and how it was making life hard for them. Mr Burton was very patient and made notes of all their complaints. I noticed the Councillor didn't write much down though.

'The Council won't know what's 'it them when 'e 'ands in that list.' Jean whispered. 'I'd love to be a fly on the wall at that meeting.'

Eventually Mr Burton bought the meeting to a close and people began to slowly drift back towards the door. I was looking around to see if there was anyone I knew when someone tapped me on the shoulder. I turned around to see a bloke a bit older than me holding out his hand and smiling. He was tall with dark brown hair and a wispy moustache.

'Hello,' he said, 'you were one of the volunteers. I saw you put your hand up. Peter, Peter Smith.' He shook my hand so hard I wondered if I'd ever be able to type again.

'Well ...'

'Good meeting,' he went on, 'what's brought you here? You must feel strongly about that wall.'

'I do. It's not fair we have to walk round just so the rich people can get their own way. Me and my friend Jean here have to walk miles further to get our bus to work.'

He nodded, 'Does it inconvenience any of your family?'

'My mum's a char and some of her ladies she does for are just the other side of that wall. She has to cycle all the way round, it makes life harder for her.'

He looked thoughtful, 'So some might say the rich people think your mother is good enough to go into their houses to clean, but not good enough to walk down their street. Would you agree?'

I hadn't thought of it like that, but it was obvious when he said so.

Jean, who'd been listening to this conversation, butted in. 'Makes you blinking mad, don't it!' she said with her best outraged voice.

Peter smiled at her then turned to me again, 'What about your father?'

'It's not a problem for him, he works in the other direction.'

By the time we'd finished chatting, the room had pretty much emptied and Mr Burton was calling us volunteers to the front.

'I must go, Mr Smith,' I said, 'I'm needed.'

'Wait. Before you go, I didn't get your name.'

'Lily Baker.'

He looked thoughtful, 'Where do you live? You look familiar, I wonder if I've seen you around.'

We compared addresses, but he lived too far away for us to bump into each other easily.

'You staying with me to chat to Mr Burton, Jean?' I asked.

'Nuh, I think I'll leave now, who knows, I might bump into Peter Smith on the way out. Did you notice his lovely broad shoulders?'

'Poor man', I thought, 'he'll soon be used and tossed aside like all her other men.'

I gathered my things and headed over to Mr Burton. Two other people joined me.

'Sit down, sit down,' Mr Burton said, pulling chairs round for us. 'First things first. Let me thank you again for so kindly volunteering to help us get rid of this wall: get back our rights to walk where we will on public highways: feel free from the restrictions of those snobby people and that construction company. But let's introduce ourselves. You already know who I am and I insist you call me Bob. We're going to be a team, so let's be on first name terms.'

He pulled out a notebook and looked at me, 'Lovely to meet you. You are?'

'Lily Baker.'

He asked our telephone number but we didn't have a telephone. He took my address instead. Then he looked at the others.

He turned to a woman sitting next to me. She was maybe a year or two older than me, and dressed very smartly in a calf length blue dress with a little white collar and buttons all the way down the front. She was carrying a matching clutch bag and her hair looked like she'd just stepped out of a salon. I wanted to dislike her, but she looked too friendly.

'I'm Rose, Rose Williams,' she said.

'And you?' Bob said, turning to the last person. This was an elderly man with white hair and a benback. He wore a flat cap, woollen trousers, a nearly white shirt and braces. If he had a jacket, he wasn't wearing it.

'I'm Fred Gardiner and I live right next door to that wall. Damned nuisance if you ask me. Apart from anything else, it blocks out the early morning sun to my kitchen.'

Bob handed each of us a piece of foolscap paper. Looking down, I saw it was a list of the skills required to get action going.

'Spend a minute looking down the list,' Bob said. 'Think about your skills and consider how much time you have to spare. Then I'm looking to find the right people for the right task. I'll give full backup to all of you.'

There was a minute's silence as we read the list, then Fred, the elderly man, said, 'I can write a good letter, and I'm happy to stand in a demo march as long as it doesn't last too long. My back will give up otherwise.'

'I can type a bit,' I said, 'only about 15 words a minute though.'

Rose took a while thinking about it. 'I work in a bank, so I can't be seen to be attending demos or anything, but I can probably do a bit of fund-raising. I have a lot of contacts.'

In the end I agreed to type the petition forms and Fred and I would take a share of the estate each, going door to door to get as many signatures as possible for a petition. Fred said he would also cover the corner shop and the post office.

Bob clapped his hands, 'We've done well and you, my fearless fighters, my soldiering soldiers, my amazing army, we need a goal. So let's aim at three quarters of the households on the estate signing the petition within ten days. Trouble is, we'll need help, that's a lot to do. Do any of you know anyone else who can help?'

I knew just the person.

~

That night I got cracking typing the petition forms on the paper Bob gave me. I sat at the kitchen table after tea, tapping away. I soon got better at getting the rejects in the bin from five feet away.

'It looks very wasteful, Lil,' Mum said, 'can't you be a bit more careful? What're you doing anyway?' She took all the paper out of the bin and smoothed it out. She read it then tore in into smaller square and threaded through a bit of string ready to hang next to the W.C.

I'd been concentrating so hard I had to stop a minute to take in what she said. Did she think I was deliberately making mistakes or what? And I was definitely getting faster.

'You know I told you I was going to that protest meeting to try to get the wall knocked down. Well, I'm only on the Steering Group.'

'It sounds really interesting.'

'Sort of, but it just means a lot of work. I'm typing petition forms so me and a couple of others can go round the estate getting signatures. Bob, the bloke in charge, wants us to get three quarters of house-holders signing it in the next ten days. At this rate, I'll still be typing the forms then.'

'You know, Lil, I'd love to help, but if my ladies I do for see I'm getting involved, I might lose them and we need all the money we can get. I don't know where it all goes.'

'Dad still keeping you short?'

She sighed, 'Same as always.'

'Mum, d'you even know what he earns?'

'No love, but It must be a lot more than he's giving me, and if he knew I did the odd extra hour's cleaning now and then, he'd dock it from my house-keeping straight away.'

I got out my purse. 'I know you don't want any more rent money Mum, but here's a couple of bob extra and I'll give you that every week, no arguing.'

She looked sad but took the money and put it in her purse.

I decided to ask her something I'd always wanted to know. 'Mum, was Dad always like this? So mean and nasty?'

She looked away for a minute, her face a study in sadness. 'No, love, he was a good man when we met. Cheerful and generous. I couldn't believe my luck that he wanted me.'

I was gobsmacked. 'Really? I can't imagine him like that. What happened?'

She stood up and busied herself tidying the

kitchen. 'War. He was at Passchendaele In France. He was too young for the beginning of the war though. Thousands and thousands of men died and a lot of them that came back weren't the same person who'd gone away. What they saw changed them. That's where your Dad got the scar on his head, too. They told me he was unconscious for two days when that happened.'

I felt cold just at the thought of what he'd suffered. 'It must have been dreadful. You must have been so worried.'

'At the time I didn't know about it. News doesn't always travel fast in wartime.'

She bit her lip. 'It's horrible you and me have to live with the consequences though. It's awful for us but awful for him too, that's why I've put up with it so long. He'll never talk about what happened, most of them don't, but he has terrible nightmares. He thrashes around and wakes up in a real sweat almost every night.'

I couldn't believe I'd never known any of this. 'Couldn't the doctors help?'

'I don't think they properly understood what happened to the men in those days. Not sure they do now. They called it shell shock because they thought it was the noise of the constant shelling that caused problems.'

I struggled to remember what I'd learned about it

at school, 'Didn't they execute some men who had shell shock, saying they were cowards?'

'Yes, looking back now it seems so dreadful. I couldn't get your dad to talk about what happened to him, perhaps it bought back too many unhappy memories.'

As I lay in bed that night I began to think differently about Dad. I'd read bits about Passchendaele and it sounded like several sorts of hell. Over five hundred thousand British troops died at Passchendaele. My Dad must have seen some awful things: bodies torn to shreds, bombs exploding around him, men drowning in the mud of the trenches. It was a wonder anyone came out sane. And then he got hit in the head too. It must have affected his brain somehow.

But did it mean it was okay for him to be so nasty to me and Mum? Didn't he have some responsibility to get help so he didn't make our lives a misery? Would he be happier and behave better if we were consistently kind to him? Would we even be able to keep it up in the face of his violence? He seemed to have good mates at work. That meant he must act normal some of the time, so didn't me and Mum deserve better behaviour too? Should she really sacrifice her happiness for the rest of her life because of what happened to him years ago? I tossed and turned long into the night, my mind a whirl of conflicting emotions.

~

A few days later I showed the petitions to Mr. Burton. He looked at them carefully then gave me a smile bright enough to bring out the sunshine.

'These are great, Lily, and on time too. What job did you say you do?'

'I sew sleeves on shirts at Richardson's,' I said. 'It's so boring, but it's regular.'

He held his head on one side. 'It sounds like a dead-end job. Who's above you?'

'Mavis is our supervisor, she's okay, firm but she's fair enough. The big boss is above her.'

'When will you get a chance to apply for Mavis' job?'

I'd never even considered it. Mavis was in her thirties and seems happy enough with the job. I couldn't see her leaving in a hurry.

'In twenty or thirty years, I suppose,' I said, feeling a bit stupid. All this time I'd been saying I was going to improve myself, but I hadn't thought beyond typing and my evening class. I began to see I needed a plan.

A frown appeared between his eyebrows. 'You're worth more than that, Lily. You can't waste your life sewing on sleeves. You need a bit of ambition. You've got some good skills there. Keep practising that typing and look for office jobs. I'll keep my ears open for you.'

4. INFIDELITY

HAVING A ROMANTIC OR SEXUAL RELATIONSHIP WITH SOMEONE OTHER THAN ONE'S HUSBAND, WIFE OR PARTNER

'So, are you going to help me, Jean?' I asked as we headed to the Dream Palace.

'What does it pay?'

'The petition? Nothing. You'll be helping everyone in Sunbury and you'll be helping yourself most of all. We won't have to walk all this extra way. Come on, we might see some good looking lads by the time we've knocked on all the doors.'

That did it. We started next evening. As we set out, we noticed all the trunks of the trees that lined the roads had been painted white.

Jean went and touched one. She got a white hand for her trouble.

She wiped her hand on some grass at the base of the tree. 'What the 'eck's that all about?'

'Don't you ever listen to the news, Jean? It's for

the black-out in case the war starts, so we can find our way round when it's dark.'

'What? You mean we can't have any lights on at all? What about if there's no moon?' she asked.

I shrugged, 'Dunno. I suppose we have to wait for our eyes to adjust and hope for the best. I don't know how the old people will manage though. They have more trouble seeing in the dark.'

Jean let out a low whistle, 'Blimey, what about the old folk who are deaf as well. They'll never hear cars or bikes coming. There's going to be a lot of accidents.'

I nodded, 'I bet it'll be easier for robbers to get clean away too. The police'll never be able to see them. But enough of that, let's get on with the job, or we'll be here all night.'

Jean and I got to our first door; time to start collecting signatures.

'I dunno what to say,' Jean said as we approached the first door. 'You'd better speak.'

So for the first few houses I spoke and most people were happy to sign, but then I noticed how long it had taken. Everyone wanted to have their say, to tell me the hardship the wall was causing them, and it was tricky getting away from some people.

'Jean, you're going to have to do some on your own or we'll never get done at this rate.'

We door-knocked for two hours, then went back

to her house to add up the signatures and have a cuppa. Our total was pitiful, we'd knocked on doors in three roads and the number of signatures we'd collected wouldn't have impressed anyone.

'Trouble is,' said Jean, 'between the chatty ones and the one's what's out, we're not getting far. We'll 'ave to give up.'

'No, we're not, we'll have to try harder and rope in some more help. I'll see if Fred can go and stand outside the Doctors' when he's not at the Post Office.'

'And ask him if they know where the best looking lads live.'

When we got to the Post Office Fred looked excited. 'Seen the paper then?' he asked me.

I was confused. Had war been declared? Was the war against the wall won?

'No, should I?'

He grinned so widely you could see both his teeth. He reached under his chair for a paper and waved it under my nose. 'You did a real good interview.'

I looked at him, 'Interview? What interview?'

As I spoke I looked at the newspaper. It was a report of the wall meeting. Half way down I read:

Local resident Lily Baker, who is one of the Steering Group, said the rich people on 'the other side of the wall' believed her mother was good enough to clean their houses, but not good enough to walk down their street.'

Jean was reading over my shoulder. She turned and looked at me. 'Did you know 'e was a reporter?' she asked.

'No, of course I didn't. I wouldn't have spoken to him otherwise. Wait a minute, you went out looking for him. What did you tell him?'

Her outraged face appeared again, 'Nothing, honest. Don't go accusing me. You said those words.'

'No, I didn't, it was you who agreed with what he said. Now he's saying it was me.'

''e's a lying toerag. I promise Lil, when I left I never found 'im. 'e'd gone. I never said another word to 'im.'

'Oh, my word,' I said, 'I hope my mum's ladies don't see this or she may be out of work.'

~

The day before the next meeting Jean and me went to see Fred again. He was still sitting outside the corner shop.

His face lit up when he saw us. 'How've you been getting on, my lovelies?' he asked. 'Your Mum get in any trouble 'cos of that article, Lil?' I shook my head. I showed Mum what the sneaky reporter had written and she was worried, but to our relief nothing had happened and she still had all her ladies.

Fred spoke again, 'Get many signature yet?'

We groaned in unison. 'It takes so long, people want to chat or they're out,' Jean said.

Fred shook his head, 'You girls got to get the knack of getting away fast. Watch me.'

We stepped back and saw him stop the next person who came out of the shop. The way he spoke got a bit more formal and he got the signature he asked for. Then when the lady wanted to have a moan he said, 'Do forgive me, Love, but I've got to catch other people if we're going to get this wall knocked down.' And with that he looked away and shuffled his papers noisily.

The lady went away without another word.

'Got it?' he said. We had.

He'd been getting loads of signatures. I can't imagine anyone getting past him without a fight; for a little old bloke he could be very determined. We compared notes and we hadn't got as many as Bob hoped, but it was a respectable pile of forms between us.

When we left him, Jean said, 'We've worked our socks off, what with the petition and the other jobs. Let's 'ave a night out - there's a Swing Band playing at The Roxy tonight and I'm in the mood for dancing. We don't need no blokes. We'll see what comes up.' She gave a dirty giggle and I couldn't help joining in.

So at eight o'clock we were at The Roxy in our finest, hoping some lads would ask us to dance. Mum had just finished making my outfit and it was my first chance to show it off. It was a lovely blue sweetheart neck dress with a wide belt and figure hugging skirt that swirled at the bottom. It swished when I walked.

I was just picking up my bag when Dad walked past on his way to his weekly old boy's club. 'You look like a cheap tart,' he said as he brushed past me. I tried to ignore him, but it still got me down. I wondered what it would be like to have a dad who thought you were something special instead of something the cat dragged in.

'He's a miserable git, and he's wrong. You look fabulous.' Mum said, and I hugged her as I said goodbye.

'Don't wait up Mum, I'll be fine.'

The Roxy was packed when we got there. The dance hall was big; goodness knows how many people it held. At one end there was a stage where the band played against a backdrop of plush blue velvet curtains. Either side of it were these enormous organ pipes that went floor to ceiling, all fancy with a metal pattern. Down each side of the hall were tables covered in white clothes and chairs, but almost all of them were empty and I could see why. People were up and dancing to the band playing a Sam Costa number *Snake Charmer*. My feet started tapping as if they had a mind of their own.

'Come on, let's dance,' Jean said, grabbing my hand. She has a figure that is all curves and wears clothes to show it off. Most of them are hand-me-downs from her big sister and an aunt, but her Mum is a whiz at altering them and you'd never know they weren't brand new or the latest fashion.

I felt a bit stupid. Girls don't usually dance together much in these big dance halls, it's usually couples. But if you wait to be asked to dance, well, you might hug walls all night. We were just learning how to jitterbug. It was a good laugh but took a bit of practice. We danced to two or three numbers then sat down to catch our breath. We gave our orders for drinks, listening to *A Gypsy Told Me* while we waited. We hadn't sat down for more than five minutes when two lads came and plonked themselves down next to us without so much as a by-your-leave. They looked like brothers, both with straight brown hair parted the same way.

'I hate to see a couple of pretty girls like you on your own,' one of them said combing his hair as he spoke.

I gave him the once over and didn't like what I saw. He had a know-all face, like he was doing us a big favour talking to us.

'We're not on our own. We're together,' I said with enough frost in my voice to make icicles. I immediately turned away to speak to Jean. She kicked my ankle hard, 'What're you doing?' she said out of the side of her mouth. 'Let 'em pay for the drinks before we get rid of 'em.'

Jean and I have different values about some things. I don't like sponging off people and apart from that, I knew it would be harder to get rid of these two once they thought we owed them something. Ignoring the pain in my ankle I stood up, grabbed her by the hand and dragged her to the dance floor just as *I won't tell a soul* was starting. By the end of the next number the blokes had gone. Mind you, I had to pay for the drinks to stop Jean moaning.

We were just sitting there looking round when I noticed there were two balconies, like boxes in a theatre. A couple in one were so wrapped round each other you couldn't have got a ciggie paper between them. I could only see the back of the bloke's head, but the way he was kissing the woman I was surprised she could breathe. I took a sip of my lemonade and glanced up again a minute or two later. My breath caught in my chest as if I'd been punched. I nudged Jean and nodded with my head in the direction of the balcony.

'You all right?' she said, 'you've gone white as a sheet.'

'That's not … is it?'

She looked up. 'Bloody 'ell,' she said, 'it is. Hasn't got an identical twin, 'as 'e?'

It was my dad. And the woman he was with was certainly not my mum.

Jean and I looked at each other. 'What're you going to do?' she asked.

Murder him, was my first thought. My poor Mum at home doing the housework and the ironing after a day's cleaning people's houses, believing he was at his Old Boy's club and here he was. Here he was with some floozy. And he had the nerve to tell me I looked like a tart.

We kept looking at them. Dad was sitting there looking mighty pleased with himself. He had a spotless white shirt on, washed by Mum, of course, and a tie I hadn't seen before. She wore a dress with pink roses on it. It was so low cut it must have saved on a lot of fabric. Dad's arm was round the floozy's shoulders in a way that showed that they knew each other pretty well. With his other arm, he regularly took gulps of his pint. I thought about how much it cost to get in the dance hall, the cost of the pint and the cocktail the floozy had, and wondered how many hours Mum had to work to earn that much.

I'd kill him.

Jean clapped her hands in front of my face, 'Lily! Wake up. What're you going to do?'

We talked it over some more and decided I would hide in the Ladies and Jean would go up and make sure he saw her but not show she'd seen him. She often popped into our house, so he knew what she looked like. He'd guess that if she was there, I would be too and hopefully he'd get the jitters and clear off. That way, we could still enjoy our evening out. But, how could I enjoy it after that? I thought about all the times he'd told I could do nothing right, always trying to make out he was always so damned perfect. I vowed there and then I would never take any lip from him. I'd stand up to him every single time he made a sarky comment. He was in for a big shock.

When I came out of the Ladies I waited out of sight until Jean found me. She was grinning from ear to ear.

'What happened?' I asked.

She giggled. 'I stood so he could see me and she couldn't. He spotted me and went so white I thought he'd slide off his chair. I saw him make some excuse to her and hurried her out.'

'Blimey, Jean, you're so brave,' I said.

'Nuh, what's 'e going to do to me? 'e's not my Dad.'

She looked unbearably smug. 'I followed them all the way. I 'ad to laugh. 'e was trying to get her out the door and she couldn't understand why they had to go. 'e was making all sorts of excuses and she was dragging 'er feet something chronic, still clutching her cocktail. They're gone now, so we can 'ave a good night.'

We sat down again and ordered more lemonade. This time I happily paid.

'Do you think I should tell my mum?' I asked.

Jean put her head on one side, 'Dunno, what's she going to do if she finds out? Leave 'im?'

I thought it through. 'I don't see how she could afford to. She couldn't pay the rent on what she earns charring, and she'd have to give up this new corporation place.'

'Let's think,' Jean said, 'if she knew, would it make a difference to how she is with your dad? Would she stand up to him more?'

I tried to imagine her doing that. 'She might, but she'd probably get a thump for her troubles.'

'Your lemonade, Ladies,' the waiter said, interrupting our thoughts.

Jean took a sip of hers, 'So your Mum can't afford to leave him and it would be too dangerous if she gave him what for. Sounds like you've got to keep quiet.'

5. ATTRACTIVE

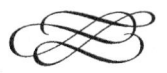

ALLURING, ENTICING, GOOD-LOOKING

I was still upset next day when I headed off to meet the others in the wall steering group. I tried to persuade Jean to come with me, after all, she'd helped to get the signatures. But she had a date with a boy she picked up after I left the dance hall early the night before. We had the meeting at Bob's house. It was on the edge of the estate and was two bedroomed. It didn't look like he was a house proud man or had a woman to look after him. But he'd made the best of what he had with some nice pictures on the walls.

'Welcome, my soldiers, my fighters, my pugilists,' he said after we'd sat down. The brightly coloured waistcoat was gone. In its place he had a white scarf slung round his neck.

Bob looked at the man sitting next to him,

someone we hadn't seen before. He was very good looking, nicely dressed too. Striped jumper under his jacket and his cap at a carefree angle.

'This is my nephew, Victor. He's a busy lad, but he'll help when he can.'

Victor smiled and caught my eye. He winked and I blushed like a schoolgirl.

We told Bob how we'd got on. He was pleased with the number of petitions and Rose had raised a whole £20.3s.6d. We all gave a cheer when we heard that.

Victor had plenty to say for himself. He smiled widely each time someone said they'd completed one of their tasks and said, 'Good show,' or 'Jolly good.' Even so, I couldn't decide if I liked him or not. Somehow his smile was a bit forced and didn't always reach his eyes. But he said all the right things, so I decided I was probably imagining things.

Bob caught my attention again, 'Anticipating your success, I've arranged to see a council official at 5.30 next Tuesday, and I'm looking for one of you to come with me. Who'll be my sergeant at arms?'

The silence was so palpable it was like drowning in slow motion.

He held out his hands, 'Come on, my soldiers, you don't have to do a thing.'

'What's the point of us being there, then?' Fred asked.

'I told you, it looks better if two of us go. I'll do the talking and one of you can just hand over the petition sheets.'

After a long hush when all I could hear was the blood pounding through my ears, I caved in.

'Okay, I'll do it. I'm working at the Dream Palace that night anyway. It's only ten minutes walk from the Town Hall. I won't be able to hang around though or I'll be late for work.'

We all left the meeting at the same time. Somehow Victor was walking alongside me.

'See you later, uncle Bob.' he called to Bob, and kept walking my way.

'Where'd you live, then?'

I told him. 'Great,' he said, 'I'm going that way. We can keep each other company.'

All the way there he made me laugh with stories of people he knew or things he'd messed up. What with my dad and the horrible war coming our way, a good laugh was just what I needed.

'Fancy coming out one night?' he asked.

And that was it, my first date with Victor.

The Town Hall was an imposing building. While I waited for Bob I counted the windows across the front, 13 across and three high, and that's just the front. I guessed there must be more rooms behind. The building had a concrete patch in front of it with a few cars parked and around the whole building there was a grass area edged with flowers. The grass was cut so short it looked like you'd get shot if you walked on it.

I wondered what the people who worked there did all day, what decisions they made that affected me and everyone else in Sunbury and the town. Had someone in there agreed the wall was a good idea?

'Good evening, my trooper,' Bob said, making me jump, 'ready for our little adventure? Councillors don't have their own office, but he's told me which meeting room he'll be in.'

He handed me the petition sheets and led the way along corridors with polished wooden floors and loads of signs I didn't even begin to understand. Everything was painted a drab cream colour, the skirting boards were chipped a fair bit and the cleaner must have been short. She'd missed the cobwebs here and there. My mum would have done a much better job. With each grand doorway and each huge hallway I felt more and more intimidated. I tried to ask Bob about the councillor, but all that came out of my mouth was a pathetic squeak he didn't even hear. I'd got totally lost by the time we were shown to two seats outside one of the doors. It was marked Meeting Room H.

We had to wait fifteen minutes before Councillor Tallis appeared. Time enough to get to know every mark on the door and count the leaves on the trees we could see through the windows.

'I'm so sorry, so sorry,' he said, shaking our hands. He unlocked the door and led us into a room that was bare, apart from a huge desk, four chairs and one massive book case that filled a whole wall. The books looked identical with burgundy spines with gold lettering. The room smelt of dust and furniture polish.

'Come in, come in,' he said sitting down behind the desk. He made a show of getting out his pens and lined them up so neatly in front of him you'd have thought he was being marked for tidiness. Only then did he look up.

'As you know, I'm very interested in your cause. Sunbury estate is in my ward. More to the point though, my mother lives on the estate and she gives me ear-ache about that wall every time I see her.'

I'd learned enough at my evening classes with the Workers' Education Association to know if he helped us it would probably be because he wanted to keep his seat, but was pleased he had a personal interest too. We sat opposite him, but before we got talking there was a knock at the door and a tubby man in a scruffy suit walked in. He had a camera slung over one shoulder, and a notepad and pencil in one hand.

'Gary Matthews, Evening News. Here to write a piece in the public interest to the people of Sunbury and the whole town,' he said by way of introduction. He looked at me and Bob.

'And you are?' he said with a smile, notebook at the ready.

'Bob Burton, I'm leading the campaign to get the wall demolished.' He stood up and shook hands with Mr Matthew who then turned to me.

I looked at the photographer. 'Why do you want my name?'

He looked surprised to be questioned. 'If we use your photo in the paper we'll put your name underneath.'

I thought about my Dad seeing my picture in the paper. I could imagine his reaction.

'I'd rather you didn't take my photo, or quote me. I've been misquoted recently by the News.'

His top lip curled.'Oh, if you say so,' he said with a sneer.

Mr Tallis nodded to him and indicated where he should sit. Very quickly he was scribbling away, occasionally stopping to tap his teeth with his pencil.

Bob outlined our case again, explaining that the

property developer, Bardman's Construction, had built the wall without consulting people in Sunbury or the Council. Despite what he'd just said the councillor didn't look very interested, and twice I caught him looking at the clock on the wall. Bob saw him too and looked worried. Suddenly he turned to me, 'Lily, explain to the Councillor the inconvenience caused to you by the wall.'

My mind switched off. Blank. I couldn't think of a thing to say. How dare he, I thought, he promised I wouldn't have to do anything but hand over the petition sheets. Now he was expecting me to say something to a councillor. Me! I stumbled over my words when I spoke to my doctor, now I was supposed to talk to an official like I knew what I was talking about.

Bob nudged me and smiled encouragingly.

'Come on, Lily, you've told me about the extra walking and having to leave home earlier.'

A picture of Rose popped into my head - so calm and in control. I envied her so much. I took a deep breath and pretended to be her, or at least behave like her. That's all it was. Pretend I knew how to speak to people like a councillor.

Taking a deep breath, I sat more upright and looked the councillor in the eye.

'Well, Mr Tallis, Mr Burton's quite right. My story is not unusual. I have to walk an extra half mile to the bus stop, that means leaving home earlier, getting home later, getting wet, getting cold, getting mightily fed up. And my mother who cleans for houses on the other side of the wall has to cycle nearly a mile extra to do for some of her ladies. Imagine cycling back at the end of a day's work, and she still has all the housework and cooking to do for us too.'

'And winter's not even here yet,' added Bob, getting in his stride. 'Our old folk have to walk the extra distance to the post office and the shops. It's just too much for some of them, they can't do it. Who's going to carry their heavy bags, that's what I want to know? They're in real trouble.'

The journalist suddenly spoke up, 'Lily, what do you think is the main problem if you could sum it up in one sentence.'

I paused and wanted to say something about the wall not being fair, but knew I'd sound like a sulky schoolgirl. I needed something more grown up, especially as it looked as if I'd get a mention in the paper. Again. I remembered all I'd learned at WEA, the long words, the ideas, how the lecturer said them. I'd never do as well as him but I'd give it a go. I took another deep breath.

'The wall highlights the way in which this town has a 'them and us' attitude. It represents all that is unfair to hard working people like us. We deserve to be treated with more respect. You can say that, but just put me down as a local resident.'

I stopped and waited, my face flushed, knowing my lecturer would hardly be proud of me, but Bob patted me on the shoulder in a kind way.

'Well done, Lily,' he said quietly.

Suddenly there was a flash. That journalist had only gone and taken my photo despite me telling him not to. Didn't even give me time to comb my hair.

Bob and the councillor were still talking when I left. I had to get to the Dream Palace. No Jean that night, sometimes we did the same shift and sometimes not. Instead I was on with Betty, she'd worked there for ever and knew everything about everything.

'You seen the newspaper, Lily?' she said, waving it in my face. 'Lots of pubs are getting those televisions and some have free entertainment. Why would people come here when they can have a night out for the price of a pint? I hope our jobs are safe.'

'They won't see the big stars down at the Dog and Drake though, will they?'

Pausing for a minute, she nodded agreement. 'You might be right. I wonder how they'll be able to hear what with all the noise of people chatting and pints being pulled. Perhaps we're okay.' Then she smiled and went back to what she was doing.

Bank Holiday was on that week with Margaret Lockwood. Betty had been on afternoon shift and told me it was really good. I decided to try to watch it when I was on duty later that week.

The evening went smoothly and we were just doing the rounds of the auditorium when Betty suddenly tripped and let out a yelp.

I hurried over to find her helping an elderly man up from the floor.

'Come on, my love, you know you can't stay here the night,' she said.

He struggled to stand and I noticed one trouser leg was pinned up at the knee. Betty passed him his crutches.

'Gotta try, my love, nowhere else to go,' he said and had a terrible fit of coughing.

Betty waited for him to finish, then I noticed her put two half crowns in his pocket.

'Thank you, me dear, lost this …' he gestured to his missing leg, 'in the Great War. I won't be no use in the one coming up though.'

We saw him out of the cinema and were relieved to find it wasn't raining.

'Poor thing,' Betty said, then she stopped in her tracks. 'Oh my goodness, I'm so stupid,' she said. 'Someone was looking for you this afternoon. A bloke. Now what was his name? Edmund? Eric?'

My heart started to beat faster.

'Could it have been Edward?'

She clapped her hands. 'Yes. Tall chap, quite a looker. Asked after you 'specially.'

'Did he leave a message?'

'Let me think. My memory isn't what it was …'

I was almost hopping up and down waiting for her reply.

'Hang on, hang on. He must be a soldier 'cos he just said he had a 24 hour pass and had to get back to barracks. Didn't say where his barracks were come to think of it.'

'Is that all?'

'He'll drop in again next time he's in town.'

My shoulders drooped and my heart felt so heavy it seemed my chest was caving in. If Edward was interested he'd have left a note. I thought maybe I'd try going on a foursome with Jean again.

∼

I got home that evening dog-tired, and disappointed. It had been a very long day and it looked like we wouldn't get much help from the councillor for all his talk about his mother giving him ear-ache. Worse still, I'd got my hopes up when I heard that Edward had called into the cinema, but they went down faster than a punctured tyre when he didn't leave a message. He probably just wanted to see the film, and being in the Dream Palace reminded him of me, but not in a romantic way.

At the door I took off my shoes as usual and noticed the light was on in the kitchen. It always meant one of two things - Mum equaled good, Dad equaled bad. This time it was bad. He sat reading a newspaper, an empty beer glass by his side. I could see the headline about Hitler, but he was reading the sports pages. He looked up when I walked in, a sneer on his face.

'What time d'you call this, then?'

I'd heard those words a million times. I'd get them put on his grave. Usually, I answered seriously, explaining for the umpteenth time it was my evening for my cinema job. That was even though I knew he'd still call me all sorts of horrible names: tart, prostitute, whore. I might've been almost old enough to get married without permission and to vote, but I'd never got over being frightened of him and his vicious tongue. Then I remembered the promise I made to myself never to be scared of him, and anyway things had changed.

Now I saw him with new eyes.

Adulterer.

Here was him trying to tell me what I could and couldn't do, all in the name of 'you've got to know right from wrong' when all the time he was out with another woman. Or more than one for all I knew.

I stood my ground and didn't answer him.

His newspaper rustled as he put it down on the kitchen table with a thud.

'I said, what time do you call this then? People will think you're a troll coming in this time of night. Look at ya, big bags under yer eyes. Been on the game, have yer? Never knew anyone so stupid.'

I didn't move a muscle. I stood up straight and looked him in the eye.

'I'm not the one who gives out to men. Not married men, 'specially.'

His eyes narrowed. 'What do you mean, you stupid cow?'

'I don't believe in going out with married men. Not like some women Mum would want to know about.'

Before I had time to get out of the way he stepped towards me and slapped me round the face. Hard.

His chin jutted forward and he leaned right into my face. His breath smelled of beer and fags. 'You keep your mouth shut, you bitch, or you'll get what's coming to you.'

I spat in his face, then quickly stepped back, picked up my things, and walked upstairs, desperately hoping he wouldn't hit me as I walked away.

'You come back down here!' he shouted after me.

But I could tell his heart wasn't in it.

I went in the bathroom and saw how red my

cheek was where he'd hit me. I ran a flannel under the cold tap then held it to my face hoping it would stop any bruising. I looked at myself in the mirror. How could I get out of this house and away from this horrible man? No way I could afford rent on my own and anyway I didn't know any girls who did that. It was unheard of. For us girls, getting married was the only way to leave home and I wasn't about to rush into that seeing what it did to Mum. If me and Mum left, then we'd have handed over this nice new corporation house to Dad and have to move into some horrible rented place.

6. FAME

RECOGNITION, PROMINENCE

I met Jean the next day after we'd finished our day jobs. If the weather was kind we sometimes met up and walked part of the way home. It saved a bit of bus fare and we'd got dab hands at putting stick-on soles and heels on our own shoes. She ran towards me waving a newspaper, and she had the silliest grin on her face.

'Lil, look, you're famous! Your photo's on the front page!'

My heart sank. Surely the stupid reporter hadn't ignored me telling him not to write about me.

'Listen to this, Lil. *Attractive Lily Baker*, attractive you are! *twenty one, attended the meeting. She was wearing a black skirt and white blouse with black flat shoes. Lily, who is part of the group opposing the wall said, "The wall highlights the way in* which this town has a them and us attitude. It represents all that is unfair to working-class people. We deserve to be treated with more respect". Blimey, Lil, did you swallow a dictionary or what? Wish someone'd call me attractive on the front page of the News.'

I snatched the paper from her hand and looked at the photo.

'I told him not to do this. And look how horrible I look, he could at least have taken a decent picture.'

I read through the rest of the article and cheered up a bit. It was sympathetic to our cause. Didn't mean I wouldn't choke him if I ever saw him again though.

Jean snatched the paper back, a gleam in her eye.

'I need this, I'm setting up a foursome for us. My latest's got a friend who sounds right up your street. Give me a day or two and I'll let you know the details.'

'No need, I've been asked for a date.'

'You dark horse. Who's that, then?' she thumped my arm.

'You know Bob Burton?'

She nodded, 'Not 'im, 'e's old enough to be your dad.'

'He's old enough to be the uncle of my date, Victor. If fact, he is his uncle. Victor's a real looker and a good laugh. You're going to be dead jealous.'

She put her hands on her hips and grinned. 'What me? With my magnetic charm? No way. You think he's the one, then?'

'The one? One what?' I asked, although I knew exactly what she meant.

She grinned widely and punched my arm again, 'Come on, the one. The one you'll spend the rest of your life with.'

I punched her back. 'You and your match-making. Getting a husband isn't the be-all and end-all for everyone, you know. There's more to life than that. Anyway ...'

'Anyway, what?'

I shrugged. 'I'm not sure about him. Still, no harm in one date.'

Jean looked serious for once. 'Tell you what, I'll ask around for you. See if anyone knows anything about him.'

Two nights later we set off with her latest Gordon and Victor to see the variety show at the big pub in town. There was a magician who wore a suit with tails, his top hat on a table next to him. He did a long act with a cigarette, making it disappear and reappear, smoking all the while. Then he did some card tricks and finally pulled a dove out of the top hat. A couple of singers and some dancers were on next. In between acts Victor told us loads of funny stories about people he knew. He also told heaps of jokes and laughed at other people's jokes. I didn't need to worry about having anything interesting to say with him around.

We enjoyed a slow walk back to my home. It was a balmy mid-summer evening. The sun was below the horizon, but threads of pink still laced the sky in the fading light. The street lights clicked on, and soon insects circled pointlessly round them, and leaves on trees nearby shone dimly. The air felt like a caress on my skin.

'What do you think?' Victor asked. 'Will you go out with me again? I'd like it if you would.'

7. ANTIDOTE

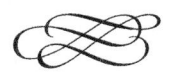

SOMETHING THAT NEUTRALISES AN UNPLEASANT FEELING

A week later we had another steering group meeting at the Lyons Corner House. This time the white scarf was gone, and Bob was wearing a yellow tie instead. I could just imagine what my Dad would've said about that. Victor wasn't there, he'd told me he wasn't much interested in what he called politics. I must admit I was a bit disappointed.

'My troopers, my soldiers, my warriors,' Bob started as the Nippy waitress brought our cups of tea. 'I've heard nothing from Councillor Tallis …'

'Give the man time, it's only been a week,' Fred interrupted.

'Fred, you're right and I appreciate your point of view, but we have to get this sorted and soon. There's a war coming. I don't know if you've seen the news, but lads aged 20 and 21 are getting called up.'

'Does that include Victor?' I asked.

He gave me a knowing look. 'Don't you worry yourself. He's twenty three so too old for this call-up.'

'It's all getting very frightening,' said Rose, her pretty face crinkling into a frown. 'They're talking about moving all the paintings from the National Gallery to somewhere safe.'

'Well, wherever it is, I want to go there too,' Fred said, lifting his cloth cap and scratching his head.

Bob tapped his pencil. 'Back to business. We need to get this sorted before people are too busy thinking about war to worry about our wall. Look how the Great War put back women's suffrage for years and years. No, we have to get this sorted out now or it will get ignored.'

'So what are we going to do then?' Fred asked.

Bob reached inside the carpet bag he always seemed to carry and produced a hammer.

'This is what we're going to do,' he said, waving it around.

'What, some woodwork?' Rose asked.

'You're not old enough to remember this, but when women were trying to get the vote, they got up to all sorts of protests and we're going to copy one of them. We're going to get as many people together as we can. Each person will have a hammer, I've only got two so they'll have to bring their own. Then we're going to go to the wall a week Saturday, and the whole lot of us will start to bash it as hard as we can.'

Rose took one of the hammers off him and tested its weight. 'But surely hammers like that won't knock down a big wall,' she said.

Bob took the hammer back and stroked it as if it was an old friend. 'I don't suppose it will, but that's not the point. I'm going to give a nod to the press, they're always looking for a good story. Lily and I met a reporter at the Town Hall last week. He can come and take pictures.

'Not of me, he's not,' I interrupted.

He patted my arm. 'We'll make sure of that. If we play our cards right, I reckon we'll get on the front page of the weekly news, might even get in the national press if we get a big enough crowd. If it doesn't get Councillor Tallis going, we'll take stronger action.'

We spent ages trying to think of ways to get people to come out and join in the action. In the end Rose came up with the answer, 'Let's make it a street party. Everyone can bring a bit of food and drink, I'll borrow some urns from the church hall to make the tea …'

'Wonderful idea, Rose. I can get trestle tables

from the club,' Bob said, 'and let's have fancy dress. That'll get their attention.'

'We should invite the Councillor, too,' I said, 'if the press is going to be there, he'll have a chance to make a speech and puff himself up into a big I-am.'

'Great idea, Lily. Can you type up the posters? We'll need at least one in each street and one in the post office and one in the shop.'

Rose spoke up, 'We've got a duplicating machine where I work. Leave it to me and Lily.'

There was silence for a minute as we thought this through.

'I might be able to spring a few surprises,' Bob said, tapping the side of his nose. He wouldn't be drawn to tell us what they were though.

Back at home Mum had the kettle on, bless her.

'How'd it go?' she asked, spooning tea into the pot and getting out the cups and saucers.

As we sat down, I told her all the ins and outs.

'Sounds like you're really enjoying it all,' she said.

'I surprised myself. Never thought I'd speak out in a meeting.'

'Yet there you were, having your say.'

I smiled, 'Bob and Rose are pretty good at making you feel one of them.'

Mum poured boiling water over the tea leaves,

'Lily, you're as good as them any day. I'm really proud of you.'

～

A week later a huge crowd joined the street party. It had rained earlier and I kept looking anxiously at the sky, hoping the downpour would stop. It happened with half an hour to spare. The roads were washed clean and the air smelled fresh, with fragrance from the roses in the gardens drifting through. Headlights from the occasional car made the roads glisten, and lights from some houses cast a romantic glow on the street. The smell of chicken cooking somehow found its way from the other side of the wall. Like most people from our side, we only had chicken at Christmas.

To my surprise, as well as us Sunbury people, there were about twenty undergraduates wearing red shirts or fancy dress here to support our cause. They all looked healthy with smooth hands and smiles showing straight white teeth.

'They're in the Communist Party too,' Bob said with a wry smile, 'a rare breed, rich people with a social conscience. Let's be grateful for them.' He made a point of going to thank them for coming.

As the afternoon wore on I was reminded of the

parable of Jesus feeding the five thousand. It seemed like one minute there were ten bare trestle tables, and the next they were laden with food. There was a mountain of sandwiches: fish-paste, cheese, jam, you name it. There were heaps of cakes, pork pies cut into wedges, and even unseasonal mince pies. It was the biggest street party since the Coronation of King George VI a couple of years earlier.

The beer was the first to go.

People had done themselves proud with their fancy dress. I counted at least five Hitlers; about a dozen flapper girls; several people in old fashioned bathing costumes I suspected were made from dyed bloomers and vests; kings, queens, Robin Hoods; and some spivs with trilbys and narrow painted-on moustaches. The children were having a great time dressed as pirates, fairies, Rupert Bears, princesses, robbers and goodness knows what else. I wore Suffragette colours and Mum made me a sash with 'Votes for Women' to wear across my front. I also had a badge Rose had made for all of us in the steering group. It was quite big and it said *The Wall Must Fall*. At least a dozen people came up to chat to me when they saw it and they were all on our side and not just here for the knees-up. I felt proud to be part of something so important for the estate.

Mum and Dad were there. Dad wasn't in fancy

dress, but Mum had wrapped a sheet around herself very cleverly so she looked like a Greek Goddess. She had a belt covered in gold paper round her waist and had made a crown of bit of foliage. You'd have thought her and Dad were just a normal loving couple. They walked up together arm in arm. Dad had his hand on her back while he spoke to other people, and she was polite to him. But after a couple of beers Dad started to get mouthy, and made sarcastic comments about her. I sat talking to some people opposite them and every time Mum passed an opinion on anything he'd chip in with 'Don't listen to her, she's just a char, what would she know?' Or 'She talks out the back of her head.'

I could feel my anger rising, but didn't want to spoil the event by making a scene.

'Mum,' I said, leaning over to get her attention, 'I could really do with some help down the other end of the tables. Got a minute?'

She gave me a little wink and walked round the table to join me.

'Come and meet Jean's mum and get away from him,' I said. 'Mind you, you won't be able to join in the Glamorous Grannies competition like her.'

Mum looked shocked, 'Surely Jean's never had a baby.'

I chuckled, 'I hope not. No, it's her brother's

wife. They emigrated to America a year before we all moved here.'

I went back to find Jean who was wearing the prettiest flapper dress of the lot. It was black with lots of fringes and she'd got some long black beads to go with it. Round her head she had a black band of ribbon with a feather on one side.

'Where d'you get that?' I asked, looking down at my own sad effort.

'My aunt's 'ad it in the back of 'er wardrobe since she was a young girl. Great, ain't it.' She did a twirl and all the tassels spun out like those seats on long chains in rides at the fun fair.

On the green at the other end of the street a brass band started up, Bob's surprise I supposed, and they led a procession of people all around the estate. Regular Pied Pipers they were, leading a Conga of kids and adults in various stages of drunkenness and excitement. As we walked round people came out of their houses and joined the line or waved Union Jacks and shouted encouragement. Soon people were dancing and singing and kids were running riot. Fred surprised us by grabbing Rose and doing a waltz with her, and she surprised him by kissing him on the cheek when they'd finished. Then smelling his breath, she hurried away.

It was the perfect antidote to all the worry about Hitler.

PICTURE HOUSE GIRLS

I noticed several flashbulbs going off.

'National press,' Bob said, his chest puffed right up. 'I reckon there's a couple of hundred people here. We'll wait till things calm down a bit and then get on with what we're here for. I've seen a lot of hammers tucked in pockets.'

I looked around and he was right; I could see three men with hammers from where I stood. 'There's a lot of bobbies, too. I must have seen at least twenty. Mind you, some of them have had a beer or two. They look in a good mood.'

It was a couple of hours before people calmed down a bit and then Councillor Tallis, who'd only just turned up, stood on a chair and called for attention. Bob handed him a megaphone. He looked very smart and official in a suit and tie.

'Ladies and gentlemen,' he said, 'I am fully behind your fight to get this wall demolished. It cuts you off, like caged animals from your entitled thoroughfare. In a country fit for heroes that will soon need heroes again, this is a public shame. The people of Sunbury are kept behind this wall like prisoners in a Concentration Camp.' He paused so he could be sure everyone was listening. 'Come what may, I intend to fight to get this wall knocked down.'

There was a huge cheer and people started singing 'He's a jolly good fellow.' Cameras flashed, drinks were downed, and me and the others in the steering group patted ourselves on the back. Now we'd get somewhere. Then the councillor held up his hand and called for silence.

'Now the leader of this protest, Bob Burton, wants to say something.'

Bob took the megaphone. It was hard to tell if he was wearing fancy dress or not. He was wearing a red trilby, red shoes and a blue and white striped tie with a crumpled black suit.

He tapped a glass to get attention. 'My army, my fighters, my heroes, I am proud of you all for coming here today to support our fight. This wall has stood for too long, a symbol of the oppression of the people in Sunbury by the people the other side of that wall. The people of Sunbury will win this fight, demolish this abomination. Are you with me, Sunbury?' He paused and some people shouted 'yes'. With great exaggeration he put his hand to his ear. 'Can't hear you. ARE YOU WITH ME, SUNBURY?' His voice was much louder this time.

There was a deafening 'Yes' from the crowd. When the noise faded he continued, 'People of Sunbury. Now is the time for action.' He produced his hammer out of his bag and waved it in the air. 'All of you with hammers, can you make your way towards the wall. Don't do anything yet. Wait for my command.'

There was a great shuffling of people as men, and

a few women, came forward with their hammers. I was disappointed it was only about thirty people when we had such a big crowd. Bob saw my turned-down mouth.

'It's enough to look good in the papers, Girl.' he whispered.

He turned to the crowd again.

'Right, my soldiers, on my word, move forward.'

He turned. In front of him was the wall, but now, directly in front of it was a line of policemen, their arms linked, forming a barrier. Shocked, Bob stood as still as a lamppost.

In the middle of the row of policemen was some sort of police bigwig with a lot of gold buttons and braids.

He took the megaphone from Bob and turned towards the crowd.

'It's been a great afternoon, Ladies and Gentlemen and I know you want to see this wall demolished. I don't care if you knock it down, but I want to make it clear, you must not touch any of my officers.'

There was a chorus of complaints. He held up his hand for silence. 'I repeat, you must not touch any of my officers. That's either directly or through bits of masonry falling on them.'

There was more grumbling.

'DO YOU UNDERSTAND, LADIES AND GENTLEMEN?' he repeated.

The complaints started quietly again, but rose louder and louder like waves on a seashore in a storm. Some men started to move forward.

Coward that I am, I looked round for somewhere to hide.

Bob quickly took control. He took the megaphone back and shouted, 'Listen to me, my army, my heroes, my hammer wielders. We cannot risk injury to the police or any of you being arrested. Councillor Tallis has given us his word, on record in front of the press, that he will get this wall demolished.'

'Yeah, but can we trust 'im?' someone shouted.

Councillor Tallis stood up, 'I can't personally knock it down, but I promise to do my best to influence the relevant people to get it demolished.'

'Yeah, says you,' the man shouted again.

'Can't believe a word you damn politicians say,' shouted someone else.

The councillor waved his arm in a *quieten down* gesture. He took the megaphone.

'I will show you how sincere I am. Next week I am meeting with the head of the council and the council's solicitor. Now, in front of you all, I invite Bob to come with me. He'll let you know what happens and I promise, I'll be fighting for you.'

Bob took over again, 'Thank you Councillor, I accept your invitation.' They shook hands on it, then Bob turned back to the crowd.

'The gentlemen of the press are here for a good picture. Inspector, if we promise not to hit the wall, will you ask your men to step aside?'

There was a moment's pause and then the policeman gave the order to his men who slowly moved to the ends of the wall, but no further.

Bob nodded to the reporters and turned to the crowd again. 'The important thing today is to get things moving and stay within the law.'

Someone booed and Bob held up his hand to quieten him. 'Those of us with hammers will walk to the wall and hold up the hammers. Do not go near the police officers. I repeat, do not go near the police officers. We just hold up the hammers while photos are taken.'

The people with hammers shuffled forward and got in place. Bob spoke again, 'The matter doesn't end here, the wall *will* fall. Hold up your hammers for the photos, then let's enjoy the rest of the day.'

He nodded to the band who struck up a cheery tune. I could feel the atmosphere relax. The photos were taken and hammers put away.

Bob thanked everyone for their co-operation, put away his hammer and turned off the megaphone. He looked at me and wiped his brow, 'Phew, never imagined they'd give in that easily. Thought we'd have a punch-up on our hands. Oh, by the way, you're coming to the meeting too.'

The failure to knock down the wall wasn't the end of the street party. We had all the competitions to judge and got Bob to judge some and Councillor Tallis judged others. As well as the Glamorous Grannies, there was the best kid's outfit, the prettiest girl, and not forgetting the pram race. Men pushed women dressed as babies in bonnets and shawls down the road. The fastest pram won, although a couple turned over, throwing the big babies into the road with howls of laughter. Finally, we had a massive sing-song. All the old tunes were remembered from the Great War, a chilling reminder of what was to come. *'Sister Susie's sewing shirts for soldiers ; Keep right on to the end of the road ; When I send you a picture of Berlin,'* and loads more I hadn't heard before.

When we'd all run out of energy Bob got onto his megaphone. 'Please everyone, we've had a lovely day. Please help us to clear all this up.'

A lot of people had already gone, but a dozen willing souls set to and it was cleared up quicker than I could have thought possible.

Ever since I'd spotted Dad at the dance hall, I'd wondered how to find out more about his affair. I was thinking of it as an affair, but the truth was I had no idea if it was. He could have just picked up that ... strumpet, that night. Maybe he picked up women regularly, although it was beyond me to understand how anyone would find him even vaguely attractive. Maybe he found easy women who were willing to put up with him for the evening for the price of a few drinks. Any more than that didn't bear thinking about. Bad enough thinking about him and Mum doing, well, you know what, I certainly didn't want to think about him and anyone else. Yuk.

I'd got nowhere with finding out more. I couldn't follow him when he went out for his supposed Old Boys' evenings. I'd seen plenty of films where followers hopped into shop doorways, or hid behind a newspaper, or bent to tie a shoelace, but none of those tactics would work in our street. No shops, not enough people to hide behind and he'd recognise me even if I was bending down. And there was no way I had enough money to pay a private detective.

'What're you going to do, once you find out?' Jean asked me when we were discussing it at the Dream Palace one evening.

Good point, I thought, what was I going to do? He already knew I knew, though it had never been discussed again. I could challenge him, but that would make the air at home even more poisonous. Who knows, he might even move out. It would be a blessing because me and Mum wouldn't have to put up with his constant moans, but I knew she'd never manage for money. Her cleaning jobs and what I gave her would never pay the rent and all the bills.

So I'd got a big fat no-where with my investigations and my heart sank whenever I thought about my poor Mum being cheated on.

Then something happened to change all that.

My bus home after the Dream Palace shift got diverted because of road works. It was late and a light drizzle freckled the windows, and street lights blurred. I was sitting thinking about the film I'd just been watching (or watching in bits as we had to do). It was a really funny comedy, *Calling All Crooks*, with Douglas Wakefield. We stopped at a bus stop and something half caught my eye. Right opposite the stop a front door opened and a man walked out. Deep in thought about the film I didn't take much notice as the man hugged and kissed the women, clearly saying goodbye.

Then my heart jumped.

It was my dad.

I almost threw myself under the seat in front, terrified he'd get onto the same bus. He couldn't have missed me, I was sitting downstairs and quite close to the door. He knew I knew, but that was different from him being caught in the act.

Only the fear of looking crazy kept me where I was in my seat, although I put my hand up to my face hoping it would hide me a bit. My mind raced – how would I deal with it? Would he pretend he couldn't see me? Would he shout and make a scene thinking I was snooping on him?

But luck favoured me. The woman said something and Dad turned around and chatted to her again. I could see she was about thirty and had blond hair, but couldn't see much else.

The bus just started pulling away when Dad kissed her on the lips and strode off towards home with a jaunty step as if he owned the world.

I felt sick all the way home.

~

The next time we had a day off, Jean and I decided to perm each other's hair. We got together in the lean-to at the back of her house. None of her younger brothers and sisters were there for once. Just as well or the ammonia in the perm solution might have knocked them out.

'You first,' Jean said, taking me to the kitchen sink. She filled it with warm water, got out a jug and ordered me to bend over the sink. Within no time my hair was shampoo'd and ready for the next stage.

I sat on a kitchen chair and Jean put a threadbare towel round my shoulders. I held the rollers in a box on my lap.

'This stuff really stinks,' Jean said as she got the perm mixture ready. 'We'll have to rinse it loads of time or no-one will come near us for weeks.'

She started to put rollers in my hair and almost pulled it out at the roots. 'Hey,' I whimpered, 'that hurts. Have mercy on my head!'

As she worked, we had time to catch up on news. 'How's your mum?' she asked, 'still waiting on you hand and foot?'

'Not any more, she doesn't. Weeks ago I realised how tired she always is, so I do my share now.'

''Bout time, I been doing my share since I was about five. Any news about your Dad?'

I told her about what I'd seen from the bus.

'Feckin' 'ell. Whatcha going to do about it?' she asked, stabbing my scalp with one of the roller pins.

I considered her question. If only I knew. I wished I'd never seen anything. If only we could unknow what we know, life would be easier sometimes.

'It's like this, I don't know what good it will do even if I find out more.'

Her jaw dropped, 'Don't be such a silly bird, 'course you got to find out. You never know when some bit of information might be useful. Now come on, what're you going to do?'

'I don't know. What can I do?' I said, rubbing a sore spot on my forehead where her hand had slipped. 'The only thing I can think of is to pretend I'm still doing the petition about the wall. Knock on her door and try to get her chatting.'

'Spot on, that'll work. Mind you, you'll 'ave to knock on a few other doors in case she spots you going straight to 'ers and gets suspicious like.'

By now she'd finished putting the rollers in my hair and was preparing the stinky perm lotion.

'Let's talk about more cheerful things,' she said, 'which film star do you want to look like?'

∼

So a week later, carrying my clipboard and petition form, I started knocking on doors, my hands trembling. It was a chilly day with heavy cloud and I was glad I'd been pessimistic and worn my winter coat.

I began five houses down from *hers*. The first two answered my questions quickly. They weren't much interested because they didn't live in Sunbury so the wall didn't affect them. The third was elderly, a retired military man who wanted to tell me all about his battles, but never gave me a straight answer to my questions. The fourth was out.

The fifth door was nothing special, it was no different from the others in the row. The faded grey paint was scratched here and there, especially around the keyhole. But the brass knocker and letter box shone brightly.

I knocked and it sounded hollow, so I didn't expect any answer. I made to leave, then, with no warning, the door was suddenly opened by an older, grey-haired woman. She was wearing a patterned wrap-around pinny and slippers with woolly bobbles on the top. Behind her I could see rose patterned wallpaper and a tiny hall table in some sort of dark wood.

I went into my spiel about the wall. I could have said it in my sleep. She stopped a minute then said, 'I don't know much about it, Love. Hang on a minute. I'll ask my daughter.'

She shouted over her shoulder, 'Grace, come here a minute, Love.'

I was turning to a new page on my clipboard when I heard footsteps coming from the back of the house, so I didn't see her. If I had I might have run away, coward that I am.

'What is it, Mum?' a new voice said.

I looked up.

It was *her*. *My dad's bit on the side.*

I shouldn't have been surprised, after all I knew she lived there.

She was taller than me, about 5'5", dressed nicely with shoulder length wavy hair done like Ingrid Bergman. Not pretty, but a nice face, like someone you'd want to be friendly with.

I hated her on sight.

I feigned a coughing fit and the older woman patted me on the back so hard I nearly lost my balance.

'You all right, Love? Want a drink of water?'

She all but pulled me into their kitchen. Before I could say a word she handed me a glass of water and put on the kettle. Then she opened a tin and put two biscuits on a plate.

She pulled out a chair and indicated for me to sit down.

'You must be ready for a break, interviewing all these people. Here, have a biscuit and I'll make you a cuppa. How many sugars do you want?'

She was kindness itself, but I couldn't sit there with that floozy; that home-wrecker. Without a word, I pushed the chair away so fiercely it banged against the wall. I snatched up the clipboard and dashed out the front door. I ran all the way to the corner of the street before I stopped to get my breath. What had I been thinking? I was never going have enough brass neck to have it out with her. Too chicken. I wondered what they thought of me dashing off so rudely. If they told everyone, it would reflect badly on the fight for the wall. Sometimes I needed to think a bit more before I acted.

My mind was in turmoil what with worrying about it and wondering what my Dad was going to do. Desert Mum and live with this woman? Maybe she made him feel young again. Poor Mum. Poor worn out Mum.

Next day I told Jean all about seeing Dad's bit on the side. She listened with her mouth open as I got to the bit where I got invited in.

'Cor, you're braver than I thought you were,' she said, 'what d'you do then?'

'I got home as quick as I could and made a cup of tea to calm down.'

Her top lip curled. 'I was wrong, you're chicken. You should've punched 'er. Want me to go round and give 'er one?'

My eyes became saucers. 'No! Don't you dare. I wish I'd never told you now. For all we know she doesn't know he's married.'

She put her head to one side as if she were talking to a child. 'Well, you can't just let it go. What're you going to do?'

Fifteen minutes later we were still throwing around ideas but no nearer to a workable plan. It'd do no good to tell my mum. She couldn't afford to leave him. Tackling my dad would be worse than useless, he'd just deny everything. And tackling the strumpet – well, she could say we were out of our minds. It would just make matters worse for everyone.

We had to give up and wait to see how things progressed.

~

A few days later I was on my way to my shift at the pictures. My feet ached from my day's work and I wanted nothing more than to sit down and rest. But as usual, the bus was late, so once it stopped I had to hurry to start work on time.

I was walking quickly towards the entrance when I stopped in my tracks. Not a yard from the door was Edward, walking with a very elegant older woman. My heart skipped a silly beat when I saw him. I looked at him, not sure whether to say hello, but he took the lead.

'Lily,' he said, smiling, 'lovely to see you.'

I smiled but couldn't think of a thing to say.

The woman looked me up and down in my uniform as if she'd just scraped something smelly off her expensive shoes.

'And who's this, Edward?' she asked.

'Mother, this is Lily, who works part time at the

Dream Palace,' he said. 'We met a couple of months ago by accident.'

She looked at me with frosty politeness. 'How lovely. Nice to meet you. Miss ...'

'Baker, Lily Baker.'

'Lovely to meet you. Do please forgive me, Miss Baker, but we must press on. We have an appointment.'

She may have been polite, but it was the chilliest politeness I'd ever heard. Edward hung back a minute.

'I'm sorry I missed you last time I had leave,' he said. 'I'm off to camp again tomorrow. May I write to you?'

I tried to look serious, but my big smile gave me away. 'Best write to me here,' I said.

～

The day for the next meeting with the council officials came round a lot quicker than I'd have liked. My confidence was growing a bit, but truth was I was still scared of people in authority, and the head of the Council was certainly that. And, as for their solicitor, I'd never spoken to one in my life. I wondered if he'd wear a wig and gown like I'd seen in films.

Bob and I walked up the hill towards the Council

offices, hot from the exertion and the sun which put in an appearance for the first time in several days.

'You're not going to ask me to say anything this time, are you? I asked Bob, my voice shaking.

He patted my shoulder. 'Don't you worry, my dear. We may not have to do much, after all this is the Councillors meeting their officials. We're just there to make sure everything he promised to say gets said fair and square.'

'But if he doesn't…'

'Then we'll make our voices heard. Nice and polite though. We don't want to give them any reason to turn against us.'

So once again we walked along those long corridors with blank doors, just occasionally passing someone rushing from one place to another, their arms full of files. It all seemed so important. I wondered if all my studying would one day mean I could dress like the women there did, and walk in that busy, confident way, in a smart suit and court shoes. It all seemed as if it would take a million years, if I got there at all.

Bob must have noticed my mood, 'Shoulders back, head up, my girl. Show them you're as good as they are, because you are. Always remember you are a unique person, just like everyone else. We've all got our place in the world and yours is an important one, especially today.'

I could have kissed him. He was a bit of an odd bod, but he had a great way of understanding other people's feelings and saying exactly the right thing. If only I'd had him for a Dad.

I followed his instructions and held my head up; put my shoulders back and walked more firmly. It was surprising how much better it made me feel.

'That's it,' Bob said grinning, 'you look at good as anyone here.'

We went into the meeting and Councillor Tallis told us to sit in seats against the wall as we weren't officially invited. They were, dark wood with cracked leather seats that creaked when we sat down. The chairs were up against a whole wall of leather bound books that looked like no-one had opened them for a hundred years. I must say I bristled a bit at being made to sit against the wall, but Bob nudged me and I sat quietly, holding my notebook so tightly my knuckles were white.

Councillor Tallis explained the position to the other two men and even told them what I'd said to him about the inconvenience for Mum and other people on the estate. From the look on their faces, I could tell they weren't impressed by what he was saying. The solicitor, who was dressed in an ordinary suit, was a different one from before. He patted a file in front of him.

'I'll be taking instructions from Mr Black. He's

the Head of Council. I would need to look further into the legal aspects even if it was decided action could be taken.'

Mr. Black, the big boss, nodded, his double chins wobbling. 'That's right, we can't decide anything now. We'll look into it and write to you in a few weeks.'

I leapt to my feet, 'A few weeks! That's not fast enough. Before you know it, Winter'll be here and people will have to trudge through the wet and cold to get round the wall.'

That stopped them. They looked amazed I could speak, much less say something a bit forceful. Bob tugged at my arm and pulled me back in my chair.

As if I hadn't spoken, Mr Black repeated, 'We'll be writing to you in a few weeks when we have had time to investigate the matter thoroughly.'

Then he looked at me, 'I think you have much to learn, young lady, about how these matters work.'

Although I was still hopping mad, I wished the ground would open and swallow me up. Me and my big mouth, maybe my outburst had ruined any hopes of them helping us. And Bob was going to be so disappointed in me, after all the faith he'd had in me.

As we left the room I was shaking so much I dropped my notebook and stumbled when I tried to pick it up. Bob kindly put his arm under my elbow and helped me up.

'I'm so sorry …' I started, wondering if he would ever forgive me.

'Forget it,' he said, 'I've done worse. You don't win the battles I've won against capitalist employers without putting your foot down very heavily and very regularly. It's all good learning.'

When I got home that night there was a letter waiting for me. It was such a rare event, Mum was almost hopping up and down wanting to know what it was about. It looked official with my name and address typed and everything.

I guessed what it was. My fingers trembled as I tore it open. I could hardly focus to read it.

'Well, what is it then?' Mum asked.

I didn't answer. I just grabbed her and danced her round the kitchen table.

'I've passed my exams! I've passed! Pitman's English and Typing!'

She was nearly as excited as me and hugged me so tight I could hardly breathe.

'Well if this doesn't call for a drop of sherry left over from Christmas, I don't know what does,' she said, beaming.

She stood on a chair and poked around in the back of the kitchen cupboard. After a few seconds of moving round flour, beans and other dried goods she pulled out the bottle from behind some baking tins. 'Had to hide it from your dad,' she said.

She poured us both tiny glasses. We said, 'Cheers' and took little sips.

'What'll you do with the qualifications, Lily?'

'I dunno. I've been so worried about getting them and with that and everything else I haven't thought much more. Mind you, Bob always said I should have a plan.'

She took another little sip of the sherry. 'Well, I never. My daughter, with qualifications,' she said and leaned over and patted my hand.

I laughed, 'I must have got my brains from somewhere, Mum, and it certainly wasn't from Dad.'

Later in bed, I couldn't sleep. Qualifications. No-one I knew had any. Not like these anyway. I could start looking for a job, but didn't know what sort of job they'd be used for. None of my family or friends did anything but factory or cleaning jobs - that sort of thing. Know your place was the message we got loud and clear. Don't step out of line, do what everyone else does. It was tempting to think that way, because after all, this was all I'd ever known. Okay, we'd moved, but although this house was better than our old one, with electricity and everything, it still all seemed familiar and safe. We even still had some of the same neighbours.

In the factory the next day I looked at the office staff differently. When we left for our breaks, we walked past the offices and could see them through the window. The typists always looked busy, hitting the keys so hard we could hear them through the glass. I wondered what qualifications they had. My typing speeds were getting better. Perhaps with that and these certificates, I could apply for a job as a typist. I worried the typists might be a bit up themselves. Would they talk to the likes of me? Would I feel like a fish out of water? I decided I would need to work somewhere else if I got a typing job so they wouldn't always think of me as the girl who sewed on sleeves.

8. LUCK

Karma, advantage

Sometimes it can seem as if the world is a hard place to cope with, but sometimes luck is just on your side. A few days after I wondered if I could apply for a typist's job, I walked into the office at the Dream Palace and Jean was sitting having a cup of tea with the boss, Mr. Simmons.

'Hasn't she told you?' Jean was saying, 'she got good marks, too.'

Mr Simmons looked up at me, 'This right, Lily? You passed your exams?'

I could hardly speak for grinning, 'That's right, I was ever so pleased. Now I'm wondering about applying for a typist's job.'

He raised an eyebrow, 'So you can type as well?

What speed?'

'Last time I checked I could do twenty five words a minute.'

He looked thoughtful, then turned to Jean. 'Would you leave me and Lily for a few minutes?'

Her mouth turned down and she dragged her feet like a sulky teenager as she made for the door.

'Sit down, Lily,' Mr Simmons said, patting the chair Jean had been sitting in. 'Can I get you some tea?'

It's funny, but whenever bosses speak to me, I think I've done something wrong, even if I haven't. I expect it's a left-over from being called out by the teacher at school for daydreaming. As I sat down and watched him pour the tea, my knees shook and my heart thumped fit to be seen through my uniform.

'You don't have to look scared, Lily,' he said, 'I want to put a proposition to you.'

At first my stupid brain thought he was going to propose. How daft can you get? Him a married man and forty years older than me.

'You might know my wife's been poorly on and off lately. Well, we're not getting any younger and we want to spend more time together. Never get a minute free running this place. Our oldest lives in the other end of the country and our youngest is thinking of moving to Australia. We'd like to see them regularly. See what I mean?'

I didn't really. I couldn't see what it had to do with me.

'That's nice,' I said.

'Lily, I've seen you working here for a while and always been impressed. You work hard and you think about things before acting. Not everyone does that. Now you've got your qualifications and can type, would you be interested in being trained up to help me? Be my assistant manager?'

My jaw fell open. Me, an assistant manager? It was so much higher-up than I'd been thinking.

'I ... I ...'

He got out a packet of digestive biscuits and offered me one. Without being conscious of what I was doing, I took one and put in on my saucer.

Mr Simmons patted my arm, 'I can see it's a lot to think about. But we can take a few weeks to train you up, so you feel confident and know what you're doing.'

My brain began to work again, 'But what about the shirt factory?'

He sat back and smiled. 'You'd have to leave there. This will be a full-time job although the hours won't be the same, you'll have to do some evenings and weekends. I'll pay you a little bit more than you earn there while you're training and more again when you know the ropes. What do you think?'

I didn't have to think. 'Yes. Oh, yes. I'd love to.

Thank you ever so much, Mr Simmons.'

He looked relieved. 'Tell you what. Come in to see me in a couple of days when I've had time to plan your training, then we can get started.'

My head was in a whirl. 'Should I give in my notice at the factory?' I asked, still not believing my luck.

'Yes, go ahead. Tell them tomorrow.'

I had trouble walking out of his office. I wanted to skip, hop and jump I was so excited. Jean was waiting just outside the door, her ear almost pressed to the glass.

'Couldn't hear a damn thing,' she grumbled, 'you get told off for something?'

I grabbed her hands and danced her in a circle. Her scowl turned to a smile, even though she hadn't a clue what was happening.

'What, what?' she demanded, 'what's happened?'

I had to calm my breathing before I could speak, 'You'll never guess what. He wants me to be assistant manager.'

A frown wrinkled her pretty forehead, 'What do you mean, assistant manager?'

'You know, help him manage the Dream Palace. Act as manager when he's not here. He's going to train me up.' I clapped my hands, 'I'm so lucky and it's all down to you telling him I'd passed my exams.'

She went quiet for a minute, 'But Lil, it means you'll be my boss. How's that going to work?'

I gave her a big grin. 'You'll just have to behave yourself, won't you!'

~

The bus home seemed to take for ever. I heard the pitter-patter of rain on the roof and looked out of the window. People were scurrying here and there, raising their umbrellas, the bright colours contrasting with the dull sky. They slowed down the bus because they had to shake off the rain and fold up their brollies before they got on, or open them ready for when they got off. Probably it just seemed slow because I was in such a hurry to get home. I couldn't wait to tell Mum. Luckily she was still up.

She'd just finished mopping the floor and was putting the mop outside the back door to dry.

'Take off your shoes,' she said as I walked in, 'and don't go messing up my nice clean floor with your wet umbrella.'

I tiptoed into the kitchen in my bare feet. 'Mum, you'll never guess what's happened. Mr Simmons has asked me to be his assistant. I'll be an Assistant Manager. Imagine!'

She smiled and clapped her hands. 'Lil, that's

fantastic, makes it worth all the while you've spent studying. But what about if it doesn't work out? You might not get back into the shirt factory.'

'I've been thinking about that. There's a munitions factory opening up next month. What with the war on the way and everything, I expect there'll be work there. I'm more worried about being Jean's boss.'

Mum laughed, 'Don't worry, you can keep her in line.'

We heard the key in the door and the celebration atmosphere changed immediately as Dad walked in.

His eyes narrowed as he looked at us. 'What you two doing up this late? What's happened?'

'Mr Simmons has offered me a job as his assistant manager.'

He snorted. 'What you? An assistant manager? That bloke must be off his head to think he could trust you to do a job like that. You can't even keep your bedroom tidy.'

Mum rarely argued with him. She knew it was a waste of time and she might get a smack for her troubles. This time she stood up for me.

'Ignore him Love, it's great news. What with all the book learning and things you've been doing, you'll be great at the job.'

'He's going to give me training, Mum.'

Dad sneered again, 'Training, my arse. He just

wants to get inside your knickers, you mark my words.'

I stood upright and looked him straight in the eyes. 'Get inside my knickers? Is that what adulterers do, then?'

There was a second's silence, then he looked at me as if he wished I would die. 'Bitch!' he hissed. He walked out of the room and stomped up the stairs.

~

The next day was a Sunday and I had a whole, wonderful day without work. Me and Jean had planned to go for a walk to Lyons Corner House and treat ourselves to tea and a bun.

She arrived at my house so breathless it took her three goes to tell me the news.

'Quick, come with me. Someone's only gone and drove through the wall.'

It was true. We stood looking in amazement at the jagged gap and the car looked as crumpled as tissue paper.

'Is the driver okay?' I asked Dai Evans who was standing nearby.

'It's like this, see. He drives into the wall and we was standing by yere. Thought he'd be a gonna, but he gets out right as rain and just walks off. Bit of blood on his head, mind, but nothing to worry about. Morris Minor he 'ad, good for nothing now.'

'Did he do it on purpose? We haven't planned anything like this.'

'Dunno, Sweetheart. Not being funny, but I think it was just an accident. Perhaps he nicked the car. Young thing, he was.'

'Come on,' Jean said, grabbing my arm. 'Let's walk through. Coming, Dai?'

By now there were about two dozen people standing nearby. We all squeezed round the car and through the wall, stepping carefully over fallen bricks and barbed wire. It was the first time we'd seen the bigger houses for a while. There was a lot of muttering around us as people looked at the luxury the people this side of the wall lived in. It wasn't just the houses that were better. The gardens all looked lush and green with flowers everywhere. People had done a good job on our side of the wall, but without money to spend on plants we'd had to do the best we could with cuttings cadged from each other. I was willing to bet some of these people had gardeners.

Looking between the houses, I could see some of the had Anderson shelters in their back garden in case of war.

A good few net curtains twitched and some of the posh people came to their doors and frowned at us or stood with their hands on their hips. We just laughed at them. It was like we'd been let out of jail. Jean started singing, 'Jeepers, Creepers, where'd you get those peepers ...' and before you knew it, we linked arms and everyone else joined in. We had a real good sing-song and walked right to the end of the road.

On the way back, we could see Sunbury again through the gap in the wall. What a contrast to the expensive side. I wouldn't really complain; our house was a hundred times better than the dump we lived in before. At least we didn't have to walk to the end of the garden for the smelly old lav. But the difference with this side of the wall was, well, a lot. Where our houses were joined together and all looked the same, these ones were bigger and all separate. And every single house had a car.

'Think they'll knock the rest of the wall down?' Dai asked me.

'Who knows? I can't see the people from the posh side being willing to let it happen,' I said.

Jean wrinkled her nose in disgust, 'No, you mark my words, they'll make sure that wall is put back as it was pretty quick. Money talks.'

She was right. Within a week the builders were back and the wall was repaired, barbed wire and all.

We were back to stage one.

9. ALTERCATION

ACRIMONIOUS EXCHANGE, WAR OF WORDS

Bob lifted the megaphone to his mouth. His outfit was a pink and grey brocade waistcoat, black trousers, a black trilby trimmed with a blue feather and red shoes.

'My marchers, my army, my heroes. Are you ready?'

The day we'd planned for nearly three weeks was here. Our aim was to gather as many protestors as possible, march through the estate, then stand at the wall with our banners, making a lot of noise. A lot of noise.

The sky was a perfect blue, and the temperature just right, although I noticed there were storm clouds on the horizon.

'This march will do a power of good,' Bob said looking cheerful. 'For starters, we'll get more of the people from Sunbury involved. Then the people from the streets we walk through will know we're taking action. And the press will be taking photos the whole time.'

'Maybe some of them will join the march,' I interrupted. His mood was infectious and enthusiasm bubbled up in my chest.

'You're right, my girl. Then, when we get to the wall, the noise will give them lot on the other side something to think about. It'll look good in the papers too.'

Bob called to the crowd again, 'Ready?'

Over a hundred assorted people from the estate lifted their heads and chorused, 'We're ready!'

And as if to prove the point, all hell let loose. Banners were waved saying, 'Down with the wall' or 'The wall must fall!' People started banging saucepan lids with spoons, or ringing bicycle bells or blowing whistles. One person even had a drum. The noise was enough to knock a small child sideways.

As we walked I noticed for the first time there were no police around. On our previous demonstrations there were always police walking alongside us. Most were okay, but some were a bit rough and too ready with their truncheons if they thought someone looked like trouble.

'I told the coppers about the march,' Bob said,

'and they were planning to be here. Perhaps there's an emergency somewhere.'

'Got yer speech ready?' Jean asked me. I looked at her in amazement. Me, make a speech? I'd as soon ride a bicycle to the moon. She frowned as she looked at me. 'Well, 'ave you?'

'I... I... I can't.' My mind went blank. Had Bob asked me to do a speech? Had I forgotten? I could feel heat rushing up from my chest.

Jean's face split into an enormous grin and she nudged me so hard I nearly fell over. 'Just kidding. I meant Bob.' She looked over to him. ''ave you, Bob? Got yer speech ready?'

His response was to wave a scruffy piece of paper over his head. It didn't look much but I knew he'd get people going.

We set off in high spirits. There were Mums with their little ones in prams; youngsters skipping and laughing with their mates; older people walking slowly; and a couple of people pushing bikes. The sun came out from behind a cloud and everyone looked cheerful. As we walked from street to street lots of people came out of their houses and cheered us on, and a few quickly closed their front doors and joined us.

But not all.

'Clear off, you lot. I just got the baby to sleep,' shouted one angry Mum holding a screaming child.

'Bugger off, bloody Commies,' shouted an old soldier, waving his walking stick.

'You're wasting your time!' called someone else.

Bob just waved and smiled at them. 'Ignore them. We've got right and numbers on our side.'

Our neighbour's little boy ran up to me and pulled my skirt. 'Got any sweets? he asked.

I shook my head but he held up both arms. I grabbed him and whirled him round a few times enjoying his squeals of delight. One of his shoes flew off and he thought it was the best joke ever. I felt like skipping myself - it was such a good turnout. Surely the council would take action after this. They'd been putting us off for so long at times I felt despair that we'd ever get the wall taken down.

I looked for Jean. Naturally, she was chatting to some lad and one I'd never seen before. Her eyes shone and her curls bounced as she walked. I couldn't hear what she was saying over the noise of the crowd, but I'd have bet ten bob she was twisting him round her little finger.

As we turned a corner someone started playing a trumpet and before we knew it everyone was singing *When the Saints Go Marching In*. We were a platoon of good natured protestors. Kids marched in tune, their arms swinging high, and adults did little dances as they walked. Satchmo would have been proud if he'd seen us.

We wove our way round streets, criss-crossing and doubling back, enjoying every minute. Then, as we walked, the weather started to change. Brief squalls blew paper along the road and whipped leaves off flowers; the storm clouds got dangerously close and the temperature dropped. I pulled my cardigan around myself.

As we got near the wall I was busy chatting to someone when suddenly the atmosphere changed. Feet shuffled, and the singing died as if it had been switched off. There was silence, then hoarse whispers blew through the crowd like a winter gale. I caught odd words,

'Mosley.'

'Goons.'

'… get out of here.'

'Excuse me,' I said, pushing my way between people. I couldn't see the wall for the people in front of me. One or two people grumbled, their jubilant mood of minutes ago evaporated.

It was Blackshirts.

Oswald Mosely's thugs. They were supposed to be illegal.

Six of them.

They stood with military posture, in a perfect straight line with their hands behind their backs; chests pushed forward; black shirts high at the neck. The buckles on their wide leather belts glinted. They looked frighteningly like the Nazis I'd seen on Pathe News. For the first time I understood what people meant when they said their insides turned to water. Bob stiffened beside me, his speech crumpled in his hand.

'Where's the Sheenies?' the one in the middle demanded. His neck was as wide as his head and he had tattoos on his hands.

Silence.

'I said, where's the Sheenies? The Yids? The Jews?' He produced a thick stick from behind his back and began to hit the other palm with it. Each slap loud as a thunderclap.

Bob stepped forward. 'No Jews here.'

You had to know him well to recognise the small tremor in his voice. I went and stood next to him for support. Jean appeared from somewhere and did the same.

'And who might you be?' the bully asked, his hands on his hips.

'Bob Burton.'

'Ah, The Commie.' He spoke with a flat emotionless voice, his face an inhuman mask.

He looked quickly left and right to his men and gave a small nod. As one, they produced sticks and stepped forward. Spreading out, they charged into the crowd. The hushed silence immediately gave way to shouts and screams as the marchers either fought back or tried to get away.

The leader rushed towards us, his eyes hard to see beneath his scowl. He struck Bob on the head without warning, then as Bob staggered he elbowed him in the soft side of his forehead. Bob slumped silently to the floor, blood pooling on the tarmac. His face was slack and the colour left his face. I thought he must be dead. Jean and I quickly bent to help him. I put my ear to his mouth.

'Thank goodness, he's breathing,' I said.

'Lil, I'll see to Bob, you go and 'elp the old people,' Jean said. She turned to her latest beau, 'Bill, go and get the cops and an ambulance. Quick.' Without a word, he ran off, dodging the Blackshirts like bullets.

I looked at the crowd. The Blackshirts were pushing people around shouting, 'Where's the Jews?'

They knocked an old man to the ground. He groaned and curled up in a ball clutching his head. I grabbed a young woman and nodded to her to take care of the old man. Then the Blackshirts slapped an old women round the head so hard she staggered and had to hold on to a tree nearby to stop herself from falling, blood pouring down her cheek. I helped her to the nearest house and knocked on the door. A girl answered the door, she couldn't have been more than eight, but she was holding a baby in one hand and a feeding bottle in the other. When she saw us she looked terrified. I didn't have time to calm her.

'Look after this lady,' I said, then I pushed them both in and slammed the door behind them. I headed quickly back to the fray. Some people were running away as fast as they could, others seemed rooted to the spot as if paralysed. I grabbed Maisie Smith from two doors down and pushed her towards the same house as the old woman. Then I saw a little lad who seemed glued where he was, his hands covering his eyes. I couldn't see his parents; maybe they hadn't come with him. I put my arms round him, dragged him away from the crowd and told him to run home like the wind.

Dai Evans hit one of the Blackshirts round the head with the big saucepan he'd been banging. The Blackshirt fell to the ground like a dead bird, his metal belt buckle clanging against his stick. His swear words blistering the air, Dai whacked another Blackshirt across the back so hard the man fell to his knees with a thud. I kicked him up the backside and he fell flat on his face. I was ashamed to find I could feel the appeal of violence; my heart drumming with adrenaline. It gave me such a feeling of power. The thug quickly got up and ran off cursing and clutching his bloody nose.

I noticed several people pummelling the first thug Dai had attacked. He was still on the ground. They were kicking him so hard I could hear them grunting with the effort. Adina, a heftily built young woman, grabbed the saucepan off Di and another off someone else. Holding both saucepans in one hand, she used the other to yank a Blackshirt off the man he was attacking. Moving her saucepans so she had one in each hand she pounded one side of his head with a saucepan, then the other. His head bounced from one side to the other like a toy. If you'd seen it in a music-hall it would have been funny. Then the man ducked down quickly and the saucepans clanged together making everyone jump. The bully head butted her in the stomach and ran off groaning and holding his glowing ears. I helped her up and was relieved to see she was just winded, not hurt at all. Her dress was caught up in her generous pink knickers and she yanked it out as if that sort of thing happened every day.

'What a shicer!' she said and spat loudly. She stopped and looked around, 'Looks like the schemozzle is over.'

She was right, as suddenly as the attack started, it was over. The only Blackshirts were the ones on the ground. The others had run off. But half a dozen marchers were either on the floor or nursing bits of their body.

'Bunch of shite,' someone near me muttered, slapping his hands together.

Jean was tending to Bob, her dress torn and stained claret. He groaned weakly, holding his head where sticky blood still oozed. He tried to get up, holding her hand tight.

A shadow blotted out the sun.

'What's this then, Bob?' asked the local copper patting his generous stomach and looking at the carnage around us. 'Been up to your old tricks?'

It was clear he wasn't about to go chasing after the Blackshirts. They got clean away.

∼

A week later Bob came to the Dream Palace. He was beaming fit to bust. His outfit that day was red trousers, a white shirt and a pink and green waistcoat. The only sign of his injury from the week before was a plaster on the side of his forehead.

'Got some news,' he said, rocking backwards and forwards on his toes.

I waited, excitement rising.

'What? What?'

'Well, it's like this …' he spoke really slowly.

'What? Tell me? Must be good from the look on your face.'

'Well …'

I punched his arm. 'Tell me!'

'I've just had a letter from Councillor Tallis. They're going to knock down the wall. Next month.' He raised his hands in triumph, 'We've won, Lily. We've won.'

I couldn't believe it. We grabbed each other and did a little jig, grinning fit to bust.

I took him into the office and made him a cuppa. He looked around the scruffy room with interest. 'The glamour's only skin deep in the movie business then,' he said with a wry smile.

I sat opposite him. 'Was it our march that did it, even though those Blackshirts broke it up?'

He stirred his tea. 'They haven't said, but those damn thugs certainly got us more publicity. Maybe the Council felt sorry for us, who knows. I'm not going to argue with them. We've got what we wanted.'

'All thanks to you, Bob,' I said and we toasted our success with tea.

10. WARNING

CAUTION, GUIDANCE

*L*ike all girls, me and Jean go to the Ladies at the same time in dance halls. It's a chance to see to our make-up and talk about everyone. Not that there was ever any privacy for a chat, far from it, as we were crowded in with lots of other girls doing the same thing. And all talking about the men there or the men who weren't there. The smell of make-up and perfume was enough to make anyone choke.

We stood in front of the spotted mirrors. They're really unkind. They show every hair out of place, every freckle, every spot, and everything you don't like about what your looks. Jean was doing her hair and I was trying to make my face look presentable, after getting hot dancing.

'Lil,' Jean said, twisting one of her thick curls.

'I'm going to say something you won't want to hear. Promise you won't get mad at me.'

I remembered the last time we were at a dance and my heart sank. 'Tell me my dad's not here with his floozy again.'

She shook her head, her hair bouncing with the movement. 'Nah, not that. It's about your new bloke, Victor. You keen on him? You haven't said.'

I felt a sense of foreboding. Jean was refusing to catch my eye in the mirror.

'Not sure yet. Don't know him well enough, but he's trying hard.'

'He's a looker for sure,' she said. 'I've seen the other girls all looking at him and wishing they was with him.'

She turned to face me. 'It's like this, see, it's only rumours so don't shoot me if I'm wrong, but well …'

There was a long pause. I waited.

'Jean, just spit it out. The suspense is killing me.'

'Well, I've 'eard 'e's a cad. Tries to get the girls in bed then drops them like hot cakes. Two timer an' all.'

I thought back over the evening. Victor arrived dead on time to meet me and gave me a flower which he tried to put in my hair. It kept falling out. He shook hands with Mum, paid her a nice compliment and even gave her a box of Black Magic. Then he hung on my every word when we walked to the

Roxy. When we arrived he helped me off with my coat. He couldn't have been more of a gent.

Jean interrupted my thoughts. 'Notice anything you'd get suspicious of?'

I thought back over the evening so far. 'Well, once we got here I suppose a lot of girls did say hello to him. Should I be worried about it?'

She scoffed, 'One or two looked like they'd like 'im to drop dead. And did you notice 'e was a long, long time when 'e went to the gents. No-one'd need that long unless they've got Delhi belly.'

'What are you saying, Jean? D'you think he was up to something with another girl?'

She put her arm round me, but I was stiff as a board. 'Dunno, Lil, but you just watch out for yourself. Okay?'

'Okay, but you tell me if you hear anything else,' I said, pulling away from her hug.

''Course I will, I'm not gonna let anyone make a fool of you, am I?'

We left the cloakroom, went back into the ballroom thick with ciggie smoke and the smell of beer. The band were playing *Stairway to the Stars*, a slow number that a lot of couples were dancing to, clinging closely together. We headed over to join Victor and Jean's latest bloke, but he was on his own.

'Where's Victor?' Jean asked, picking up her drink.

'Over there, behind that plant,' her beau said, nodding to the left.

I looked over and Victor was chatting to a girl. A very pretty girl wearing a low cut dress she almost popped out of at the top. She was leaning towards him with her hand on his arm and gazing into his eyes like he was Cary Grant or someone. He didn't seem to mind a bit. The music stopped and he looked around. When he spotted me his face changed, and I thought for a split second I saw a frown appear, then it changed again and he beamed at me, and said goodbye to the girl.

'Who was that then?' Jean asked him as he came to stand beside me.

'Who?'

She rolled her eyes. 'The girl who was just dribbling on you.'

Victor made a dismissive gesture. 'Oh her, she's my cousin. Haven't seen her for ages.'

I took a step away from him and he stepped towards me, putting his arm round my shoulders. I took another step away.

'Oh, come on Lily. She's just my cousin. You jealous? Hope so, it means you like me.'

He leaned towards me and whispered in my ear, 'She's not a patch on you. You're beautiful. Special.'

I could feel myself giving in, giving him the benefit of the doubt. After all, everyone deserves a chance. But I decided to make sure things went slowly. Not much chance of anything else really, with me working most nights at the Dream Palace.

Jean caught my eye and raised an eyebrow. I shrugged my shoulders and gave her a half smile.

Victor behaved perfectly for the rest of the evening. He bought drinks for me and a couple of rounds for all of us. He never even looked at another girl and he was very attentive. Once or twice during slow dances his hand started to slide to places I didn't want it to go, but he was good as gold and stopped as soon as I told him to.

At the end of the evening he walked me to my door. He was keen for a proper kiss goodnight, but I wasn't ready for that. A peck on the lips was all he got. We arranged to go for a walk a few days later when I had time off.

When I got in, Mum was still up; she was sweeping the kitchen floor. She stopped and put the kettle on. I got out the cups and saucers.

When the tea was made we sat down. 'Good evening?' she asked. 'He seems a very polite young man.' She reached over to the shelf and got out the chocolates he'd given her. 'Let's have a couple of these before we go to bed.'

I took my time choosing my favourite chocolate, but only after Mum had taken hers.

'I'm not sure what to make of him to be honest, Mum.'

She raised an eyebrow, 'Why not?'

'Well, mostly he says and does the right thing, but there's something about him doesn't feel right.'

She looked relieved. 'I didn't want to say, but I thought that too.'

I sipped my tea, 'Jean told me he can be a bit of a cad.'

'Well then, you going to see him again?'

I shrugged, 'I think I will. Just once to see what I think. He might have changed. Nothing to lose.'

It turned out I was wrong, very wrong.

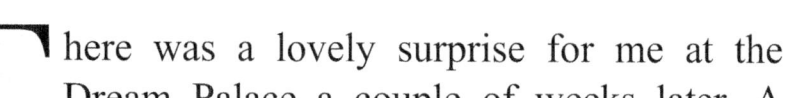

～

There was a lovely surprise for me at the Dream Palace a couple of weeks later. A letter from Edward.

Dear Lily,

I'm sorry I didn't have time to stop and talk to you when I was with my mother. She can be very impatient at times. I was pleased to see you looking so well and I hope it means you are over that horrible attack.

Life here is very busy and I am learning an enormous amount about strategy and how to motivate the men. Like them, I'm itching to put it all into practice.

Next time I have leave I'll pop into the Dream Palace and hope to see you. Perhaps we can go out for a drink or a cup of tea.

Best wishes,

Edward

He hadn't put a return address, so I couldn't write back. If I'd wanted a letter I could hug and hold close to my heart, this wasn't it.

I showed it to Jean the next time I saw her.

She read the letter and turned it over looking for more words. 'Not much of a letter, is it? Can't be that keen, then. Pity. How you getting on with Victor these days?'

'I don't see him often 'cos of the job.'

She raised an eyebrow. 'Think it'll go anywhere?'

'I don't think so. I can't say my heart races when I see him, so …'

'My heart races with every new bloke, so it tells you nothing. Still, is 'e a bit of alright?'

'What d'you mean?' I knew exactly what she meant.

'You know, cuddling up and that. I'm being polite.'

I pulled a face, 'He's a bit too keen on that, and I don't want to. In fact, when I think about it, I don't even want him to kiss me.'

'Time to give 'im the big heave-ho, then.' said Jean.

If only it was that easy.

~

The very next day Edward's mother came to the Dream Palace with a friend. She was dressed in a very smart suit, black and mid calf length. She wore a black floppy bow at the neck of her spotless white blouse. She didn't recognise me, which was no surprise, but I'd have known her anywhere. As they were waiting to go in I could overhear her conversation.

'Oh yes,' she was saying, getting her handkerchief out of her handbag. 'I remember him. Ran off and married a shop girl, no less. Broke his mother's heart.'

Her friend nodded in agreement, her little mink hat bobbing up and down, 'They've got two little ones now, both girls. Poor as church mice, not surprisingly. His father won't help out. Young people can be so headstrong, thinking that to marry someone outside their circle is acceptable.'

Edward's mother put her hanky to her nose as if there were a bad smell nearby. 'That won't happen to my boy. I've got someone lined up for him. You know the De Vere's daughter? She's recently got back from Switzerland, finishing school, you know. Very well bought up. Make an ideal officer's wife.'

Then they went in and I couldn't hear any more. My disappointment made me realise I'd been hoping something might come of it with Edward. Silly me. It's only natural they'd want one of their own kind. I pitied the De Vere's daughter having Edward's mother as a mother-in-law and resolved to put him out of my mind, letter or no letter.

~

I chickened out of dumping Victor the next time we met. Stupidly, I thought I'd give him another chance. I met him in town as arranged. If he came to the door when my dad was there, I'd just get an earful of abuse. Dad couldn't wait to get rid of me, but if he ever met any boy I had a date with he went crazy.

It was a busy evening in town with couples taking advantage of the mild air. The long light evenings and silky air made me wish Summer would last forever. But there was a looming cloud in the sky. Boards outside newsagents were full of reminders of possible war : *Women's Land Army Reformed*, one shouted ; *Mersey Ferry stops running to Rock Ferry* said another.

'It's all so worrying,' I said. 'Are you thinking of signing up? Three lads from our road have been called up.'

'I don't have to, I'm too old. I try not to think about it. You shouldn't either. Let's go to the pub.'

'I'd rather go for a walk. I spend so many evenings indoors with my job. Shall we walk by the river?'

He pulled a mock petulant face. At least, I hoped it was a mock one. 'I want a pint. Haven't had one for a couple of days.'

'Let's go for a walk first, then the pub. It'll be cooling down by then.'

He griped a bit, but we headed to the river. It meandered slowly along grass covered banks. A family of ducks swam lazily past and a butterfly drifted ahead as if leading the way. Couples strolled along arm in arm and parents pushed their babies in their prams. The smell of honeysuckle hung heavy in the breeze.

Victor and I chatted about how we'd spent the time since we last met. He'd been to the Roxy a couple of times. 'Don't mind, do you?' he asked. 'I like a dance and I can't be hanging about at home every evening waiting for you. I'd go mad.'

I stopped in my tracks and looked at him, 'Victor, are you saying you think we're courting?'

His face went red. 'Not sure I've thought it through. What do you think?'

'We've had what, a few dates. I don't think it means we're courting. But I think it means we should be honest if we are going out with someone else too. Could mean one of us gets upset otherwise.'

He was quiet. 'I'd be upset if you saw someone else,' he said. I thought he had no right to feel that way.

I waited. Bob had taught me people will often speak if you wait long enough.

'I have had one other date,' Victor said after a long painful pause. 'Nothing happened though.'

'What do you mean, nothing happened?'

'You know. We didn't …'

I managed to keep a straight face when I turned to look at him. 'Didn't what?'

His face went red, then white, then red. 'Oh, nothing. Forget it.'

Then without warning, I fell over.

It must have been a rabbit hole. To make matters worse I fell on a thick branch from a tree and badly scraped my knee. I yelped, holding back tears. Blood dripped down my leg and the graze looked dirty. Victor grabbed his hanky (clean tonight!) and very gently pulled the splinters and grass out of my knee. Then he wrapped it as best he could, tying it in a little knot. I limped all the way to the nearest pub, grateful for his kindness and help. Perhaps he was okay after all.

The pub was quiet and clean; the barman going round wiping all the tables. Two middle aged couples sat together talking quietly and a couple of men were playing darts in the next bar. When the barman got to us he noticed my knee. 'That looks sore,' he said, 'no dancing for you tonight.' He wandered back to the bar.

Victor insisted I have a whiskey 'for medicinal purposes.' I'd never drunk it before and couldn't believe how awful it was. I coughed and spluttered and ended up spitting half of it on the floor. But it did warm me and take the edge of the pain. He got me another one which I sipped very slowly.

Victor stood up, 'I'm getting another drink. What'll you have?'

I looked at him in amazement. We hadn't been there half and hour and he was going for his third drink. I wondered if he might be addicted to it, and where he got his money.

'What did you say your job is?' I asked.

His eyes slid from mine, 'Oh, you know, bit of this and that.'

'No, I don't know, what does it mean?' I kept quiet again so he would have to speak.

His forehead shone and he wiped it with his hand. 'You know, bit of buying and selling. This and that.'

'It sounds dodgy to me.'

He took my hand in his, 'No, honest, nothing dodgy, all legal like. It's just I know where to buy stuff cheap and who needs to buy it. All above board.

But enough of that, what'll you have to drink this time?'

'Just a lemonade please,' I wanted to keep my wits about me, 'then I'd like to go home and rest my leg.'

When I got home I was full of doubt. I couldn't make up my mind whether to go out with Victor again or not. He had some good points. He was good looking - Jean would laugh and say I was being shallow for listing that, even though it was high on her list. He had been kind when I fell over. He was very keen. But I still had misgivings. He was too secretive about some things and it made him hard to trust. The truth was I hadn't been out with many lads for more than the odd date and didn't really have an idea of the sort of person I wanted. I just knew he had to not be like my dad. But how would you know? Mum said he'd been a perfect gentleman when they got married.

～

I met up with Jean the next day before our evening shift at the Dream Palace. We went to the new Woolworth's cafe on the High Street. The smell of meat cooking hit our senses before anything else and made our mouths water, drawing us in. The restaurant was huge, there must have been forty or fifty tables lined up with military precision. The floor was big black and white squares and the rectangular tables were quite close together. No plump waitress would ever have got between them and one or two well-padded customers struggled to squeeze through the spaces. Every table had a menu standing upright in a silver holder thing. The noise of people chatting and walking about was colossal. We could hear a radio somewhere broadcasting the news. The talk was all about the number of women who were joining the ATS.

We looked at a menu as we walked along. 'Look Jean,' I said, 'Lamb stew is only sixpence. Can't beat that.'

'I'm going for the egg custard tart and some tea. They'll set me up for a few hours, and give me change from sixpence. We'll have to come here again.'

The place was mostly full of men who'd just finished work. From their laden plates, they didn't have a wife to cook for them at home. I thought it would happen more often if lots of women joined up.

I heard one of them, a big burley man, say, 'Bloody women in the forces. Fat lot of good they'll do. Go crying the first time something upsets them.'

I moved round so I was facing him, my hands on my hips, 'What rubbish! Have you tried having a baby? Nursing someone who's dying? Running a house-hold on not enough money and doing a job as well?'

He looked stunned that someone had challenged him, and his mouth flapped as he tried to think of something to say back. I didn't wait. I decided to leave well alone in case he got violent.

We edged past them, and went to the self-service queue.

'Excuse me,' I said when I jostled a man's arm. It was beefy and had a heart tattoo with 'Gladys' written in it.

'I'd excuse you anything, Darling,' he said with a wink.

'Seems like we never get chance to talk these days,' Jean said to me, her eye drawn to the selection of food on offer.

'Well, we have a minute here and there when we're working the same nights.'

The poor cooks were rushed off their feet. We grabbed a tray each and shuffled along. Jean never got as far as the custard tarts, the bacon butties were too temping to miss. I couldn't resist them either.

''Ere, we got our gas masks the other day,' Jean said as we shuffled along the queue. 'Got yours yet?'

'Yes, but surely we don't need to carry them unless the war actually starts.'

'Nah, we'd have 'eard if we should. My uncle has joined the Air Raid Wardens, 'e's too old to think about joining up the proper army even if we do get into a war.'

I hadn't heard of that. 'What'll he have to do then?'

'Dunno, really. Keep us all calm if there's a raid? Put out fires?'

'But they won't have a fire engine.'

She looked at me as if I was the most stupid person on earth, 'No, daft, small fires. Get everyone working with buckets of water and things. They've got girls from the Women's Royal Voluntary Service doing it as well.'

A shiver ran down my spine. 'Let's hope Mr Chamberlain can sort out something. It doesn't bear thinking about otherwise.'

We finally got to the front of the queue and handed over our money. Then we had the job of finding an empty table. Waitresses rushed about collecting empty plates and wiping tables down. I didn't envy them. My job at the Dream Palace was a doddle by comparison.

We found a newly wiped table by a window and sat down.

'Are we supposed to eat with the tray on the table, or find somewhere to put it?' Jean asked.

I looked around, 'Seems like no-one knows. Some are doing one, some the other. I suppose whatever we do will be okay.'

She took a bite of her bacon butty, margarine dripping down her chin. 'You dumped Victor yet?'

I bit my lip. 'No, I chickened out when I saw him. It wasn't a bad evening, but I'm going to have to do it.'

She put her head close to mine so no-one could overhear us.

'Yeah, no good going out with a bloke you don't want to touch you,' she said with a wink. I wasn't going to admit that I didn't really know what people got up to when they, you know what. No-one had ever told me. But I guessed Jean would never let me forget it if I owned up. But I did know it could lead to babies.

I put my hand on her arm, 'Jean, tell me you're not taking chances with the blokes you go out with? Not one of them would marry you if you got in the family way, you know that. Then where would you be?'

'Up the duff, I suppose.'

My heart sank, 'You're not, are you?'

'Nah, never go all the way. Not that stupid. Mind you, sometimes it's a bit 'ard to get them to stop.'

I pulled a face my gran would have been proud of. 'Why d'you let them start then?'

'They give you all these 'ard luck stories... *They'll be ill...*'

'Ssshh, keep your voice down, Jean!'

'… *if you don't let them go all the way.*'

Jean giggled, 'I've 'eard them all. *If I really loved them, I'd let them.*'

'*I want to wake up in your legs.*'

'*You know I love you.*'

'*… and I'll marry you if you let me.*'

'*You owe me, I bought you a drink.*'

'*You frigid or something?*'

'*Rather have girls, would you?*'

'*Come on, you know you'll love it. I'll pull out in time.*'

We were laughing so much my sides ached. 'Stop, stop, I can't breathe.'

'Seriously, though, Jean. You've got to stop taking these risks. What if they don't stop? You could ruin your life.'

She poked her tongue out at me. 'Oy, you're not my boss 'ere, you know. You can't tell me what to get up to with lads. She took another bite of her butty and a long strip of bacon fell onto her plate. 'Still dream of Edward?'

I could feel my cheeks going pink and looked down at my plate.

'And you call me stupid,' she said, ''ardly met the bloke and 'earing wedding bells. You're wasting your time. Forget 'im, dump Victor. Plenty more fish in the sea. Talking of that sort of thing, you 'eard any more about your dad's bit-on-the-side?'

'No, nothing. I'm not sure if that's a good thing or a bad thing. But he still goes out his regular nights so I suppose he's still seeing her.'

Jean slapped her forehead, 'I'm so stupid, sorry to change the subject, but my aunt Mary wrote and said I could go and stay with 'er for a week. Fancy coming to the seaside?'

~

'Come on, Lil,' Victor said, 'you'll love this pub. I've got loads of mates in here.' I wondered if he'd already been drinking, I smelt beer on him. A lot of beer. I hadn't wanted to come. My evenings off were precious and I kicked myself for agreeing to it.

It wasn't a pub I knew, and it was in a bit of town I'd never been to, but I knew it had a rough reputation. But then, I thought, so had Sunbury and that was fine. I decided to keep an open mind and followed Victor into the Coach and Horses. Old men wearing cloth caps sat at small tables playing dominoes. Women wearing hats or scarves knotted at the front sat around the edges of the room. The walls needed a fresh coat of paint and the ceiling was sticky brown from the cigarette smoke. The barman, his sleeves rolled up, had damp patches under his arms as he hurried to serve everyone. The noise was so bad we couldn't hear each other and I found if difficult to even think. The smell of beer and the fug of ciggies caught my throat and I coughed and held my hanky over my nose.

Victor looked at me through squinted eyes, 'Proper lady, ain't you. You must get plenty of smoke at that place you work.'

'I do, but I don't have to be in the auditorium so much now so I've got out of the habit.'

He pretended to doff his cap, 'Excuse me, I was forgetting myself, you a manager and all.'

I decided to ignore the dig. 'What's wrong, Victor? You seem out of sorts.'

He pulled my arm towards the bar and didn't bother to answer.

'What d'you want? Not light ale again. Go on, have something stronger. Let yourself go for once. A whiskey?'

I pulled a face. 'No thanks, it's horrible.'

He ignored me and turned towards the bar. I had time to look at him. The last couple of dates, he'd changed. Maybe my mum was right and you never know someone 'til you live with them. It was like Victor was nice at first, then the facade slipped. Each time I saw him, he was a bit less kind, less attentive. It was as if he thought he'd hooked me, so he didn't need to try any more. Even his face seemed to have changed. It looked harder somehow, and his smile rarely reached his eyes.

Leaving him at the bar, I went into the Ladies. The floor didn't look like it'd been washed for months and the washbasins weren't a lot better, with chipped and grubby tiles behind them and a speckled mirror with a corner missing. While I was in the cubicle, perched so I wouldn't have to sit on the seat, I heard a couple of girls talking as they washed their hands or did their make-up, I couldn't see which.

'D'you see that Victor is in here? I'm amazed he dares show his face.'

'Yeah, he blacked that bloke's eye last time. Just 'cos the bloke spilled his drink. It was an accident an' all.'

'Nasty piece of work. Maisie went out with him a few times. Had to fight him off in the end and when she finished with him he wouldn't leave her alone. Proper nuisance he was.'

I opened the door and went to the wash basins. The girls smiled hello and left. I took a long time washing my hands, thinking. I wondered if it was the same Victor. It wasn't an unusual name.

Tugging at my hair, which always goes frizzy in the damp weather, I left the WC and joined Victor again at the bar, jostled by other men as I wove through them. Someone whispered in my ear, 'Like to cuddle up to me, then?' And someone else pinched my behind. I turned quickly, but couldn't tell who'd done it. It reminded me of the horrible incident at the Dream Palace.

Victor was waving a ten bob note around, his elbow on the sticky bar. 'Oy, I'm waiting to be served here!' he shouted. So were lots of other blokes, but Victor's voice had a nasty edge to it. I felt ashamed to be with him.

As if he remembered me, Victor turned and called me over. 'Here, meet Jim, good mate of mine,' he said, nodding to an older man standing next to him. His cloth cap was thick with grease and dirt and his collar wasn't much better.

'Pleased to meet you,' I said.

'Good looker, ain't she?' he said to Victor as if I'd never spoken. 'Yeah, I always like 'em like that. Don't want to go out with any old slag, do I?'

Eventually it was his turn to get served. I noticed he took a good look down the bar lady's top. It was low cut and showed quite a lot, but he didn't have to be so obvious. He nudged the bloke the other side of him, one who had a tattoo of a naked woman on his arm. He said something and they both laughed and made a rude gesture.

'Two whiskeys, if you can spare the time,' he said to the bar maid.

Her look was cold as ice and she served him without a word.

'Thanks, Sweetheart,' he said when he got the whiskey, but I heard him mutter, 'Lazy slut!'

I was angry and embarrassed and annoyed with myself for not knowing what to do. It was a part of town I didn't know and I wondered if I'd be safe leaving on my own. If this lot were anything to go by, I'd be worried about walking down the street alone.

'Go and find yourself a seat,' Victor said, handing me the whiskey I didn't want. 'There's one over there. Don't mind if I go and play darts with my mates, do you?'

He didn't wait for an answer and I was left sitting between two couples who were canoodling. They didn't even notice I was there, much less want to speak. I sat on the hard wooden bench, sipped my drink slowly, and looked around. There were a lot more men than women, and most of them seemed bent on drinking as much as possible, as quickly as possible. An old couple sat in the corner, nursing half a pint of shandy each. They should've looked out of place, but somehow they looked like part of the furniture, and I guessed they'd been going there for years and years. They were shabbily dressed, but clean, and had the sort of thinness that comes from a life of being poor. Plenty of the younger people in the bar would have the same fate. It made me even more determined to keep on with my studies and make something of myself.

I couldn't see Victor as the dart board was in the other bar. About half an hour after he left me, he came back, a fresh pint in hand. 'All right there? Need another drink?'

I shook my head and he left again without another word.

It was enough. Before he could find me in the crush I got my things together and slipped outside. I thought I'd seen the last of him.

I was wrong.

11. HARASSMENT

PERSECUTION, MOLESTATION

The next day was a Saturday so I had to go to the Dream Palace much earlier than usual for the kids' Saturday morning pictures. I love seeing all the little ones come in, excited at the outing. Round our way they don't get many treats. Lots of them have hand-me-down clothes and shoes that don't fit; some smell of wee; some are dressed perfectly. No matter what, they all get a tiny bar of chocolate which they usually eat before they even get to their seats. Jean or whoever is on duty with me stands by the door with a wet cloth and wipes their hands before they can smear chocolate all over the seats. That week the film was a cowboy and Indian story, with lots and lots of shouting and cheers when the poor Indians got shot.

It was a crisp, glorious day, the sort that makes you glad to be alive. The gardens were full of dahlias and penstemons and the scent of roses made me want to stop and sniff them. They reminded me that Summer would soon be fading. A couple of neighbours waved as I walked past and old Mr Thompson, ninety years old at least, tried his usual bit of flirting.

My good mood was about to come to an abrupt end.

I turned the corner near the wall and there was Victor, leaning against a garden fence like he owned it, ciggie in hand. I tried to ignore him, but he got into step with me.

'What happened to you last night, then?' he asked.

I spoke without looking at him or breaking my stride. 'I'm surprised you even noticed I'd left. I don't want to see you any more.'

'Is this just because I was playing darts with my mates?'

I didn't answer, but kept walking briskly.

He did a little skip and hop so he was ahead of me and could look me in the face. His voice took on a tone that was half pleading, half aggressive, 'Come on, now, be reasonable, a bloke has to have his mates and I was only gone a few minutes.'

He touched my arm, and I pulled mine away with a jerk.

'Don't be like that. You know you like me, we make a good couple.'

I stopped in my tracks and looked at him face on. He looked hung over, bags under his eyes and pasty skin. Not surprising with the amount he'd been drinking. I could still smell drink on him. There was a beer stain on his shirt and his hair was lank and greasy. As I watched, he dropped his ciggie and ground it out with his shoe.

'I don't like you, and we are not a couple. We never were. We just went out three or four times. I am breaking up with you. Now leave me alone.'

He stroked my arm. 'Ah, come on, if you don't even tell me what I've done wrong, how can I put it right? I'll make it up to you. Here …'

He thrust a tiny box of chocolates in my hand. I pushed them back at him. He wouldn't take them, so I dropped them on the floor. 'Take them, I don't want anything from you.'

He picked up the chocolates, dented as they were, put them in his pocket and got out another ciggie. I was walking again and he kept matching my steps as his struck a match and lit up.

'You're beautiful. I like being seen with you. People are jealous you're my girl.'

'Well, I'm not your girl. Now go away.' I walked faster and refused to look at him again.

'You know you want to go out with me. I'm

going places. Gonna build up my business soon, start with a market stall, have a shop before you know it. Lot of shortages these days.' As he spoke his slouch transformed into an upright stance, shoulders back, and chin held high.

I didn't bother to answer him. I could just imagine his business, which'd be black market for sure. I wouldn't want any more to do with that than I would with him.

He kept trying to persuade me all the time until we were near the bus stop, sometimes aggressively, sometimes almost pleading. As I neared the stop, I was getting desperate; in no way did I want him to follow me to the Dream Palace. But then, I thought I was saved. I spotted a saviour. Ted, the city centre bobby came out of a side street. I knew him because he called in for a cuppa at the Dream Palace sometimes, usually when it was cold and wet and he wanted to warm up and have a bit of a chat. He always reminded me of that song *The Laughing Policeman*. His stomach was round and he often rested his hands on it, like women do when they are expecting.

He grinned when he saw me, 'Hello, Lily, didn't expect to see you here. Off to work?'

Just then Victor leaned over and tried to kiss me, his arm round my shoulder. I shook him off.

'Go away! I'm serious.'

He tried again with the same manoeuvre.

I pushed him away again and turned to Ted, 'This man is bothering me, he won't leave me alone.'

The bobby looked at Victor. 'Is it true?' he said, 'you bothering this lady?'

'Bothering her? 'Course not, she's my girl.'

I looked at him, hands on hips. 'I am not your girl, never was, now go away. I never want to see you again.' I turned to Ted, 'my bus is coming soon, please will you make sure he doesn't get on it.'

Victor looked at the bobby, all man to man. 'Don't take any notice of her, she's a bit hysterical, you know how girls get. She's like this sometimes and we always kiss and make up. Probably got the curse.'

Ted looked at me, 'Is this true, Lily?'

'No, it's damn well not,' I said, anger making me swear.

Victor put his arm round my shoulder again and gripped is so tightly it was hard to move away and his fingertips dug in enough to bruise.

'She doesn't mean it, officer. She loves me really, don't you?' And with that he leaned over and kissed my cheek.

I stamped on his foot, hard.

'Aw, that hurt,' he said, hopping up and down.

'See, officer, she gets violent sometimes. Does that sound like a girl who can't looked after herself?'

The bobby smiled, 'Ah, young love. Me and my missus used to have some right ding-dongs.' His eyes took on a faraway look, 'Making up was, well, enjoyable.'

He turned on his heel and started to walk away. I called after him, but he just waved over his shoulder and carried on.

Victor let go of me so quickly I almost stumbled. 'Do that again, Bitch, and you'll live to regret it.'

I couldn't catch my breath. 'Just go away!'

'You're my girl and don't forget it,' he said with a sneer, wiping his hand across his Brylcreemed hair.

My bus came along and I sobbed with relief. I jumped on, but was horrified when Victor set a foot on the platform to follow me.

Without a single thought I held onto the bus rail, lifted my foot, and kicked him off. I got him in the stomach and he doubled up, winded.

The bus began to pull away and he half straightened up. He shook a fist at me and shouted, 'I'll get you, you just wait and see.'

The conductor shouted back, 'Blimey, I wouldn't mess with her, Mate.'

Shaken and embarrassed, I found a seat a few rows back. All eyes were on me as I walked along the aisle. The conductor came to collect the fare, 'Where you going, Love?'

'Cosgrove Road, please.'

'That'll be tuppence.'

I handed over my coins and he turned the handle on his ticket machine. It needed oiling and squeaked as the ticket came out.

'Hope you don't mind me saying, Miss, but I couldn't help seeing what happened with that man. Been having trouble with him, then?' he asked.

Before I could answer, a lady on the other side leaned over. She was comfortably fat, still wearing her flowery pinny over her dress. She hitched up her generous bosom before she spoke. 'I had one like that, Love. Took me ages to get rid of the bugger, if you'll excuse my French. D'you know what he did once? He only put dog business through my letter box. The smell!'

Her nose wrinkled and her throat tightened at the memory of it.

'Didn't the police help you?'

'The bobbies? You must be joking. They weren't interested, the sods. Said it was a domestic matter, couldn't interfere between a man and his woman. You mark my words, they always take the bloke's side.'

My heart sank. What if Victor started doing

things like that? He'd make my life a misery. I felt seriously worried.

I looked at Mrs Bosom, 'I heard some girls saying their friend had trouble with Victor, he wouldn't leave her alone. How did you get rid of your pest?'

She hitched up her bosom again, her smile broadening from ear to ear, 'My brother went round there and beat him up. That did it! He ran off at a fair clip, I can tell you. You should've seen his bruises!'

The conductor had been standing there, mouth agape. 'Cor, I always say you learn a lot on the buses and today just proves it.' He looked at me, 'You got a beefy brother?'

'I haven't got a brother at all,' I said, my mouth turned down at the corners.

Mrs Bosom leaned over again, 'What about your dad?'

I almost laughed. My dad might have a tough mouth, but he was so weedy he could be knocked over with a puff of wind. There was no way he'd lift a finger to help me anyway.

'No. He wouldn't help.'

'Then I guess you've just got to hope he gives up soon. Keep a pot of pepper in your pocket to throw in his eyes if he comes near you.'

For the rest of the journey I worried. Victor knew

where I lived, and where I worked. He could just turn up any time.

~

The day the wall committee had worked so hard for finally arrived. It should have been a bright sunny day to reflect the good news that the wall was going for good, but instead it was cool and drizzly, the sky a low grey blanket.

It was a pity the wall was knocked down on a work day. Most people were out and couldn't enjoy the spectacle. I saw most of it on my way to work. It was done in a matter of minutes. A huge steam roller just ploughed through it, backed up, then went forward again until the whole lot was gone. The noise was terrific and bits of brick dust flew everywhere. I had to keep my hand in front of my eyes each time the machine knocked more down, then comb the bits out of my hair. The dust got into my lungs and I coughed and coughed. Even so, the few other people who were around cheered each time the wall got smaller. When it was finally gone, we linked arms and did a silly little dance of glee.

Then two men appeared with a lorry. One of them, a short man with a massive beer belly, came over to us, 'I've read about this wall in the paper. Bet you'll be glad to see it go.'

And with that he joined the other man and they started throwing the bricks into the back of the lorry. The road needed to be redone where the bricks had left a scar as a reminder. The only bricks left were the bits between the houses, and you could hardly see them. The workmen said they'd be removed the next day. Just watching the wall fall felt like we were being let out of prison. It put a spring in my step and no mistake.

Celebrations started almost as soon as people got home from work. Time and time again we'd see people walking slowly, dragging their feet as they came from the bus stop. Then they'd see the hole where the wall had been, and their steps were lighter and smiles transformed their tired faces. We let them know there'd be a knees-up at seven o'clock. The drizzle stopped and the evening turned fine; the world was washed clean.

Some people nipped home and got out their fancy dress again, others just turned up as they were, keeping their kids up late and bringing beer and pop with them. We had a great impromptu party. Not surprisingly, none of the people from the other side turned up. An entertainer from the pub came with his accordion and some people danced. *South of the Border* was requested several times. We had a right laugh walking backwards and forwards through the gap like a load of crazy people, cheering as we went and no doubt confirming all the horrid beliefs the snooty people had about us.

Bob turned up half way through. He looked weary but triumphant. His blue flat cap was at a jaunty angle and matched his tie which was knotted with the biggest knot I'd ever seen. He went round like a real politician, kissing babies and shaking everyone's hands. People couldn't wait to clap him on the back and congratulate him.

After a while he called for attention. 'My protesters, my army, my soldiers. The demolition of this wall shows that sometimes the right things happen. Sometimes the little people are not put down by those with money. This is a victory for justice, for equality, for what is right. Let's give ourselves a well deserved round of applause.'

The cheering and clapping went on for ages, until someone started singing 'For he's a jolly good fellow,' and Bob was carried back and forth a few times in the gap where the wall had been. When they put him down, he came over to me. 'You played a good part in this Lily, you and the others in the Steering Group. You've done something you can be really proud of.'

And he was right, I was proud to have been part of getting something done. I walked taller when I finally headed for home. I didn't leave it too late because I had something very special to do at work the next day.

Mr Simmons had decided to have a Film Premiere, or at least a local Premiere. 'It'll be good publicity for the Dream Palace and cheer people up with all this gloomy war talk,' he had said. 'You're going to help me give them a night to remember.'

I gulped, 'Me? But I've never done anything like that before.'

He winked and grinned wickedly. 'You will now. In fact, I'm putting you in charge.'

I could hear the blood pounding in my ears; my knees wobbled and I held onto a chair for support.

Mr Simmons chuckled and patted me on the shoulder, 'I can see I've worried you. You'll be fine and surprised at just what you can achieve. We'll spend a good bit of time planning and we'll write down everything that needs to be done. We'll work out who else will need to help you and what you'll pay them and you can report to me every couple of days. I'm planning the Premiere for three weeks time.'

'Three weeks? Three weeks?' my voice squeaked, 'There's so much to do!' I said.

'Easy,' Mr Simmons replied, 'make a list, and it'll be a long list, mark my words. Then put it in order, what needs to be done first, second and so on. Write a date beside each. The problem is sticking to it when you're busy. But it's the system I use.'

He could see I was still worried, 'Oh, and you can help a bit by getting things to be auctioned. We'll need a few big things to draw the crowd, I'll sort those out. Do you think you could try to get some smaller things?'

'But how would I do that?' I asked, feeling completely clueless.

'I'll give you a list of businesses I've got links with. There's the printers for a start, they could offer to print some cards for the winner. And they are the people to contact quickly to get invites printed. They'll help you with the design too - they know what they're doing.'

I hesitated, 'So I go to the businesses and ask them to give us something to auction?'

'It'll be easier than you think. They know me and once you tell them it's for local children they'll give you something. I'm only suggesting you visit six shops. Have a think as well if anyone or any business could offer their services as a prize.'

Going to the shops to ask for auction items turned out to be as easy as he said. Each shopkeeper thought for a minute, and I suspect they were trying to think what hadn't sold or had made the least profit. But I came away with a promise of a basket of fruit to be delivered on the morning of the auction, a fancy teapot, a joint of ham, a necklace and bracelet set, a pair of cufflinks and a book. Twice when I was walking round I thought I spotted Victor out of the corner of my eye, but decided I must be imagining it.

For three weeks we planned and acted, and planned and acted. Mum said she'd love to come but there was no way I could get her a ticket and anyway, she wouldn't have a smart dress to come with. 'No decent man either,' she muttered.

Then I hit on a solution.

'We'll need help. The food's being done by the bakers down the road so there's no cooking, but it will need to be put on trays and then offered round. Want to do it? We'll pay.'

Did she ever! I had my first waitress, and found the other two amongst the part-time usherettes who were happy to come in for a bit of extra overtime. I knew they were all good workers and had confidence in them.

On my way to work that day, I kept going through everything to be done in my mind. I even stopped twice and got out my list. Every couple of minutes I told myself it would all be fine. With all the planning we'd done it should all go smoothly, I thought.

How wrong can you be?

I was met at the door by one of the waitresses. She had deep frown lines on her usually smooth forehead. I hadn't even put my stuff down when she came hurrying over to me.

'Mavis is sick, she can't come in. We can't possibly manage without her. It'll all be a disaster,' she said, looking as if it was all her own fault. She put her head in her hands, 'Things will go wrong, people will think the Dream Palace is useless. I might lose my job. I can't afford to do that. I've got to feed my kids.'

I had no idea how we were going to manage, but spent a few minutes reassuring her anyway. At that moment, Mum came in and saw my worried face, 'What is it, Love?' she asked.

'Oh, Mum, Mavis just sent a message. She can't come. How are we going to manage? There's still so much to do.'

She was silent for a minute, then her face lit up. 'I know, we'll ask Vera across the road. She's been a waitress and she's always short of house-keeping. Let's see if we can grab a boy and get a message taken to her.'

Finding a boy who wanted to earn sixpence wasn't difficult, but the half hour waiting for Vera to turn up was nerve-racking. I must have looked at the clock a dozen times. What if the lad just ran off with the money? What if Vera couldn't come? What if? What if? But we just had to get on with it. We tidied and prepared all the plates for the food ready for when it arrived, and made sure everything was perfect.

And then, bless her heart, Vera turned up looking every inch a waitress in a black skirt and white blouse. She hugged me and Mum.

'Right,' she said, 'what needs doing?'

I looked at the clock. 'That's strange, the food should have been here twenty minutes ago. I'll nip to the bakers' and see what's what.'

I put on my coat and walked down the road, noticing the weather was clear and the air balmy and fresh. I was relieved that all the people coming to the Premiere wouldn't have their clothes dripping wet. But my positive thoughts evaporated when I got to the door of the bakers'. My heart fell to my knees. The door was locked and a big notice said:

DUE TO BEREAVEMENT,
CLOSED UNTIL FURTHER NOTICE

I'm afraid I was so worried about my own problems, I didn't have much spare sympathy to feel sorry for whoever had died and who was left grieving. Panic set in and my brain wouldn't work. Then I overheard two women who were also looking at the sign.

'Poor Albert,' one said, 'his heart, I expect. Been

playing up for years. Good job there's another bakers' round the corner.'

My brain clicked into gear and I ran round the corner like I was in the Olympics. I told the baker how many people we had to cater for and asked advice on how much to buy.

He scratched his head, got a pencil from behind his ear and made notes on a scrap of paper. When he finished he looked up with a smile, 'We can do it, Miss. I haven't got enough loaves for that many people, mind,' he said, 'sorry Love.'

My heart sank faster than the Titanic. 'Oh no, what on earth am I going to do?'

'Let me think. Does it have to be sandwiches? We've got some rolls here. Cut them open and just put a filling on the top. You get two out of each roll that way and they'll look really special. Cut up some pork pies into dainty little wedges, too. Grab some tomatoes for a bit of colour and it'll be looking fit for a king.'

I could have kissed him. Sensing my panic, he worked really quickly and soon I was heading back to the Dream Palace balancing a tray of bread and rolls a bit precariously. I handed them over to Mum and headed back out to buy marge and fillings.

When I got back to the Dream Palace Mum and the others were having a well earned rest. They'd been inspecting everything to make sure the place was spotless and everything was it its right place.

I tried to look sympathetic, but probably failed badly. 'Up, quick,' I said, 'no time to lose, we've got to make sandwiches for everyone.'

They looked at me in disbelief, we all looked at the clock and groaned. But soon we had a real system working. One cutting, one buttering and one filling. We dragged the projectionist down from his box and got him laying the food on the platters so they looked appealing. We made a great team.

Just then Mr Simmons came in, all dressed up in his DJ looking very distinguished. 'What's all this then? You're not supposed to be making the food.'

I explained what had happened. 'I hope it's good enough,' I said, 'it's the best we could do.'

He smiled and patted my shoulder, 'Don't you worry yourself, you've all done wonders. Thank you for your hard work, Ladies. No-one will know what they were supposed to get, will they? Go on, all of you, you've got time for a quick cuppa before everyone arrives.'

We sat sipping our tea and eating a cake I'd bought at the bakers'. I didn't think Mr Simmons would mind in the circumstances.

Vera took a mouthful of the cake. 'Mmm, lovely. Think any royalty will come tonight? It'd be so exciting, something to tell the grandchildren.'

'I don't know, but I think the boss would have told me if we had. I just got the total numbers of people, not their names. Me, I'd rather have a film star.'

'Cary Grant,' Mum said without hesitation.

'No, James Stewart, he's so kind and gentlemanly,' Vera replied.

'What about Henry Fonda?' one of the others said.

'Funny how we've all chosen men. I wonder why.' I said. We all grinned.

After our tea we went back to the foyer. The premiere was a big deal. Well, a big deal for our part of the country. An absolute first. And it was a great film too. *Pygmalion*, a comedy with Lesley Howard and Wendy Hiller. I wondered how the boss had arranged it. Every time I asked he just winked and tapped the side of his nose.

As I was checking my list yet again Jean walked by, lipstick in hand.

'Come here, you look pale enough to faint clean away, you daft thing,' she said.

I tried to smile but it seemed like the muscles in my face were too tense to oblige. The butterflies fighting to get out of my stomach didn't help a lot either.

'Smile!' Jean said in a voice that meant no arguing. I swear she sometimes forgets I'm her boss here. Before I knew it, she'd put bright red lipstick on me.

'Look at yourself in the mirror,' she said, turning me round to face one of the huge mirror panels in the foyer. I'd never worn such a bright colour and was amazed at how it changed my whole look.

'See. Told you,' Jean said, 'You look just like Margaret Lockwood.'

I didn't, but it still made me feel good that she said it. I checked my outfit, a smart dark grey skirt and jacket we found in a jumble sale and Mum'd helped me alter to fit, and then went to turn up the music so the guests were greeted by something cheerful. Noel Coward it was - Jean had the job of changing the records, although I'd had to have strong words about her not putting on only her favourites.

The boss's wife, Florence, was next to arrive. She was wearing a wonderful dark pink dress that suited her colouring perfectly. It was floor length with a V neck down to her waist but a glamorous lace inset protected her modesty. The suit I'd thought smart a minute ago was suddenly dull and boring.

'All ready?' asked the boss.

'All ready,' I said, the shake in my voice betraying me.

Florence looked around. 'It all looks very chic,' she said, 'I love the sparkling lights. Did you design it, Darling?' she asked Mr Simmons.

'No, Lily did it.'

'I didn't,' I interrupted, 'Jean chose the designs and colours. She's ever so good at that sort of thing.'

'Are we showing Pathe News before the film?' Florence asked, her forehead crinkling. Mr Simmons shook his head.

She smiled like a load had been taken off her mind. 'Thank goodness. The constant talk of threatening war is so depressing it keeps me awake at night. Not appropriate tonight at all.'

Mr Simmons patted her arm, 'Tonight is all about enjoyment, my dear.'

I was relieved that our first guests arrived then, before the conversation got even gloomier. It was the Mayor looking splendid in his suit and big gold chain of office. His wife seemed timid beside Florence.

Mr Simmons tapped me on the shoulder, 'I forgot to tell you. A man called Edward came in yesterday. He was looking for you. I told him your shifts this week. I hope it wasn't the wrong thing to do. He said he'd wait at Lyons Corner House tomorrow at three o'clock and hope to see you there if you can make it.'

My smile was answer enough.

Then, so quickly that I couldn't even begin to tell who came when, the foyer was full of couples dressed to the nines. I'd never seen such glamour except on the big screen. I felt privileged and intimidated being there. What a long way from the shirt factory, or my home come to that. I couldn't forget I was just one of the staff, but even so I felt exhilarated to be part of it all.

Just like Mr Simmons had taught me, I kept an eye on things - 'playing the room' he called it and I noticed he did the same. We wanted to make sure everyone felt special, especially as there was going to be a charity auction after the film. I'd never heard of one of them before.

Several times I had to duck out of the way as photographers mingled with the guests ready to dazzle them with their flashes. Each time one appeared people stopped chatting and posed, glass or cigarette in hand, looking like film stars themselves. As I walked among them my arm brushed against soft velvets, smooth silks, glittering beaded fabric, and brocade.

I overheard a dozen snippets of conversation:
'Yes, the dress was from....'
'That awful man Hitler ...'
'I'm so worried my son will sign up.'
'... workers' march tomorrow...'
'I hope the film ...'

The chatter of so many people got louder as they refilled their glasses and soon the music was drowned out, so Jean might as well have played just her favourites.

Mum and the other waitresses walked quietly amongst the guests offering tiny sandwiches. I smiled as the guests tried to juggle their glasses and food while still trying to look elegant.

The projectionist appeared discretely on the stairs giving me the nod that he was ready whenever we were. I quietly told Mr Simmons. He went over to a half size replica of the MGM gong he got from goodness knows where. He'd paid Jean overtime to clean it up and the bumps on it dazzled as they reflected the lights around us. Looking like he thought he was one of those athletic Gongmen, he struck it twice and the room gradually quietened.

'First of all, I'd like to thank you all for coming to this special event. We are honoured to have the creme de la creme of the town here this evening. I've seen the film and I just know you're going to enjoy it. And I hope you'll all be feeling so warm hearted afterwards you'll generously support our charity for poor children in this area.'

He spoke enthusiastically about the Dream Palace for a couple of minutes then said, 'With no further ado, Ladies and Gentlemen, please take your seats for this very special premiere.'

It took a while for people to put down their glasses, but eventually they all took their seats and the film began.

I sat in a seat right at the back, ready to deal with anything that needed attention.

Jean and I had watched the film all the way

through with Mr. Simmons the day before. I smiled when we learned about Pygmalion from the big writing on the screen at the beginning of the film.

Pygmalion was a mythological character who made sculptures.
He made one of his ideal woman - Galatea.
It was so beautiful he prayed to the gods to give her life.
His wish was granted.

'Wish I could make me a perfect man,' Jean said. 'The one I've got ain't up to much.'

Poor Jean, her luck with men never seemed to improve, but at least she got rid of them when she realised they were rotters. Not like my Mum. It made my thoughts turn to Edward. I smiled at the thought of seeing him next day.

'You never know someone 'til you've married them,' Mum always said. Bit too late by then, that was the trouble. And living in sin was, well, sinful even if I had a lot of trouble believing in God. I didn't know anyone who lived together without being married. You'd be the scandal of the town. But then I stopped and thought for a minute. My dad wasn't living with his fancy bit, but they were a sort of couple. And rumour had it that Mrs Briggs down the road wasn't really a widow. Her husband was said to be living with someone else in London, large as life and no-one to know they weren't married. Perhaps he'd even married her as well.

I slid out of my seat fifteen minutes before the end of the film. Jean, bless her, had already got all the things to be auctioned out of the office and into the foyer. They were on a makeshift table covered in scarlet velvet cloth. There were several pieces of jewellery, a couple of cut glass vases, tickets to a show, a carriage clock and two oil paintings as well as the things I'd gathered.

To my surprise Mr and Mrs Simmons came out of the screening immediately after me. She looked pale and sweaty and was clutching on his arm for support.

'Lily,' Mr Simmons said, a deep line between his eyebrows, 'you'll have to do the auction. I need to take my wife home.'

'But ... but ...' I started.

'I'll have to leave it to you,' he said, already making for the door, 'we've discussed it, you know what to do.'

I wanted to argue that I wasn't up to the job, but another look at Mrs Simmons bought me to my senses. 'You go, I'll manage,' I said, with my fingers crossed behind my back.

I found Jean and told her what she needed to do to support me.

While everyone filed out of the auditorium I ran

through what I needed to do, twice. Then, feeling the biggest fraud on the planet, I hit the MGM Gong and waited until everyone stopped talking.

'I hope you all enjoyed the film, Ladies and Gentlemen,' I said with a smile I was amazed I could produce, 'now it is my great pleasure to encourage you to bid generously for these wonderful items here.' I gestured to all the items on the table.

I decided to pretend that I was Mr Simmons and I knew him well enough to know how he'd handle the crowd. So I cajoled, I flattered, I joked, I bullied. Strangely, after the first couple of items, I realised I was feeling a buzz of enjoyment, especially as they were cheerful and willing to bid. People often ended up bidding far more than the item was worth, but they could feel good about doing good and everyone there could afford it anyway. It was the perfect way to round up a successful evening.

Next day Mr Simmons came in with a big bunch of flowers as a thank you for the success of the Premiere.

'How is Mrs Simmons?' I asked.

He patted my shoulder, 'Thank you for remembering, she's much better today. Just a stomach upset. Remember how your knees shook when I told you you were going to organise the Premiere?' he asked.

How could I forget? It seemed like yesterday but also a year ago, so much had happened.

'You helped me a lot, Mr Simmons, I couldn't have done it without you.'

'Don't underestimate yourself, Lily. You needed help because you'd never done it before. If you had to organise another big event, you'd sail through. Did you see all the coverage we got in the press? It's terrific. Got to be good for business.'

12. ACQUAINTED

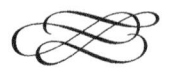

FAMILIARISED, INFORMED

*E*dward was as true as his word and was waiting at Lyons Corner House as arranged, looking very smart. Seeing him made my heart run faster, and my knees went weak when he smiled at me. He shook hands rather formally and we looked at each other shyly. I'd thought about him so much, but the truth was we'd hardly spent any time in each other's company. One thing I'd remembered right though, was how gorgeous he was, lovely eyes and a touch of Cary Grant's chin and dimples.

'Hello, Lily,' he said, 'we finally meet again. I'm so glad. I've thought about you often.'

I blushed and got horribly hot, 'I've thought of you too. You were so kind when you rescued me.'

He gave a broad smile, 'You're worth rescuing.'

We hardly knew where to start, so much had happened to me since we met, and I realised the same would be true for him.

I told him all about my promotion at the Dream Palace and he seemed genuinely impressed. 'That's terrific. It's hard for girls to get promotion. You'll be running the place yet.'

The Nippy came just then, smart as ever in her black skirt and blouse with a white apron with a frilled edge and her black and white hat on exactly right. I'd heard Lyons were real sticklers for the uniform being worn correctly. She held her little notebook and pencil at the ready.

'What can I get you? Miss? Sir?' she asked.

'Lily, what would you like?' Edward asked.

'Just some tea, please.'

'Tea for two and,' he looked at me, 'two Chelsea buns. Would that be okay?'

I smiled agreement. I couldn't often afford cakes so it would be a treat.

We talked about the situation with Mr. Hitler.

'There's going to be a war,' Edward said, very decisively.

'But most people I know think Chamberlain will sort it out, and President Roosevelt is trying too. Surely even Mr. Hitler wouldn't go to war and risk losing so many men.'

Edward frowned and shook his head, 'I wish it were as easy as that. Hitler is up to all sorts of things. He's violated the Munich agreement and invaded Czechoslovakia. And Britain and France have promised Poland independence. Hitler has invaded that country and he's not going to give it up without a fight. I think he wants to take over the world.'

'But so many rich and famous people seem to think National Socialism is a good thing,' I said.

He rubbed his forehead, 'I'm afraid they have no idea what Hitler is really up to. Or perhaps with some of them it suits their purposes.'

I was beginning to feel very ignorant. 'What purposes?'

'Rich people often want to preserve the status quo and make sure the workers don't get restless and demand more money or better working conditions. And some of them hate the Jews and are happy with what they hear is happening to them in Germany and Poland.'

Just then the Nippy came with the tea and Chelsea buns. Edward thanked her and gave her a tip. She gave him a big grin in return.

The Chelsea buns were still warm and the smell of cinnamon and peel made my mouth water. Far too quickly to be ladylike, I picked one up. It was soft and squidgy; several currents falling out as I took a big bite. I closed my eyes and let out a little 'Mmm' as the flavours burst in my mouth.

Edward laughed. 'I like a girl who likes her food,' he said.

A soldier came and sat at the next table and brought me back rudely to earth. I felt a real frisson of fear thinking about another war. I was too young to remember the last war, but my parents and everyone of their generation did. They often talked about it. Millions died. The thought of it happening again was terrifying.

Edward tried to reassure me. 'If it happens, it won't be as bad as the last one. I've read gas masks are being made in huge quantities for people in this country, so we don't have to worry about a gas attack. That's something.'

'I don't know if that makes me feel better or worse. Why would the government spend money having them made it they didn't think there would be a war?'

Edward gave a sad grin and shrugged his shoulders. 'Let's not talk about it any more. Our tea's getting cold and I can't wait to start on the bun. I'd better eat it quick before you get your hands on it.'

He cut his bun in halves. Mine was almost gone. As we stirred our tea Edward looked up. He looked very serious.

'Lily, I hope you won't think I'm being presumptuous, but may I speak plainly?'

I nodded, wondering what on earth was coming.

He suddenly went as red as I had earlier and brushed back his hair with his hand. 'I mentioned I've thought of you often, and we've got to know each other a little bit better today. I just wanted to say … gosh this is hard … that if circumstances were different, I would ask you out.'

Although I'd hoped for this, I was still surprised at him being so open, so forward.

'What do you mean, if they were different?'

'You know the army can move me around any time it wants. We've been told our next posting will be anywhere in the UK, or abroad. That's not much help and I can't ask you to wait for me when we hardly know each other. And so much of my time is taken up with army work, and trying to pass my exams to get to the next promotion.'

I didn't know what to say. If I said I would wait, it would put pressure on him when he was busy. I sighed a little too loudly.

He put his hand on mine. 'What is it, Lily? Are you angry with me?'

'I'm probably not the right person for you to go out with anyway, even if you were stationed near here.'

A frown wrinkled his lovely forehead. 'What on earth do you mean?'

'Your mother and her friend came to the Dream

Palace recently. Your mother didn't seem to recognise me, not surprising when we met so briefly.'

'I don't understand,' he said, 'what's that got to do with us?'

'Well, I overheard them talking. Her friend was talking about someone who had married a girl beneath him and how awful it was.'

He raised his eyes to heaven, 'That'll be Mrs Roberts, she's a dreadful snob. I always try to avoid her when she calls on Mother.'

'That's as maybe, but your mother didn't contradict her. Quite the opposite. She said she'd never allow you to do that, and she had a suitable wife all lined up for you.'

He made to say something, but I held up my hand to silence him.

'No, Edward, she's right. We come from different sides of the tracks. I'd feel awkward with your people and probably embarrass you all the time. I can't imagine what you'd think of mine. We live in different worlds.'

He turned over my hand and held it tight. 'My mother is always trying to pair me off with some girl. She'll be talking about Lucy White, the daughter of another of her friends. We've known each other for years.'

My heart sank. 'There you go, then,' I said with a shaky voice.

'Lucy and I have never been attracted to each other for a second. In fact, she is secretly romantically involved with someone her mother wouldn't approve of. He is, wait for it, an artist! It's hard to think what would be more shocking in Mrs White's eyes. As far as she's concerned men have to do manly jobs not mess about with paint brushes. I promise you, there is not the least danger of me marrying her.'

I was thrilled, so Edward was free, not that it meant he would be seriously interested in me.

Edward grinned widely, 'Ah, you like a bit of gossip. Well, here's some more that will delight you. I've heard Mrs Roberts' other daughter is about to elope with a much younger man.'

I giggled, delighted at the idea of the snobby Mrs Roberts getting her comeuppance.

Edward smiled too. 'Delicious, isn't it? I'm sworn to secrecy, so please don't tell anyone. Mr and Mrs Roberts may just get over it because the younger man will inherit a title and a lot of money one day.'

I was serious for a moment, remembering what she'd said about the man whose family cut him off. 'That's a big step. If he doesn't inherit soon, I hope they'll have enough to live on if Mr and Mrs Roberts refuse to have anything to do with them.'

He squeezed my hand. 'We've rather got off the subject. Lily, may I call on you when I'm in town?

PICTURE HOUSE GIRLS

You are under no obligation to wait and if you go out with someone else I will just vanish from your life. I wish the timing were better.'

All too soon Edward had to go back to his barracks. We separated at the door of Lyons Corner House and I turned towards the shops to buy some new stockings. I hadn't gone a hundred yards before Victor stepped out of a doorway and grabbed my elbow so hard I yelped.

'Think you can go out with someone else?' he asked, his voice full of menace. 'You're my girl, and don't forget it.'

I yanked my arm away and faced him. 'I am not your girl. My life is nothing to do with you. Go away.' And with that I walked quickly away and got myself in amongst other shoppers. But Victor caught up with me again, his face cajoling, his voice one minute pleading, the next angry.

'You know you don't mean it, you care for me really.' He thrust a bar of chocolate in my hands. I dropped in on the floor and walked quicker. He scurried forward and stopped dead in front of me, blocking my way. I tried to get past him, but he kept dodging left and right so that I couldn't go forward.

I looked around. A burly, middle aged man was walking past. 'John!' I said, 'lovely to see you.' And with that I put my arm through his. I hadn't a clue who he was and he looked baffled, which wasn't surprising.

'My name's not …' he started.

'Just keep walking,' I said out of the corner of my mouth, 'this man is bothering me.'

He looked at me, then at Victor. 'Lovely to see you, too,' he said loudly. 'Let's go and have a cup of tea somewhere.' He marched me off, chatting loudly about the weather. Victor stopped and was soon left behind. When I was sure he couldn't see me, I apologised to the stranger and thanked him for his help. He was so sweet and wished me well in getting rid of Victor. Then I bid him farewell and went into a big shop where I could keep an eye on the door. Twice I saw Victor walk past, looking this way and that; he wasn't giving up easily. I walked past counters filled with wonderful things I couldn't afford to buy: perfumes that made me stop in my tracks and sniff the air; richly dyed silk scarves I longed to stroke; fur coats; cashmere cardigans; exquisite leather court shoes; and wonderful lingerie. I finally found the stocking counter and the woman serving was chatty so I took a risk. I told her what was happening and, wonderful person that she was, she took me through to the back of the shop so I could leave by the staff entrance. It meant going through some stockrooms that couldn't have been more different from the luxurious shop. Drab off-white walls, boxes piled everywhere and looking like no-one had cleaned it for a month.

We both had a good look round before I dared step outside, but there was no sign of Victor so I headed off towards home. My head was full of how to get rid of him. The police didn't seem like they'd help and I was reluctant to ask anyone, even Edward, to beat Victor up as the lady on the bus suggested. In any case, they could go to prison for doing that. My head went round and round, but I simply couldn't think of a way to get rid of him that wouldn't make him angry. And I wondered what he would do if he was.

13. BLUNDER

ERROR, GAFFE

A few days later the local papers reported something that made my heart sink.

COUNCIL BLUNDER
Wall to be rebuilt

'The News has learned that the local council will have to rebuild the wall it recently demolished in Sunbury. Bardman Builders' solicitors have informed the council that the wall was built on land Bardman's owns and therefore the council had no legal right to demolish it.

No spokesman from the council was available for comment, but we understand the builders are demanding the wall be rebuilt immediately.

The wall was built by Bardman Builders after the

residents in the private houses at one end of the street complained that they were disturbed by people from the local authority estate walking through their road. There have been vigorous campaigns from the residents of Sunbury who say they have to walk an extra half a mile to reach local facilities because of the wall.'

I ran to the phone box in the pouring rain to call Bob.

'What are we going to do?' I wailed. 'War's getting nearer and no-one will be interested then.'

'Let's have another meeting and start all over again. It's wretched news, Lily, but never give up.'

A week later we were back in St. Matthews Church Hall. It looked the same, the same notices, the same clock, the bunting a bit dustier. But the sun wasn't shining, and the storm clouds outside reflected the mood inside. I noticed there were fewer young men. One good thing I saw was that more people chatted to others near them. I hoped our street party and other activities had helped to bring people together.

Before Bob could even start the meeting a man stood up and shook his fist.

'What're you going to do about that wall, then?' he shouted. 'All our bloody protests come to nothing. Bloody waste of time.'

Bob held up his hands. 'I'm with you, comrade,

all our work come to nothing. And first of all I'd like to thank everyone for coming tonight. Let's see what we can do to get this wall knocked down again.'

'Too bloody right,' the man muttered.

The meeting was shorter than the last one and I hoped it didn't mean that people were giving up. Maybe they were thinking of the bigger fight looming in Germany. No-one said much, and those that did moaned. Bob's request for more volunteers to continue the fight got no takers this time. People trudged out at the end looking as gloomy as I felt. Perhaps they'd just got used to walking the extra distance to the shops and the buses.

The sub group met again when everyone had gone. I went into the kitchen and made us all some tea. As I waited for the kettle to boil and reached for the tray, I thought we could do with something stronger to lift our spirits.

Rose was speaking as I handed round the cups and put the sugar bowl down.

'What on earth can we do if Bardman's own the land the wall is on?' Rose's usual smile was replaced by down-turned lips.

Bob lifted his tartan cap and scratched his head, his shoulders slumped. 'Never give up, Rose. Where's there's a will, there's a way. We're a bit down-hearted at the moment, but we'll find a way round it. Don't suppose you can raise enough money to buy the land?'

'I'd love to,' she said with a wan smile, 'but getting £25 first time took a lot of doing. I suppose we just go back to doing what we did before.'

'More or less. We still have the petition so we can get more names for that. We'll have to think of some different ways to get attention to our cause. Any ideas?'

'Throw ourselves in front of a racehorse?' Fred suggested, putting three heaped spoons of sugar in his tea.

'Been done,' Bob replied, 'and the end result wasn't too good.'

Fred blew on his tea and took a cautious sip, 'I reckon the protest is dead and buried. Might as well give up now and accept the rich have won as usual.'

Bob steepled his fingers, deep in thought. We all looked at him expectantly.

'Dead and buried. Dead and buried. Good idea, Fred. Tell you what, let's walk through the town centre carrying a coffin. It can signify the death of freedom of movement through our streets.'

I caught his enthusiasm, 'It can be draped with a slogan about our campaign. And marchers can dress all in black or have black armbands.'

Bob was grinning now, his back upright, shoulders ready for action. 'Very photogenic too. The press'll love it. And the council will hate it. Bad publicity for them, especially if people are put out in any way. We'll have to ask for another meeting with Councillor Tallis as quickly as possible.'

Rose suddenly spoke, her smile back, 'I've got an idea for another way we can get attention, and soon. The Chamber of Commerce are having a big award ceremony in two weeks time for local businesses.'

'What sort of award?' Fred asked, tipping a generous amount of tea into his saucer and slurping loudly.

'You know, employing the most people, doing the most for the community, that sort of thing.'

Fred grunted and spat out some of his tea, 'You've got to be joking, we don't want to be awarding them Bardman's anything. They…'

'Ssshhh,' Bob said, 'let her speak.'

'How about we break into the ceremony and give Bardman's an award for being so mean and lily livered? My dad's going to the ceremony and if I ask him he'll get me a ticket. I can let you all in somehow.'

'I like it,' Bob leant over and patted her on the shoulder, 'we'll have to think of a fancy name for the award, but we can sort that out later.'

'What will the award be?' I asked. 'Bricks wrapped in pretend pound notes?'

'Yeah, a wheelbarrow load full. They've made a

load of dosh out of them big houses. How about a dustbin, 'cos they're a load of rubbish,' Fred replied. 'Wait, I've got a better idea. How about a chamber pot, cos they're a load of shit 'eads, 'scuse my French. A full one. We can tip it over the boss man's head, and a big badge for his dinner jacket that says '"I'm a greedy bastard," 'scuse my French.'

Fred laughed, demonstrating the size of it - the size of a tea plate.

Bob smiled, 'Great ideas, you really are my creative army, I knew I could trust you.' We all basked in his praise.

'Let's meet again on Monday to plan further. Two weeks isn't long. I've got to go now. Rose, can you phone me tomorrow so we can talk about the venue and think about how we'll get in, etc.'

~

The night of the Award Ceremony came round with breathtaking speed. We'd had three meetings and dragged Jean into our plot. As always, she took a bit of persuading.

'It'll be fun, Jean. Honest,' I said, my fingers crossed behind my back.

We were round at her place minding her littlest brother and sister: Trixie aged 3, a tiny version of Jean with the same blond curls and George, aged 5 whose hair was cut so short he looked almost bald. He kept getting nits. They were playing in the back garden where George was trying to teach Trixie how to use a yo-yo, without a lot of success. I had to admire his patience.

Jean listened to my attempts at persuasion and curled her lip, 'I've heard that before. Your idea of fun and mine aren't always the same. Spit it out, what d'you want me to do?'

'First off, can you ask around here and at work and see if anyone's got any sheets so old they're willing to give them to us? We could do with two. They won't get them back.'

'Shouldn't be 'ard. We've got one upstairs that's been topped and tailed so much you could read a newspaper through it. What do you want them for?'

'I'll explain later. Let's get the sheets first. You're a hero. I've got heaps of other stuff to do myself and it'll be one thing off my list.'

Just then there was a scream from the garden and Trixie came running in, crocodile tears at the ready. 'Jean, Jean, George hitted me with the ho-ho.' she cried, rubbing her head where a tiny red mark could be seen.

Jean pulled her into her arms and kissed the hurt. 'You'll be okay, Sweetheart, you're a tough nut. Talk to Lil for a minute while I go and tell George off.'

She got the sheets within a few days, but talking her into the second favour took a bit more doing.

We were in the office of the Dream Palace for the next episode of getting her involved. I told her to sit down and reached for a bag of clothes.

'We're doing a special sort of demo for the wall and I need you to dress up and pretend you're Fred's wife.'

Her eyes widened and her jaw went slack. 'What, Fred? Fred what's 93 if 'e's a day and 'as breath like a donkey's arse?'

Well, when she put it like that, it didn't sound so good.

'Ah, come on, you won't have to kiss him or anything. Just walk next to him. We'll make you up to look old. And there's an outfit for you here.'

Flinching in readiness, I handed her the bag of clothes.

She took out a faded, moth-eaten brown dress. She shook it out and the creases stayed exactly where they were. 'You've got to be kidding,' she screeched, 'This must have been old in Queen Victoria's time. Like when she was crowned.'

She sniffed it. ''asn't been washed since from the smell of it. Where the 'ell did you get this?'

'It was left over after the jumble sale,' I said, wishing I'd thought up a good lie.

'Huh! Not surprised, no-one'd even want it for a

ha'penny.' She reached into the bag again and pulled out a scrumpled brown felt hat. She looked at the hat, looked at me, then looked at the hat again. Finally, she stared at me as if she hoped I would burst into flames and burn in hell. She stood up, threw the hat on the floor, and jumped up and down on it. 'I ... will ... not ... wear ...that ... blinking ... 'at...' she said, breathless from the activity.

I kind of thought that might be her reaction, and reached in my bag for another hat. It was still pretty awful but elegant compared to the first. It was a cunning trick, but it worked. She grudgingly agreed to wear it, on condition I treated her to tea and a bun at Lyons Corner House.

∼

It was a dark night, no moon or stars, just cloud so low it felt as if we could touch it. It was perfect for sneaking into the Award Ceremony. Rose was already in the Hat and Feathers as planned. The Chamber of Commerce had spared themselves no expense for their event. Although she would let us in, she wouldn't take part in the protest itself in case we needed her help in the future. Couldn't blot her copy book.

We were a small group of protestors. Bob was dressed up as Master of Ceremonies; strange to see him without some outlandish clothing. Mind you, some would say today's get-up was no stranger than what he usually wore. I was dressed up as Lady Muck, in a fancy frock in dark green velvet and a hat my Mum had borrowed from one of the ladies she did for. As finally agreed, Jean was dressed as a poor granny, her dark, dowdy clothes the opposite of her usual look. She was under orders to walk with a bent back and look old. We sprinkled talc on her hair and put it in a hairnet under the second worst hat. Fred didn't have to dress up or make himself look old. He just wore his own clothes. He looked like a poverty stricken old man naturally, because he was. He was Jean's pretend husband.

We got a few looks on the bus, but we laughed and said we were going to a fancy dress party. Goodness knows what they thought our big, rolled up sheets were about. Fred kept putting his arm round Jean, and she kept backing away from his breath. In fact, we laughed a lot on the journey, but truth be told the laugh was to cover up our nerves. All except Bob, he was an old hat at this sort of stuff.

We got off the bus and crept towards the side of the pub, like a load of cat burglars.

'This way!' Bob said in a stage whisper. 'Don't make a sound! Don't even breathe.'

I swear I heard Jean say, 'That means you, Fred.'

I looked around and couldn't see the door, 'Which way do we go, Bob?'

'Hold on to my coat tails and follow me crocodile style.' We dutifully grabbed hold of each others clothes and took a couple of steps before Fred fell over.

'You lot walk faster than me,' he grumbled, rubbing his knee.

I heard Jean groan, 'Come on, get up Fred. No time to waste.' And I heard his heels scrape on the ground as he was pulled upright.

We crept round the side of the pub, feeling our way past parked cars, bikes and a motorbike and side car. Nerves made us giggle as we tip-toed, and we made more noise telling each other to hush than the giggles. We were almost there when I walked into a dustbin I hadn't seen in the dark. It made more noise than a horse and cart galloping through. We all froze, ears flapping like wings. After what seemed like hours of holding our breath, but was probably only a minute, we decided our luck was in and no-one had heard us. Pushing the door an inch at a time we opened the back door. I don't know about the others, but I was terrified. My knees shook and I badly needed to go to the WC.

'What if we get arrested?' I whispered, wondering if I'd get the sack.

Bob patted me on the shoulder, 'Be brave, my

girl. We'll just do our bit and leave while they're trying to take in what happens. The press will already be there anyway, but I've tipped them off. All keep your heads down and your hats covering your face and you won't be recognised. Lily, your hat has a veil, pull it down.'

'But Bob,' I said, 'you can't cover your face with what you're going to do. They'll recognise you.'

'The most they can do is keep me in the cells for the night. I've had worse. What's our offence? Trespassing? I don't think they could make that stick. Anyway, they won't want to give us more publicity.'

Before I had time to tell him I was still scared, we heard a click and the side door opened.

Rose came in, pale with nerves. 'You can hide here,' she whispered, 'I'll leave the door open a crack so you'll be able to hear what's going on. Turn the light off though in case it gets anyone's attention.'

Bob gave her a hug. 'We'll appear in between awards just as planned. Nothing else for you to do. You're a star, a hero, a wonder.'

Rose gave him a worried smile and headed back into the room. She looked lovely in a long, red, tightly fitting dress that hugged her slim figure.

We were in some sort of windowless storeroom. It was really stuffy and smelled like a jumble sale. The walls were lined with stacked chairs leaning at a crazy angle. Christmas decorations spilled out of a bag in one corner and a huge pile of table-cloths sat on the floor. We stood still as statues - scared to breathe. All except Fred who was still trying to get Jean to kiss him. She clouted him soundly round the head and turned to me. 'My mum was right, she said they're never too old 'til they're in their box,' she whispered.

We could hear the speakers in the dining room in between the rounds of applause and the clinking of glasses. Companies seemed to be getting awards for so many different things I began to wonder if it was just an excuse for a lavish knees-up.

Then our perfect opportunity arose. We heard the announcer say, 'Thank you ladies and gentlemen, and many congratulations to our winners. The rest of the awards will be announced after you've had desert. I can tell you it's a delicious banana cake that just might be laced with a spirit or two.'

'Get ready,' Bob whispered out of the side of his mouth.

The applause died down and Bob said, 'Now!'

My knees shook so much I thought I'd fall over.

From behind the scenes, I called loudly, 'Pray silence for the Master of Ceremonies.'

The room hushed again.

Bob walked out, looking magnificent in his Master of Ceremonies outfit. He strode to the centre of the stage and tapped on a glass to get attention.

'Ladies and gentlemen,' he said, 'there is one more award, a very special award to be given out before you start that delicious desert.'

From the wings, I could see a look of confusion on some of the faces at the tables. The waitresses, hands laden, stopped in their tracks. This wasn't supposed to happen, but Bob looked so convincing I guessed no-one felt they should say anything.

The room was big and rectangular and smelled of money. All the tables had dazzling white tablecloths almost down to the floor and each person had several sparkling wine glasses and silverware. Elegant chandeliers twinkled like diamonds. The bigwigs were at the top table on the stage at the end near us and the members of the Chamber of Commerce and their wives, were at long tables.

Bob was in his stride. 'This is a very special award, as I was saying. It is for the company that has done the most for uniting communities across our town. The award goes to…'

He paused for a few seconds. The room still with anticipation, all eyes on him, glasses suspended half way between table and mouths.

'The special award goes to Bardman's the Builders! Give them a big round of applause everyone!'

The Bardman's people stood up, smiling with surprise and delight. The boss, a big man with a stomach to match and a thick moustache, looked like he might beat his chest with pride.

'Thank you, Ladies and Gentleman,' Bob continued, 'here is their special award!'

He handed them an official looking scroll with the word 'Award' in big letters at the top. The rest couldn't be seen by the people in the hall, but it wasn't complimentary.

When he'd handed it to the manager of Bardman's, he gestured towards where we were standing, and we were on, hearts thumping and knees shaking. I went first in all my finery, my shoulders back and my head held high. I was holding a pole. Attached to the pole were two sheets sewn together. As I walked on, directly in front of the bigwigs on the top table, the banner gradually unfurled. We'd rehearsed this many times, so the unfurling went perfectly. We'd painted a wall on it, brick by brick. And the words 'The Wall Must Fall' in big red letters. Jean and her 'husband' looking poor and worn out, held the pole at the other end. As I stood there I could see Mr Simmons from the Dream Palace. He knew it was me and gave me a wink.

There were a few seconds of confused calm and several flashes of light as the photographers got their shots. The bigwigs' mouths flapped like landed fish and their eyes grew wide. The applause that was loudly enthusiastic when Bob announced the award, faltered then stopped altogether. There was a moment of awkward silence because no-one understood properly what was happening. People started to talk amongst themselves and the volume rose.

Then someone shouted, 'Get them off!' and two or three men stood up and started to move towards us.

We'd prepared for this. We dropped the banner and ran as fast as we could the way we'd come, half carrying poor old Fred. We closed the adjoining door behind us and pushed a chair under the door handle. We'd only run a few yards, but I was struggling to find my breath.

To my surprise there was a car waiting outside.

'Didn't think I'd make you wait for a bus for a getaway, did you?' Bob grinned. 'Hop in quick.'

We dived into the car in a heap and my hat got a bit crushed in the process. Once in we couldn't stop laughing.

'We did it!'

'Did you see their faces!'

'Wait 'til you see the papers tomorrow!'

Our driver, who turned out to be Bob's brother, drove out of there as if we'd robbed a bank and had a posse of cops after us. We swerved round corners, bumped into kerbs and screeched to a halt at crossroads. None of it mattered. We'd pulled off a great bit of publicity.

Bob had insisted we have our normal clothes in bags when we first arrived, and his brother had them in the car. We went to the Dog & Dragon to celebrate, after changing into our normal clothes in their WC. It was a small pub, with wooden benches against one wall and just three tables and chairs in the middle. A gaggle of old men in their cloth caps sat on the bar stools nursing their pints. The price list was on the wall next to the dart board.

Bob held his arms out wide. 'My champions, my warriors, my clowns, you all deserve a drink and I'm getting them in. What'll you have?'

Jean and I had half of cider each and the men had beer. While Bob was paying, Jean and I dragged two tables together so there was room for us all. We were still so excited from our adventure we could hardly sit still and kept talking about what happened as if we hadn't all been there.

Fred came towards us with his pint. 'I'll sit next to you, wifey,' he said, heading for Jean.

'Oh no, you don't,' she said, 'I'm not your wife, nor anybody else's. Clear off.'

His face fell but after two sips of his beer his usual humour returned.

Two days later Bob popped into the Dream Palace. He was waving the local paper in the air.

'Seen this, Lily?' he asked with a massive grin, 'we got some great coverage.'

I read it with a growing sense of excitement. 'Think it'll do any good?' I asked.

'I'm hopeful, my girl. Now, are you coming to the next meeting?'

14. HOLIDAY

BREAK, VACATION

'We're so lucky Mr Simmons let us both have this week off,' Jean said as we lugged our cardboard suitcases to the station. She was all dolled up in her best clothes as if we were going to a dance - not sit on a smoky train.

'Thank goodness Mum could help out,' I replied. Since she'd stepped in at the premiere, Mr Simmons had called on her once or twice when he was short of people.

'Bet she's glad of a chance to get away from your dad too, not to mention the extra money.'

'Are you certain your aunt won't mind me coming?' I asked. I could imagine what my father would say about me asking a friend to stay.

'Too late now if she does, you daft thing,' she said, 'but don't expect anything posh.'

I smiled at the idea. 'I'm not used to posh.'

'No, I mean really not posh, no inside lav or anything. ''ope you like spiders 'cos the lav's down the garden. And I'm not sure if she's even 'ad electricity put in yet. But you'll soon see. Come on, we need to get a move on or we'll miss our train.'

We hurried through light drizzle, not enough to put up an umbrella but enough to make you damp and sticky. It was mid morning and buses trundled by; old ladies with shopping trolleys dragged their groceries behind them; Mums pushed big prams in and out of puddles, or dragged whining kids by the arm.

We were surprised to find the station much busier than usual; we had to push our way towards the ticket office. Most of the men in the crowd milling about were in crisp, new uniforms. The recent call-up laws meant all single men aged twenty to twenty two were conscripted.

Jean leaned over to me. 'They look too young to shave, much less fight in a war,' she said.

I nodded, 'I wonder if they'll all come back. Gives you the shivers just thinking about it.'

Eventually Jean and I got to the front of the queue. The ticket man didn't look up, all we could see was the big bald spot dotted with dandruff. 'Where to?' he asked, not even looking up.

'Two third class to Weston-Super-Mare, please,' Jean said.

'Barbed wire,' he said, still not looking at us. Jean looked at me, looked back at him and made a 'he's crazy' sign.

'Barbed wire,' he said again.

Jean put her head on one side, 'What do you mean, barbed wire?'

He slammed down his pen and looked up for the first time, scowling. Then I saw his scowl vanish and his eyes light up when he saw Jean. It always happened, men of all ages found it hard to take their eyes off her. 'Hope you're not planning to go swimming, Sweetheart,' he said.

Jean gave him one of her dazzling smiles, and put one hand on her hip like a model. 'Think I'd look good in a costume, then?'

I nudged her. 'Jean, we've got a train to catch.' I whispered in her ear, ready to kill her.

She looked about to carry on the flirtation so I pushed her aside. 'Can you tell us what you mean, please?' I asked the ticket man.

His expression changed and he looked weary, the frown lines back. 'Beach is covered in barbed wire, I heard some soldiers talking about it. Still want to go?'

I looked at Jean and we both nodded immediately.

'Yes please, two tickets, third class.'

By the time we'd paid, we had to hurry out onto the platform, but we needn't have worried, there was no sign of the train.

There were even more soldiers out there, and a couple of women in uniform, looking very smart and businesslike.

There were loads of civilian women and children, too. They'd probably bought penny platform tickets to see off their men. The noise was tremendous, what with the chatter, the smoke burping out of train funnels and the rattle of the wheels on the track.

Jean nudged me, 'Think we'll get a seat?'

I shrugged.

She was having a good look at the lads in uniform. 'Maybe one of them'd let me sit on 'is lap if not,' she said, 'I wouldn't mind that at all.' One of them caught her eye and winked.

'Jean, I'm not going to have to spend this holiday keeping you out of trouble, am I?'

'Nah, we'll have some fun, just you and me. Mind you, they do 'ave a dance once a week and we can't pass up on that, can we?'

The train pulled in with a screech of metal on metal, and everyone on the platform shuffled into place to grab a seat.

'Come on, Lil, let's push our way forward,' Jean said, and with that she dragged my arm, but we didn't make much progress because of our cases. They bumped into everyone and stopped us weaving our way through the crowd. We needn't have worried though, the soldiers were perfect gentlemen and let us through with many a smile and a wink, not to mention a couple of wolf whistles. The smell of their damp uniforms mixed with the engine oil and smoke.

Puffing and panting we dragged our cases into a carriage already occupied by a family of four: Mum, Dad and twin boys who looked about three years old. Two soldiers got in with us. I made to put my case up on the luggage rack.

'Let me,' one of the soldiers said. 'Can't have a lady lugging heavy cases.' Like we hadn't just lugged them to the station. I smiled sweetly and thanked him. His mate, blushing furiously, did the same with Jean's case. She kissed him on the cheek for his trouble and he blushed even more.

The mother with the family looked at him, looked at Jean and gave me a knowing smile. I raised an eyebrow and grinned back. The soldier who helped me was older, probably in his mid thirties. His uniform had seen some use so I guessed he was a regular soldier. I looked at the corridor and could see soldiers sitting on their kitbags, standing having a ciggie, or pushing down the windows to wave goodbye.

The older soldier smiled at everyone. His hair was thinning a bit at the front, giving him a widow's peak, and he had a gap between his front teeth big enough to slide a half crown through.

'Hello, all,' he said, 'Jim's the name. Guess with all the hold-ups on the trains we're going to be spending quite a bit of time together.' He leaned forward and shook us all by hand, even the three year olds who looked startled, then giggled shyly.

Jean asked him where they were going. Jim hesitated. 'Not allowed to say, careless talk and all that. But we're getting off a bit before the end of the line, then we have to get another train. Late night for us, I reckon.'

The journey took an hour and a half longer than it should have done, with many unexplained stops. War hadn't been declared yet, but it seemed we were all starting to experience a small part of what was to come. But Jim kept us all amused with lively stories of his life before the army.

15. ACCIDENT

MISHAP, SETBACK

*J*ean's aunt's cottage was like something out of an old fairy tale, perhaps Red Riding Hood, though I didn't spot any wolves hanging around. It was a tiny wooden house, set back from the lane by a narrow path bordered with Delphiniums. The scent of the roses round the door was heady. Jean took me straight round the back, pointing out the lavvy which was a few yards from the back door. It was built of ancient bricks with a crooked tiled roof and a wooden door hanging open. Ivy and clematis climbed around it. I could see ripped up squares of newspaper on a bit of string ready for use. I could also see an old wooden sign that read *The Lord seeth all*. I hoped not.

The rest of the back garden was given over to fruit and vegetables. Apples and plums hung heavy on their trees, ready for bottling and jam making. Cabbages, carrots and leeks looked ready to pick. In the corner was a chicken run surrounded by barbed wire to keep out the foxes.

Jean knocked loudly at the back door, shouted hello and walked in. Her aunt was bent over the kitchen table mixing pastry in a blue stripped bowl. Her face broke into a wide smile when she saw Jean. She stopped what she was doing, brushed her floury hands on her apron and held her arms wide for Jean to rush into her embrace. Only then did she seem to notice me.

'Lil, it is Lil? I've heard such a lot about you. Call me Aunt Mary,' she said, and gave me a hug almost as generous as Jean's. She was even shorter than me, soft and cuddly and smelled of soap and cooking.

'You must be worn out after your journey. Sit down, sit down.' She turned and started to put cups and saucers on the table.

The kitchen was old-fashioned but warm and cozy. The wooden table was in the middle of the room and bore the scars of long use. A pile of logs rested near an iron range with two small ovens, and delicious smells drifted from them. A bunch of wildflowers in a jam jar on the windowsill looked pretty in front of the thin, flowery curtains that moved lazily in front of the open window. Beneath it was a deep, crazed sink like we used to have in our old place, and under it a curtain on a wire hid the Vim and scrubbing brushes. A fat, ginger cat slept in a rocking chair in one corner, twitching from time to time as if it were dreaming of mice.

We were soon sitting round the table drinking tea and eating Aunt Mary's light-as-air scones with her home-made strawberry jam. Jean talked for so long about her family goings-on she had to keep topping up her cup 'cos her mouth got dry. When they'd exhausted the topic, I asked about the barbed wire on the beaches.

Aunt Mary's smiling face became serious. 'Someone's been having you on, Dear,' she said. 'There's nothing like that here, although the postman told me lots of troops have started coming as suddenly as anything. Jean'll be pleased about that,' she said, and gave Jean a mock smack on the wrist. 'It breaks my heart to think we might have another war. I lost two brothers in the last one. I want you girls to be very careful when you're here.' She started to gather the crockery together, 'But enough of that gloomy talk; get your cases and go up to your room while I get tea ready.'

We had to go up stairs that were little more than a ladder, and then walk through Aunt Mary's bedroom to get to ours. The ceiling sloped with the shape of the roof. Two narrow beds lined the room, each covered in a crocheted bedspread. Rose-painted chamber-pots peaked out from under them. There were pegs on the wall for our clothes and a chair under the window with a candle in a stubby candlestick on it. Looking out we could see the back garden and trees in the woods behind. I sniffed the country air; It was heaven after living in town.

'What shall we do tomorrow?' I asked Jean, 'and don't say go looking for handsome soldiers. Mind you, Edward said in his last letter that he was being posted not far from here.'

Jean's mouth dropped open, 'Why aren't you meeting him then?' she asked.

'He's busy doing his training and anyway, this is our holiday, so I didn't suggest it.'

'I wouldn't have minded, you daft thing,' she said, 'no harm in keeping an eye open for him though, is there?'

I thought the odds on bumping into him were very small, but hoped I'd be lucky.

Jean stood up suddenly. 'Let's help Aunt Mary with her chores, then go for a walk into town. I haven't been here for ages and it'll be good to see it all again.'

~

Next morning the cockerel woke us up far too early. Jean rubbed her eyes, 'If you want a bath you'll have to boil some water and use the tin bath. It's in the lean-to at the back of the house. Aunty will show you everything.' Our old house was just the same and I was grateful again for the modern conveniences we had now.

The smell of breakfast cooking enticed us downstairs and we soon demolished the egg, bacon and fried bread Aunt Mary put before us. When we'd finished we asked how we could help. Aunt Mary gave us a list of tasks. We got the eggs from the chicken run; we picked vegetables for dinner; cleaned the downstairs windows and washed up the breakfast things. After inspecting our work, Aunt Mary handed us a pack of sandwiches and sent us out for the day. The sun was shining although there were clouds in the distance.

'Don't trust the weather,' Aunt Mary said, 'take an umbrella, it's going to rain. Might even be a storm, so look out.'

We didn't believe her for a second but took the umbrellas just to please her. She was right about the barbed wire. We headed for the beach and there was none, just miles of soft sand. It was bliss to take off our shoes. Paddling at the water's edge, I could feel the smooth ripples made by the outgoing tide. The waves rippled gently, the air washed with the smell of salt. Seaweed was washed up here and there and it was the deep green sort that has pods you feel you could pop. I shaded my eyes and looked out to sea. Children were swimming and playing and further out three boats sailed silently along, triangles of bright colour twisting and turning in the wind.

Like a couple of kids we collected shells and wrote our names with them in the sand. Families were enjoying the sun, too. Dads with knotted hankies protecting their bald heads ; Mums fussing around keeping an eye on the kids; and grannies and granddads snoozing on deck chairs. The Punch and Judy show was near the pier and a donkey took children up and down the beach. Some jumped up and down on the poor animals back while others looked terrified and begged to get down. Then, looking up, I saw that the heavy clouds were closer and noticed a cooler breeze on my skin.

By lunchtime clouds had come over the sun. People put on coats or drifted away from the beach, wondering how to kill time until they were allowed back into their B & Bs. Not much beach was left because the tide had come in. Jean nodded towards the pier, 'Come on, there's seats on the pier and we can eat our sandwiches there and have a go on the penny arcade after.'

We walked through the amusement arcade. There

were lots of machines where you could win a soft toy if you were very lucky, but probably wouldn't. A bit further on there were rides like the ghost train where teenagers squealed with enjoyable fright, or the merry-go-round where children laughed with excitement. We bought a bottle of pop each and sat and ate our sandwiches watching it all happen.

Jean paused mid-bite. 'Ever wonder if this is all there is?' she said.

I looked round, confused. 'All what is?'

She waved her arm around to include everything we could see. 'You know, all this. A week's 'oliday a year if you're lucky. Bored to death in the shirt factory with a monster for a manager who loves nothing more than finding fault. Going out with stupid lads who just want to get in your knickers.'

I nudged her, 'Hey, speak for yourself. I don't go out with stupid lads.'

She nudged me back, 'Oh yeah, what about that Victor then? 'e wasn't catch of the year, was he? And you 'aven't got him off your back yet, 'ave you?'

'Jean, I could do with some advice about Victor. He's being a real pest. He's followed me a few times. Sometimes from a distance, but making sure I can see him, and a couple of times walking next to me and trying to get me to talk to him. I never do after the first time. And twice he's left presents for me at work.'

Her forehead furrowed. 'You kept quiet about it being quite so bad.'

I could feel my face drop, 'Got any ideas what I could do to stop him?'

'Murder?' she offered.

'Love to, but I'm looking for ideas that won't get me landed in jail.'

We kicked around ideas for a few minutes but couldn't come up with anything that sounded like it would really work. Then Jean clapped her hands, 'You said he'd done this sort of thing to someone before. Why don't we find her and see what she did?'

'But what if she got someone to beat him up?' I repeated the story Mrs Bosom had told me on the bus that day.

She looked at me disapprovingly. 'Let's cross that bridge if we ever find it. When we get 'ome, we'll try to find 'er. Can't be that 'ard if we go to the pub you told me about.'

It wasn't really a solution, but at least it was an idea and I'd been stuck for one of those up to now. I could feel the tension leave my face and I smiled at her.

'Thanks, Jean. You often have great ideas.'

'Yeah, but what we was talking about earlier. Doing something a bit worthwhile. I 'aven't got any ideas for that yet. It's all right for you. You've been going to them classes and got them certificates. Now you've got a decent job; doing something worthwhile.'

'Jean, I'm hardly brain of Britain. You're every bit as brainy as me.'

'I might be but I've never done anything worthwhile. I don't know where you get your get-up-and-go from. I bet it was your mum so you didn't end up with 'er life and someone like that miserable dad of yours.'

I thought of my mum's life and hoped it would get better one day so she could have some happy times without him. I could feel a tear tracing a line down my cheek and bit back a sob, 'Poor Mum, perhaps she'll stand up to him one day.'

'Yeah, I hope so too, she's nice.'

She threw away the crust of her sandwich. It was immediately claimed by fighting seagulls. She almost had to shout to be heard over their squabble. 'I'd like to do something with my life. A bit more than working in a shirt factory.'

'Like what?'

'I dunno. Gotta think about it. Something that counts - that 'elps other people.'

'I don't know if being an assistant manager at the Dream Palace fits the bill, so you don't need to feel jealous.' For the first time, I stopped and thought about the purpose of my work.

Jean pushed my shoulder and laughed, 'You jok-

PICTURE HOUSE GIRLS

ing? Going to the flicks is the only pleasure a lot of our customers get in their life. If war starts it'll be even more important.'

As she spoke a group of kids ran past, laughing and clowning around. They were carrying buckets and spades, some clutching shells and others holding hands in case they got left behind. The pleasure of watching them made me realise how true Jean's words were. Having fun was as important as breathing.

'You're right,' I said, 'it is important, but other jobs can be even more important. You've just got to find the right one. If war does come along and it's anything like the last one, us girls will have a lot more choices.'

I stood up, put my sandwich wrapper in my bag and grabbed her hand, 'Just stay away from those boys in case you have a nasty accident!'

Then out of the blue there was a loud bang and we jumped so high we nearly left our seats. It was quickly followed by a flash of lightening and the heaviest rain I'd ever seen.

Jean peered through the door, 'Blimey, that's some storm. Good job we've got our brollies, though the wind'll turn them inside out.'

As we sat, the storm got wilder, the wind whipped trees around and big waves crashed over the wall. We saw one family set off from the pier, but the wind was so strong the parents struggled to drag their children round the corner, with the kids' feet slipping and sliding in the wet and their bodies being buffeted by gusts of wind so strong you'd have thought a boxer was laying into them. After tugging them with both hands, the parents finally got them round and they set off, heads down against the rain. It was raining so hard the drops formed bubbles and bounced off the road like tiny balls like marbles.

Me and Jean had a cuppa at the cafe on the pier and waited for the rain to stop, but after a while we gave up.

'I reckon we might as well go back. This looks set in for the day,' I said.

'Oh, Lil, I'm so sorry your first day is such a wash out. Perhaps tomorrow will be better.'

The wind was too strong to use our umbrellas so we wrapped our jackets round ourselves and lurched out into the rain. Like the family we watched, we struggled to get round the corner of the pier and had to link arms to manage it. We walked along the deserted promenade at the foot of the cliff. Jean decided to make a game of it and started to skip ahead loudly singing *Jumpin' Jive:* '*The jim-jam-jump is a jumping jive'*. I grinned at her zest for life and sang along with her although her crazy dancing meant she got a bit of a way in front.

Then three things happened at once.

There was an almighty clap of thunder.

A blinding flash of lightening.

And a massive wave which smashed over the sea wall, rose up like a sea monster and caught Jean, dragging her off her feet and towards the cliff. Despite the racket of the weather, I heard the noise her body made as she hit the sea wall with force.

'Jean!' I shouted. I ran over and knelt beside her. She was drenched and lifeless; her skinny form so white it was like a marble statue. Blood poured from a cut near her hairline and stained her hair, and I could see one arm had lost a lot of skin. I couldn't breathe for fear. I had no idea what to do. She looked dead and I had never felt so useless. And all the time more waves lapped at us and I was terrified another freak one would get us both.

Then Jean gave a feeble cough. She was alive! I didn't realise I'd been holding my breath, but gave a big breath out. But Jean didn't move again, although thankfully I could see her chest moving up and down.

'Help! Help!' I called, hoping against hope someone would hear over the rain and storm. I cradled Jean in my arms. Should I drag her all the way back to the pier? Would I do her harm as I dragged her? Would anyone ever walk along the promenade in this downpour? The rain was still torrential. I counted the time between the next lightening and thunder and could tell the storm had moved slightly away but not enough to take the rain clouds with it.

My thoughts were still all over the place when a sopping wet little dog ran up, barked at us and then, turning round, barked the other way. I looked in that direction and saw a woman wearing proper rain gear running towards us. I cried with relief and send a silent prayer of thanks to God.

Without a word the woman knelt and began to examine Jean, feeling her head and neck, then her arms and legs. She was gentle yet confident. All the time the rain beat down and we both had to wipe our faces many times.

'I'm a nurse,' she shouted after a couple of minutes. 'She's unconscious, but I can't feel anything broken. Run back to the pier and ask them to get an ambulance. Hurry.'

Jean and I had only walked a couple of hundred yards but the run back to pier seemed like miles. The rain lashed against my face, water dripping off my hair and my nose. Twice I slid over and took some skin off my knees. But then at last I was at the Pier, dodging holiday makers as I looked for my goal. It took a couple of precious minutes to find the manager's office. I knocked three times without a response and was just coming to the conclusion he was elsewhere when I heard a bored 'Come in.' He was a portly man in middle age. He leaned back in his chair, reading a newspaper. A beer and a full ashtray sat on the desk in front of him. An untidy pile of papers on his desk threatened to slide on to the floor and the room smelt of stale food and sweat.

As I rushed in, he ignored me, finishing what he was reading before he looked up.

'Quick! Quick!' I cried without introducing myself, 'phone an ambulance. My friend's been hurt and she's unconscious.'

He put the newspaper down and nodded to me to sit in the chair opposite. I was far too tense to sit and stood bouncing up and down on my toes. 'Hurry!' I said, my breath ragged. My command seemed to have the opposite effect.

The man took a big swig of his beer, wiped his mouth with his sleeve, then said, 'Now calm down, Missy, and tell uncle George all about it.' Then he patted his knee as if I should sit on it.

I nearly leapt across the desk and choked him. Instead, I went round the side of his desk, picked up the phone and thrust it in his hand.

'Phone an ambulance. NOW!' I said in my sternest voice.

He did.

~

The journey to the hospital seemed to take forever, with me holding Jean's hand all the way although she didn't know I was there. Her hand was limp and clammy as if it was no longer part of her. The ambulance screeched to a halt with such suddenness I was thrown on the floor. I heard the ambulance men running round to open the rear doors and things moved very quickly after that. We ran through the corridors to the x-ray department and then on to a cubicle where Jean was thoroughly checked by a doctor.

'She's got concussion,' the doctor said, 'but there are no broken bones. We'll keep her in for a night or two to make sure she has no brain damage.'

My jaw dropped, 'Brain damage? You mean she might be daft or something?'

The doctor made to walk towards the door. 'Let's not walk before we can run. One day at a time. We'll see how she goes tonight and assess her again in the morning.'

Jean was put in Victoria Ward, a long room that smelt strongly of disinfectant. There were about twenty beds lined up against the wall with military precision. It was like a morgue, with patients asleep, reading quietly or staring into space. Two women in adjacent beds in the far corner were speaking quietly. Everything was so regimented it could have been an army barracks; I expected a Sergeant Major to appear at any minute barking orders to get well immediately, and stop taking up bed space.

The Sister's desk was in the middle of the ward, pencils and papers all placed very tidily. Not a thing was out of place. I almost felt scared to walk on the floor or speak out loud. A nurse was walking quietly around, going from bed to bed taking temperatures and pulses.

I sat looking at Jean who was as pale as the sheets. She had a bandage on her head and another on her arm. She looked asleep but I knew she hadn't come round yet. It wasn't sleep.

As I watched I remembered Aunt Mary had no idea what had happened. She didn't have electricity, so she certainly wouldn't have a phone. Before I had time to work out what to do about it the Sister strode over to me, her starched uniform swishing with every step. Her fanned hat made her look like a strange crested bird.

She tapped me on the shoulder. 'I'll have to ask you to leave now, myear, visiting hours have finished,' she said with a sympathetic smile.

'But my friend's just come to the ward. She's unconscious. I don't know what's going to happen to her.'

'I know it's hard, I'm sorry, but the doctor will do his rounds later. Don't try to visit her again until visiting tomorrow afternoon. Two o'clock until four o'clock. Patients need their rest, you know.'

She stood there and nodded to my bag to indicate she expected me to go immediately. Even though she'd been sympathetic, I hated her. Like a difficult teenager I grumbled and picked up my bag very slowly. I kissed Jean's cheek and whispered, 'Be well, Jean, I love you,' then turned to go.

As I left the hospital I noticed the storm had blown itself out. Rain still spotted the windows and the world was a dozen shades of soggy grey. I stood in the doorway of the hospital wondering what to do. People hurried here and there and two ambulances drove further into the hospital grounds. Aunt Mary needed to be told but so did Jean's mother. Should I send her a telegram now? Would I be worrying her for nothing? I'd never sent a telegram before and wondered if I had enough money. In the end I decided to go back to the cottage and ask Aunt Mary what to do.

I was walking back past the shops, head down, still worrying, when I heard someone call my name. Confused, I looked around and saw several soldiers on the other side of the street. One of them was waving and started to cross the road. I thought my eyes were playing wicked tricks on me. It was Edward, lovely Edward.

'Lily, what are you doing here?' he asked, a big smile on his face.

I tried to answer him but instead I burst into tears, the tension of the last few hours overcoming me. He took me in his arms and waited without saying a word until my sobs finally stopped.

'There's a cafe over there,' he said, 'let's get a cup of tea and you can tell me what's happened.'

'But what about your friends?' I said, looking around.

'They've gone on. We were just having a night off duty, they'll be fine without me.'

I blew my nose and wiped my eyes as we crossed the road and went into the cafe. It was small, but spotless, with seaside pictures on every wall. A delicious smell of freshly cooked bread made me feel suddenly hungry. Edward noticed. 'Tea and toast okay for you, or would you rather have something else?' he asked. A cheerful elderly waitress with her hair in a net came over. She had brightly rouged cheeks and deep red lipstick. They clashed somehow with her wrinkles, although her smile more than made up for it.

'What can I get you? Miss? Sir?'

'Tea, toast and jam twice, please.' Edward said.

She wrote our orders on a tiny notepad and vanished to the kitchen.

The tea and toast were long gone by the time I'd

told Edward all about Jean's accident. He looked thoughtful.

'So the sister said the doctor would see Jean after you left. Is that right?'

I nodded.

'So why don't we go back to the hospital and see if he's still there. If we ask firmly enough, we can get him to tell us how she is.'

I kicked myself for not thinking of that. 'It's a good idea, but he may not tell us anything. We're not relatives.'

He grinned, 'We are now. You're her sister and I'm her brother. Now, what's her surname?'

~

Back at the hospital we waited in a short queue to speak to the receptionist. About a dozen people were waiting in uncomfortable looking chairs. I could see one woman clutching her bandaged head, another was carefully holding her wrist, a third had a tea towel wrapped round his hand, bright spots of blood dripping occasionally to the floor. Before I had time to look more, we moved up the queue and were in front of the receptionist. She was a plump, middle aged women with a pen resting over one ear and another in her hand. Her desk was a mass of forms and notebooks she kept rifling through.

We stood for a few seconds, but she didn't look up. My mum would have said she was being ignorant.

'I'd like to see the doctor about my sister, please,' I said.

She didn't look up. 'What doctor?' she asked.

'I think it was Dr. Thompson.'

She still hadn't looked up, but instead continued working on her paperwork.

'Think or know?'

I wasn't sure, but I'd had enough of this. 'I'm sure, we need to see Dr Thompson.'

She finally looked up and her pen fell on the desk. 'He's busy,' she said. She hadn't checked in any way.

'In that case, we'll wait,' said Edward with a firm but pleasant tone.

She looked up, surprised, 'Um, it might be a long wait.'

Edward gave her a smile that would have melted an iceberg. 'We have time. I'm sure you'll do all you can to help us. We're very worried about our sister. She's had a horrible accident.'

Seeing his smile, a blush crept up from her neck. 'I'll see what I can do,' she said.

She left her desk and walked briskly down a long

corridor, her well padded bottom jiggling from side to side like two balloons filled with water. A few minutes later she was back, breathless from hurrying to give us the news. Ignoring me, she smiled sweetly and spoke to Edward, 'If you'd like to come with me, I'll show you into a room where the doctor will see you. He will probably be ten or fifteen minutes.'

Edward rewarded her with another smile and a jokey kiss of the hand. She giggled like a schoolgirl.

After she left us, I turned to him. 'I'm seeing a whole different side of you,' I said.

He grinned, 'Most people are helpful if you approach them in the right way.'

I couldn't help but think that his posh voice had something to do with it too.

We sat in silence waiting for the doctor. I picked up a dog-eared magazine on a little table but couldn't concentrate on it. I kept looking at the clock but it was as if the hands refused to move.

It was thirty five long minutes before the doctor arrived. He was tall and reed thin. His white coat had a few spots of blood down the front and the stethoscope round his neck was crooked. He stood in the doorway as if dazed and I wondered how many hours he'd been on duty. Then, seeming to come round, he shook his head and came towards us. We stood up.

'The receptionist tells me you are the brother and sister of Jean Norman,' he said.

I held out my hand. 'Yes, I'm Lily Baker and this is my brother Edward. Please, how is Jean?'

He shook hands with us both and indicated to sit down. He sat with a relieved groan, took off one shoe and rubbed his foot.

'How was she when you last saw her?' he asked.

'Still unconscious.'

'Then I've excellent news for you,' he said with a smile. 'About half an hour ago she came round. She's a bit dopey but it's only to be expected. She was quite rational and there's no reason to think she won't make a full recovery. Her cuts and bruises are only superficial.'

My shoulders sagged with relief and Edward leaned over and squeezed my hand. I wanted to hug the doctor there and then.

'That's wonderful. How long do you think she'll be in?'

He paused, 'Hard to say for sure, but if all goes well she could be discharged tomorrow or the next day. Why not phone in the morning and see what the situation is then? Will you be able to collect her? We couldn't let her go without someone with her after that sort of injury. And she'll need to rest for a few days.'

'I'll be able to collect her and look after her,' I said.

'I must tell you that if you notice any difference

in her, either physical or mental, you must bring her back immediately.'

I nodded, 'I promise. I won't let her out of my sight.'

He stood up, his mind already on the next patient. 'Then all's well. Best of luck.' He walked out of the door without even a goodbye.

'I'm so glad,' Edward said, taking my hands in his, 'you must be very relieved. I have to get back to the barracks now I'm afraid, but I think I could get away for a couple of hours tomorrow morning. Would there be any chance of meeting you?'

I thought quickly. Visiting was in the afternoon only, so I couldn't see Jean any sooner. I knew she'd approve; she was always trying to improve my love life as she called it.

'I'd love to,' I said, trying not to grin too idiotically, 'where shall we meet?'

I set off to Aunt Mary's with a spring in my step. Instead of having terrible news, I could tell her all would be well. And I'd tell her about Edward too.

Early next morning I walked to the phone box at the end of Aunt Mary's lane. As usual, it took me all my strength to open the kiosk door. The little mirror invited me to check I looked good for the call, as if the person the other end could see me. Crazy. I put my coins in the slot, dialled the number and inspected the doodles on the phone directory as I waited. When the hospital answered I pressed button A and asked for Victoria Ward.

After a delay long enough for me to have to put in more pennies, I finally got through to the ward. Jean was doing well and they expected her to be discharged next day. I almost skipped back to Aunt Mary's cottage to tell her, then headed off again, this time to meet Edward. Aunt Mary and I would meet at the hospital for visiting time. What had seemed like a catastrophe yesterday, had turned out well. Apart from Jean's sore head that is.

The storm of the day before seemed like a mirage, and the new day was bright and mild, the sky as blue at Edward's eyes. Occasional fluffy white clouds drifted lazily by and seagulls squawked loudly as they dived for dropped chips.

'Can I hold your hand?' Edward asked.

I smiled and reached for his. 'I'm so glad to see you. You were such a help yesterday.'

He put his head on one side, 'Is that the only reason?'

I play punched his arm, 'No, silly, it's lovely to see you.'

He stopped and turned to face me. 'Lily, last time we spoke about it, I said it wasn't right to ask you to wait for me, but I've got to know you better so, well, do you think you could? Is it okay for me to ask?'

'What? Wait for you?'

He ran his hand through his hair. I was beginning to recognise it as a sign of nervousness. 'Yes. Although I remember you had seen another boy a few times.'

I grinned, 'Mmm, Victor. He's long gone, we only saw each other four times then I gave him the big heave-ho, although he doesn't seem to quite believe it yet.'

He frowned, 'What, you mean he's still pestering you?'

'Yes, he's being a nuisance, following me sometimes and other things. I heard he'd done the same thing to someone else. Doesn't like being dumped.'

An army lorry went by, full of soldiers looking too hot in their uniforms. A couple of them whistled at me and I smiled as they went by.

Edward looked serious, 'Do you want me to do something about this Victor? I don't know when I get leave next, but as soon as I can.'

I thought about it. Some men take things more seriously from men than from women. But I wanted to sort this out myself. 'No, I'll deal with him. Let's not talk about him any more, it'll ruin our time together.'

Our two hours went as quickly as snow on a summer's day and we clung on to each other when it was time to say goodbye, not knowing when we could meet again. There was an army camp about five miles from home. I thought for the millionth time it was a pity he couldn't be posted there so we could see each other more often.

As I walked back to Aunt Mary's my euphoria at Edward asking me to be his girl deflated. Was he just saying this because he might soon be going to war and wanted someone at home to think about? If he wasn't scared of dying alone, would he want someone like me, or wait for a more suitable girlfriend? I'd heard so many stories about hurried marriages during WW1 that had gone terribly wrong. I didn't want to make the same mistake. Not that he'd proposed anyway.

∼

Aunt Mary looked different at the hospital; it was the first time I'd seen her without her pinny and she looked years younger. I'd thought she was quite plump but in her flowery cotton dressed she looked trim and attractive for her age. Her face lit up when she saw me and she linked her arm through mine, asking me about my date with Edward.

'He sounds like a good one,' she said, 'hang on to him.'

We were soon at the ward and had to wait a few minutes with other people for visiting time to start.

Once the door was opened we all pushed forward like we were in a race. Jean was sitting up in the immaculate bed looking far too well to be there at all. A bandage round her head made her look like a pirate and was rather fetching.

'I've been thinking,' she said after we'd settled down. 'I've been watching these nurses and they do a great job. A lot more worthwhile than working at the shirt factory.'

Aunt Mary lit up, 'I was a nurse in the Great War.'

Jean's mouth dropped open, 'You never said.'

'Well, time moves on, don't want to bore people with my old stories.'

Jean took her hand, 'But I'd love to know more.'

'I was a VAD really…'

'What's that?' Jean asked.

'A nurse for the Voluntary Aid Detachment. They called us VADs, less of a mouthful. We were all volunteers and went to field hospitals. Then, as the years went on we got used for more and more work, not just nursing, and I ended up near the front in France. I wouldn't want to tell you the awful things I saw. Young men in their prime, dead or ruined. If you're thinking about being a nurse you need a strong stomach. It's not like nursing in peace time. You'll see men with missing arms or legs, or their guts hanging out. Or going mad because of the awful things they'd seen.' She paused and stared into the distance for a minute. 'In 1917 I did an exam and used to do the x-rays. When you get home tomorrow I'll tell you all about it.'

For the rest of our holiday Jean had to rest, so we took it easy staying round the cottage or going for gentle walks. We helped Aunt Mary with her chores and I particularly enjoyed collecting the eggs each morning. I even got to know her chickens by name. My favourite was Maisie, a white chicken who Aunt Mary said was a Leghorn.

Every day when we sat down for a cuppa Jean would beg her to tell us about her time in the VADs.

'I don't like to talk about it much,' said Aunt Mary. 'In some ways it was a great time. Us girls got to do lots of things that people said only men could do. But the other side of it was the terrible death and destruction.'

Jean put her hand on her aunt's arm, 'So when did you join up, then?'

'About half way through the war. I'd done a bit of nurse training with the Red Cross, so the VADs accepted me. They needed a lot more nurses then because so many young men were coming back injured or worse. In a way I was lucky though.'

'How do you mean?' Jean asked putting more sugar in her tea.

'The VADs who joined up early in the war got a

rough time. The doctors and professional nurses used them as skivvies, just getting them cleaning, swilling out bedpans and horrible jobs like that.'

She stood up and went to fetch the cake tin. She paused and spent a while looking out of the window at the clouds scudding by. I wondered what horrors she was remembering.

When she spoke again it was more to herself than us, 'I remember one young man, Tom his name was…'

She broke off with a sob and stood up wiping her eye. 'You got those eggs in yet, Lily?'

~

To my surprise Jean listened intently to the talk about nursing and she talked a lot about the nurses who took care of her after her accident. I began to think she might really do something about becoming one. If a new lad didn't distract her, that is.

But one thing put a dark shadow on the holiday. It happened on the Thursday. The postman came bright and early as usual, stopping at aunt Mary's for a quick cup of tea. Jean and I came downstairs, only half awake.

'Good morning, young ladies,' the postie said,

'and a beautiful morning it is, all the better for seeing you two.'

He put down his cup and reached into his sack, taking out a small parcel wrapped in brown paper and string. 'Which of you two ladies is Lily Baker?'

I frowned, 'That's me. Why?'

He thrust the parcel into my hand with a little bow. 'Someone loves you enough to send you a parcel,' he said. He stood up and put on his cap, its Royal Mail badge glinting in a ray of sun through the window.

'Well, I must be going or I'll never finish my round at this rate. Thank you for the tea, Mary. Much obliged.' He grinned, kissed her hand, got his bag and walked out of the cottage. A second later we heard him pick up his bike and ring his bell as a jaunty goodbye.

Jean and Aunt Mary looked at me expectantly while I examined the parcel. I didn't recognise the writing, so it certainly wasn't my mum's or dad's. Apart from Jean's family, I couldn't think who else would know aunt Mary's address.

'Well, ain't you gonna open it?' Jean said. 'I'd have ripped that apart in a second.'

Aunt Mary saw me hesitate. 'What's wrong, Lily?' she asked.

'A lad I went out with a few times has been pestering me and I'm worried this came from him.'

She put her head on one side, 'It's bad to be pestered, but why are you worried about the parcel?'

I pulled a face, 'A lady told me that a bloke who was pestering her put dog business through her door. What if that's what's in here?'

Before I could do anything else Jean grabbed the parcel out of my hand and sniffed it, her face comically screwed up. 'Nah, it's not dog-do.' She handed it back.

'Here, let me open it for you,' Aunt Mary said. She carefully unpicked the knot in the string which took ages, then along with the brown paper, put it in the kitchen drawer. She handed what was left back to me. It was something wrapped in newspaper. My heart racing, I opened it so slowly you'd have thought it was an unexploded bomb.

It was a bracelet.

A pretty bracelet with an unusual pattern on it.

'Well, he must really like you,' Aunt Mary said.

Jean just grabbed it out of my hand again. 'Cor, this looks expensive. D'you think it's gold?'

'One way to tell,' Aunt Mary said, 'hand it back.'

She rifled amongst the bits and bobs in her drawer and found a tiny magnifying glass. She inspected the inside of the bracelet. 'I'm no expert, but I think this mark here means it's gold,' she said.

'You lucky...' Jean started.

I went from feeling numb to feeling hot with fury.

How dare he keep bothering me this way? What right did he think he had?

I slapped my hand on the table, 'No, it's not lucky. I don't want the damn thing.' I threw it across the room and it bounced on the stone slabs. Jean bent and picked it up.

'Keep your hair on, you could've dented it.' She put in on, and moved her arm this way and that, admiring it. 'I'll have it if you don't want it.'

I took two deep breaths, then held out my hand. 'No, give it back to me. I'm going to return it to him. If I keep it he'll think I like him or he's got one over on me.'

Jean's face dropped. 'Ahh, what a pity.' She reluctantly removed it from her arm and handed it back.

I took it and put it in my bag.

'But couldn't it have been from Edward?' Jean asked.

'I didn't give him this address. It's from Victor. There's something else, something worse. He sent it here. How did he find out where I am? He must be spying on me somehow.'

∼

I dreaded going back home, wondering what surprises Victor would have in store for me. So it was with a heavy heart we got ready to leave aunt Mary's.

'No need to walk all that way with your suitcases,' she said. 'Mack the milkman will be here in a minute, and he'll give you a lift sure as eggs is eggs. His depot is near the station and I'm last on his round so the timing will be okay.'

Half an hour later we heard the clip-clop of the milkman's horse coming into the yard. Although the milk was also delivered by a milkman and a horse round our way, I'd never gone near one. I was scared by how big and powerful the horse was.

'Go on, give him a stroke,' Mack said, 'he won't hurt you. No, hang on.' He reached round the milk cart and produced a wrinkled apple. 'Give him this and you'll be his friend for life. Make sure you put in on an open palm, mind, or you won't have any fingers left.'

For the first time I could see why people get so fond of horses, but there was no time to delay more. We said sad farewells to Aunt Mary with many promises to visit again soon. Mack rearranged the empty milk crates so there was room for us to sit at the back of his cart, legs dangling like schoolgirls. Sitting there I felt like a runaway, one of those lads

I'd seen in films who jump onto moving trains. It was a bumpy ride over country lanes but the beautiful scenery made up for it. The sky was a clear blue with just the occasional wisps of cloud. The grass and crops we passed waved in the gentle breeze and the smell of hawthorn trees followed our route. I began to feel hypnotised by the sound of the clip-clopping of the horse's hooves, broken only by his occasional snort and the chirping of birds in the hedgerow.

Jumping off at the station we thanked Mack and patted the horse before heading to our platform. It was packed with families looking sunburnt and soldiers heading who knows where. Posters urged us to visit Kew Gardens, or Devon or Dover or other places that looked heavenly. Another showed a boy playing cricket and advised *Potatoes - feed without fattening and give them energy.* Yet another shouted *Keep warm, but use coal and coke separately.* We couldn't see any film posters and wondered what film would be showing when we got back to the Dream Palace.

We were soon alerted to the arrival of the train by the clackety-clack of the wheel on the tracks. It was crowded but the bandage on Jean's head guaranteed us a seat. We sat in a crowded compartment opposite an older man whose right sleeve was folded over at the elbow. I looked at Jean and saw she'd noticed too. He got off at the next station.

'Really think you could cope with blood and guts?' I asked her.

She grinned 'I'm sure it's 'orrible, but I've grown up looking after five younger brothers and sisters. I've dealt with loads of cuts, broken bones and cleared up plenty of blood, sick and diarrhoea,' she said.

16. INFURIATE

AGGRAVATE, PROVOKE

Next day, the wolf who hadn't been at Aunt Mary's wandered into the Dream Palace.

Victor.

I was busy concentrating on paying a pile of invoices when he knocked on the office door and walked in without waiting for an answer. He looked cleaner than last time I'd seen him; he was wearing a crisp white shirt and blue tie with a black jacket. I looked at him and couldn't understand how I had ever thought him good looking. Now all I saw was his sneaky, threatening personality.

He walked up to the desk and leaned with one hand on it, one leg crossed casually over the other. 'Have a good holiday, then? How was the weather?' he asked.

I sat back in my chair. 'I'd like you to leave,' I replied.

He gave a vulgar grin, 'Come on, you don't mean that, but if you're busy I can come back when your shift is finished. What time's that?'

'I'd like you to leave,' I repeated, pushing my chair back.

He gave an exaggerated sigh. 'Look, I don't know why you girls think it's a good idea to play hard-to-get. We can tell when you're keen, so it's a waste of time. Come on, what time shall I meet you?'

I glared at him. 'Never. Go away.' I stood up, intending to edge him towards the door, but he took a step closer and stroked my arm. Repulsed, I took a quick step back.

'Did you like the bracelet?' he asked, smiling. 'Good quality, that. Cost a lot of money.'

Yes, but whose money? I wanted to ask, but was determined not to engage him in conversation.

'I'm not keeping it. Where shall I send it back to?'

He looked around the office, 'Got it here, then? Can't leave it alone?'

'No, it's not here or I'd give it to you now.' I pointed to the door. 'Leave!'

I would have walked out but in the tiny space I couldn't get past him without getting close enough for him to grab me. All I could do was move so the chair was between me and him.

He quickly stepped forward and sat in the chair, reaching over his head to try to get hold of my hands. I moved away but found I was in danger of getting caught in a corner. I glanced around for a weapon but couldn't see anything suitable.

He looked over at me. 'You know, nasty things can happen to ungrateful girls.' Without another word, he picked up the glass from the desk and dropped it to the floor. Shards flew in every direction. One hit my leg and a trickle of blood ran down my stocking.

'Get the hell out of here!' I shouted, pointing to the door. 'I never want to see you again!'

He stood up, jaw clenched, face turning beetroot. I could see a pulse throbbing in his temple. He took a step towards me and I held my breath ready to fight him off.

Then, without warning, the door opened and Jane, one of the usherettes, walked in. 'Everything okay in here?' she asked, 'I thought I heard shouting.'

I took a deep breath, getting myself back in control, 'Victor is just leaving. Aren't you, Victor?'

He looked as if he might not move.

'Jane,' I continued, 'can you hang on, there's something we need to discuss.'

Victor took a step towards the door, running his hand along the desk and knocking a pile of invoices on the floor. 'If you're talking about me,' he said, 'make it good.'

He closed the door behind him with exaggerated care and I fell onto the chair, deflated as a burst balloon. I put my head in my hands and fought tears.

Jane put her hand on my shoulder, 'What …' her question got no further because we heard a thud and the front door rattle. We both raced to see what had happened. Victor was no-where to be seen, but he'd thrown some film leaflets across the floor.

As Jane and I picked them up, she asked, 'What's that all about? I hope you didn't mind me coming in.'

'Jane, I could have kissed you. That bloke, Victor, won't leave me alone. He's convinced himself I want to go out with him.'

She frowned. 'Well, he's got a very strange way of going around it,' she said. 'Have you told the police if he's bothering you?'

'I would if I thought it would do any good.'

But the next day I decided I would tell the police, even if I was wasting my breath. I'd never been in a police station before and tried to imagine what it would feel like to walk into one in handcuffs escorted by a policeman each side. I hoped it would happen to Victor. The room I entered was about twenty feet by fifteen feet. A wooden desk blocked the way between the front door and the rest of the room. Behind it stood a police officer and behind him were several desks. They all had piles of paper in trays and a telephone. One or two had policemen working at them. The windows were so high they reminded me of school; no chance of being distracted by the view. The room smelt of dust and old socks.

A policeman finished what he was writing before looking up. Dandruff showered his shoulders and he had what looked like an egg stain on the front of his uniform jacket.

'Yes, Miss?' he said.

'I'd like to report a man who won't leave me alone,' I said, realising how feeble it sounded. I could imagine what he'd be thinking. Stupid girl, can't even get rid of a bloke when she wants to. Perhaps she doesn't even want to, but likes to make a drama out of everything.

'What do you mean, he won't leave you alone?' he asked.

'He follows me, he sends me presents I don't want …'

He chuckled, 'Most of us can't get presents we do want. Hope you like them.'

I looked at him stony faced. 'No, I don't. He turns up where I work, he follows me, he won't leave me alone.'

'Well, Miss, can't say I would either. What law

do you think he's breaking? Seems to have good taste to me.'

If looks could really kill, he'd have shrivelled up in a second. 'I'd like to speak to your superior,' I said.

He held up his hand as if he was directing traffic. 'Hold your horses, Missy. No need to get all uppity when a man pays you a compliment.'

I refused to be drawn. 'I'd like to speak to your superior.'

He put his hands on his hips. 'Well, he's not here. Do you want to leave a message or come back when he's here?'

I took a deep breath, 'When will he be here?'

'Can't say as I know. He doesn't tell me his comings and goings. Busy man, he is.'

I turned round and walked out.

∼

Two days later I was off with Bob to the meeting with Councillor Tallis. Bob was wearing a baby blue flat cap, a matching waistcoat and red shoes. I couldn't imagine where he even found the things he wore, I'd never seen anything like them in the shops. We'd heard nothing concrete from the Councillor and the excitement I'd felt after the article had waned.

'Be of good heart, my warrior,' Bob said, trying to cheer me up. 'The council can get a Compulsory Purchase Order if there is a compelling case in the public interest.' Bob recited this like he'd learned it by heart. 'The trouble is, they don't seem to have done anything about it. We're here to make sure they do.'

Like before, we walked down endless corridors, important people striding by, their arms full of files and papers. But I found I wasn't feeling as nervous or intimidated as I had before, and Bob noticed it.

'Are you going to say more this time, Lily?' he asked.

'You have your say and I'll chip in if necessary,' I said. Braver or not, I wasn't ready to take the lead yet. I didn't understand enough about the legal side of things and Councillor Tallis was sure to have their solicitor with him.

We were only kept waiting a couple of minutes then shown into the same room as before. The sun shone through the tall windows throwing long shadows on everything.

Councillor Tallis said, 'It's a bit stuffy in here,' and opened one of the windows before he sat down, inviting us to do the same. This time we got to sit round the desk to join in the conversation, rather than being assigned to hard chairs against the bookcases.

Councillor Tallis introduced us to the council solicitor, Mr Saunders, a tall thin man without a single hair on his head even though he only looked to be in his thirties. He constantly rubbed his head as if he hoped to find he suddenly had a full head of hair. He cleared his throat every time before he spoke.

'Thank you both for coming,' Councillor Tallis said, 'let's see what we can do about this wall.'

Bob shook hands with both men. 'Thank you for seeing us. I understand the council can get a compulsory purchase order if there is a compelling case in the public interest.'

Mr Saunders suddenly came to life, and rubbed his head, 'Hmm, that's right Mr Burton, we can. However, we have to prove there is a compelling public interest and Council Members have to be convinced.'

'Can we go back and demand they look at it again?'

'Hmm, yes, but we would need a different, better argument. They won't change their mind if we just go back with the same one. Do you have any further ideas?'

Bob looked thoughtful, 'I'm wondering about the effects if war is declared. Hitler has invaded Poland, the Emergency Powers Act is already in force and no-one believes that Hitler will resolve differences with dialogue.'

'Hmm, yes, it's all very worrying, but how does

this affect Sunbury and its people? If it doesn't do so, we can't use the possible impending war as an argument.'

My heart was thumping so loud I was surprised they couldn't hear it. 'May I speak?' I said.

They all looked at me as if they'd forgotten I was there. I felt a blush start to rise from my neck, but gave myself a good talking to. I sat up straight and looked directly at them.

'There is an army barracks not five miles from Sunbury. There is already an increase in army lorries and trucks moving around the town. You must have noticed them. The road with the wall runs directly from the barracks side of town, and a little bird has told me it will be an evacuation route. If the wall were removed, army movement would be much easier. Lives could be saved.'

As one, they sat back in their chairs. Councillor Tallis steepled his fingers, Mr Saunders rubbed his head, and Bob grinned widely at me. For a minute no-one said anything.

Councillor Tallis looked at the solicitor. 'What do you think, Mr Saunders?'

'Hmm, I think, hmm, the young lady may have something there. If war is declared it could make a compelling case. The next council meeting is in a month...'

I interrupted. 'Will it be sooner if war is declared?'

'Hmm, yes, it probably will be. There will be much to be decided. May I ask you and Mr Burton to write to me about this? I can then show it to the meeting on your behalf.'

Bob spoke up, 'Councillor Tallis, with respect, I know how these things work. Miss Baker and I will write to you within the next couple of days, but if you were to have a private word with each of the committee members ahead of the meeting you may have more chance of convincing them when they're all together.'

When Bob and I were out of sight of the council buildings he laughed and patted me on the back.

'Fantastic, Lily, you had a great argument and put it across well.'

At home that evening I found Mum in the kitchen making a pie for our tea. The smell of steak and kidney made my mouth water. Mum looked tired, but then she did most days. As she rolled out the pastry I told her about the meeting.

'That's great, Lily, it sounds as if you've been really helpful,' she said with a smile. 'I've got some news too. I've been along to the Filling Factory.'

'What's that?' I asked, wondering if it was something to do with pie filling.

She put the pastry on top of the pie plate and

trimmed round the edge with a knife. 'You know, the new munitions factory in Gladstone Road. They call it the Filling Factory. They fill the bombs and things with explosives.'

'It sounds dangerous,' I said, grabbing the left-over pastry and rolling it out again. 'Can I make some jam tarts with this?'

She got out a fork and made a pattern round the edge of the pie. 'You know where the jam is. Well, I was saying, the filling factory. I've got a job there, start week after next, so I won't be doing the cleaning jobs any more. My ladies aren't a bit pleased but I've got to put myself first like they do. The factory's nearer, it pays more and I won't have to cycle all that extra way because of that wretched wall.'

Just then we heard Dad's key turn in the lock. 'Sshh, not a word,' she said, turning to put the pie in the oven.

He walked in and hung up his hat and coat in the hall. 'Get me some tea, Woman.' he said without looking as he walked into the living room and turned on the radio.

'Get it yourself,' I muttered under my breath, but old habits die hard and Mum was already filling the kettle.

I picked up my coat and bag, 'Got to get to work Mum, save me some pie.' I kissed her cheek.

It was damp and drizzly outside and I needed my

umbrella. Ever since Victor pestered me I was always looking around in case he appeared again. A couple of times I saw men his build, tensed up, and then told myself I had to stop worrying. So I was relieved my journey to the Dream Palace was uneventful. My working patterns varied. Some days I went in early, did paperwork, then opened up for the shows for the day, other days I went in mid afternoon and stayed until we closed, sometimes I just worked evenings or did a split shift. I liked the evening shift because I had the whole day to myself although I was already wondering if I'd like it so much when winter came.

I could hear the soundtrack from the latest film 'The Body Vanishes' as I walked through the door. Since I got the promotion I looked differently at things, so after I hung up my coat and put my bag in the drawer in the office, I checked to make sure everything looked clean and tidy. I straightened some leaflets and got a cloth and wiped some fingerprints off a mirror. I thought how proud Mum would've been if she could see me.

Just as I finished and headed to the door Julie, one of the part time usherettes, came out of the auditorium.

A middle aged widow with three children, she could only work evenings when her sister looked after the kids. Her uniform hung off her and I felt sure she spent her wages feeding her children and went without herself. I gave her extra shifts whenever I could.

She grinned when she saw me. 'Got an admirer then?' she asked, following me into the office and sitting down to rest her feet.

'What do you mean?'

'Go on, look in the top drawer, present for you. I put them away in case anyone else fancied them.'

My heart sank. I took the chocolates out of the drawer.

Julie pointed to the dent in the box, 'He'd got a bit of a nerve giving you a dented box, but perhaps he dropped it on the way here.'

'I think I know who these are from. Did he leave a message?'

'Just to say he misses you and looks forward to seeing you soon. Said his name was Victor.'

I didn't want to tell her about the way Victor was pestering me, she had enough troubles of her own. 'Here, you have them,' I said. They would have choked me.

'Really?' she said, 'I can take them?'

'You'll be doing me a favour. I hope you enjoy them.'

Julie left clutching the chocolates and I did my round of the Dream Palace, having a quick chat with everyone to see if all was well. I took Frank, the projectionist a cup of tea and a biscuit and he showed me a photo of his new baby, his third. Mr Simmons came in most days and was often in full time, but he was gradually cutting back and looked better for it. I was still excited at the faith he showed in me and the kind way he taught me how to do the job. When I'd finished my round I made a cuppa and sat down to listen to the news. What I heard made me hold my breath.

'This is London. You will now hear a statement by the Prime Minister. "This morning the British Ambassador in Berlin handed the German Government a final note stating that, unless we heard from them by 11 o'clock that they were prepared at once to withdraw their troops from Poland, a state of war would exist between us. I have to tell you now that no such undertaking has been received, and that consequently this country is at war with Germany."

~

Jean was fully recovered from her nasty accident. She was a bit pale but otherwise you'd never know what she'd been through.

I told her all the things Victor had been up to. She pulled a face.

'Time for action,' she said, dragging me along the street. 'Let's find them two girls you chatted to in the Ladies at the pub. We'll find out 'ow their friend got rid of that Victor.'

'I don't know, Jean. Now that war's been announced it seems so insignificant.'

'Don't be daft. War's not going to stop him pestering you unless he gets called up. Come on, let's find out how to get rid of him.'

It took three visits to the pub before we found them.

It was a busy night at the King's Arms. The old couple were there again nursing their halves, and a dozen men of all ages were leaning against the bar. It was noisy with a game of darts in the other bar. We could hear the thud of the darts and the cheers or jeers of the players after each one. Nearby three old men were playing dominoes, the click of the wood on the table combining with their low chatter. Me and Jean crept around as best we could making sure Victor wasn't there before we ordered drinks. I wasn't brave enough to go to pubs alone, especially the pub where I might bump into him.

''ow many more times are we going to look for these girls?' Jean asked. 'This is the third time. I don't mind coming, but maybe we're wasting our time. Could've been a one-off them being 'ere that evening.'

'You're right, we'll make this the last time. Mind you, they must have been here at least once before to know about Victor hitting someone. If we don't find them this time, we'll give up. Not like we don't have other things to do with our time. It's good of you to come with me, Jean.'

We ordered half a pint of cider each and found a table in the corner where we could keep an eye on the door.

'What're you going to do if Victor comes in?' Jean asked. 'Hide under the table?'

I looked at the table. It was big enough for dominoes or a game of cards, but wouldn't hide the both of us. Just the thought of him coming in made me feel a bit wobbly. 'We'll just have to walk out as quickly as possible and hope he doesn't see us.'

'Or we can stand up to 'im, the stupid git. We can manage 'im okay. 'e's not going to try much in 'ere, is 'e?'

I gave her a bright smile that she saw through straight away, 'You're right. We'll think of something. At least it'll be two against one.'

Fifteen minutes later a chilly draught told us the door had just opened and in walked the two girls we were looking for. One was tall, about five foot nine, with very long brown hair. Her friend was even shorter than me and looked tiny beside her. We watched as they went to the bar and ordered their drinks. Two blokes tried to chat them up and they gave them cheery backchat but went over to a table near us and were soon busy talking.

'What're you going to do, just go over to 'em?' Jean asked.

'Nothing else I can do, is there?'

I felt a bit of a fool going up to them, but I just had to know how to stop Victor's nuisance behaviour. They were deep in conversation, giggling and giving the lads the eye from time to time. I was shocked to see the short one was drinking a Guinness, because I thought only men drank that.

Jean and I waited until they paused for a second. It was a long wait.

In the end I decided we'd just have to interrupt them or we'd be there 'til closing time.

'Excuse me,' I said, butting in, 'I'm sorry to bother you but some time ago I overheard you talking in the Ladies about how Victor Burton had been a nuisance after one of your friends dropped him.'

They frowned. 'Excuse me,' the taller of the two said, 'do we know you?'

I could feel myself going red. 'No, but I overheard you talking. I've been going out with Victor and now I've finished with him he's being a nuisance to me, too.'

The taller of the two put her hand on my arm, 'Oh, you poor thing. I'm Mavis and this is Jenny.'

I could feel my tension dropping. 'I'm Lily and this is my friend Jean,' I said.

'Yeah,' Jean said, ''e's being a right pain in the

backside. 'ow did your friend get rid of 'im? Was it difficult?'

Jean spoke for the first time, 'It took ages, she thought she'd never get rid of him.'

'He got up to all sorts,' Mavis said, 'kept giving her presents she didn't want. Followed her whenever she went out, sent her threatening letters, spied on her, and goodness knows what.' She turned to me. 'Have you had all that too?' she asked.

I nodded, 'Yes, most of it. I'm desperate to find a way to get rid of him. What did your friend do?'

'You won't like this,' Mavis said, 'but he never gave up until he got another girlfriend. You'll have to hope he finds someone else.'

Jean turned to me with a grin, 'Don't even think about asking. I'm not going out with him.'

17. HAPPINESS

GOOD FORTUNE, PLEASURE, JOY

*E*dward wrote to me regularly, long chatty letters telling me all about his everyday life. I loved reading about what he was doing in the army and often laughed when he described some of things people got up to. It wasn't as good as seeing him though, and I missed him every day. When he wrote and said he'd got weekend leave I was so excited. I tried to get the whole weekend off work but couldn't get cover for the Saturday morning. He wrote:

'Don't worry about it Lily, I need to spend some time with my parents so I'll make that the Saturday morning and I'll be staying there Saturday night so I'll have breakfast with them Sunday but we can spend the rest of the weekend together. Any idea what you'd like to do?'

Although the summer was coming to an end, we

still had a lot of choice if the weather was kind. I hadn't been to the Lido all summer although it was one of my favourite places. I felt awkward at the idea of Edward seeing me in my swimming costume, but still thought the Lido would be my number one choice, and perhaps a walk and a picnic on Sunday.

The Saturday morning of his leave seemed twice as long as it normally did and I was too impatient to even enjoy seeing the excitement of the children coming to Saturday Morning Club. But eventually twelve thirty came and there he was, waiting at the door for me to finish my shift. Mr Simmons had agreed to take over for the rest of the weekend and he came out of the office with me, keen to meet Edward.

They shook hands. 'It's a pleasure to meet you, Sir,' Edward said and they chatted for a couple of minutes. I could tell from his body language Mr Simmons liked him and felt relieved.

The sun made sharp shadows as we walked along the riverside. The water sparkled and people fishing had to pull their hats over their eyes to spot the fish biting. Every now and then there was a small splash as a fish wriggled, trying to get off a hook.

'How's your campaign going to get the wall removed?' Edward asked.

'The council moves so slowly, but someone told me the wall would be blocking an evacuation route.'

'I didn't know Civil Defence had decided on them yet,' he said.

'I don't know for sure, but it gave the councillor and his solicitor something to look into. Have you ever told your mum about me and what I'm involved in with the wall?'

He gave a short laugh, 'I've told her about you, but haven't said you're on the Wall Must Fall committee. She goes blue in the face even at the thought of the wall being removed.'

I stopped and faced him, 'Edward, she's going to hate me, I just know it.'

He drew me close to him, 'Not once she gets to know you, she won't. She'll come round.'

The Lido, which was next to the river, was an elegant Art Deco pool and the blue water was complemented by the deep pink and yellow stripes just above the water line. The word Lido was written in graceful script. The changing rooms had matching doors; men at one end, women at the other. In between was the entrance box and a small cafe. Sun beds lined two of the long sides of the pool. We settled down, with me self-consciously covering my legs with my towel.

The pool was busy with families enjoying the late summer sunshine. Children were clowning around, pushing each other in and jumping on each others' shoulders. Adults were either trying to get a tan or hiding from the sun. Many were snoozing, and the occasional gentle snore could be heard in rare quiet moments.

Edward went to get some lemonades and I sat enjoying watching the children. Then something caught my eye. A child floating face down on the water, not moving, his knitted swimming trunks ballooning with air. He looked about four years old. No-one seemed to be taking any notice. My first thought was that he was messing about, but I quickly decided if he wasn't, he was going to drown. Forgetting my modesty, I threw my towel aside and jumped in, swallowing a mouthful of water. I swam over to him as fast as I've ever swam in my life, turning him over. He was as limp as a leaf on a wet pavement.

'Help! HELP!' I shouted and swam towards the steps. I pulled him behind me, struggling to keep my breath. Two adults nearby quickly came to help me and we dragged the boy to the poolside.

'Put him over your knee and hit him on his back,' someone shouted, but I'd already started to do that. It took five slaps before he coughed and spluttered. It was a wonderful sound. There was a little round of applause from people who had seen what was happening. The other adults and I all let out sighs of relief and I looked round for the parents. No-one had come to see what was happening and the boy was too young to have come on his own. The man and woman who helped me went round waking up the people who were asleep. It was the sixth person, a stick thin, middle aged man, who took some shaking, who was the boy's father. When he saw what had happened he ran over to the child, tears streaming down his cheeks. He couldn't look at us, but kept saying 'thank you, thank you,' as he cradled his son in his arms. The boy, soon over the drama, was looking around wondering what all the fuss was about.

I went and sat on the sun bed again, shaking all over. A couple of minutes later Edward, who'd been in the cafe and not seen what happened, came over with the drinks.

'What's wrong? You look shaky.' Edward said, putting down the drinks. 'Has something happened?'

'You're a hero,' Edward said when I told him about the boy. He picked up his towel, stood behind me and started to carefully dry my hair. Then he put down the towel and massaged my scalp; it was so lovely I wanted to throw myself at him there and then in public. Then he stroked my neck and I took his hand away and kissed it. 'Mmm,' I said, feeling almost woozy, 'I think you'd better stop there, before we get carried away.'

With a moan so quiet I hardly heard it, Edward sat down again next to me and held my hand. 'I'd love to get carried away with you,' he said.

I pretended to smack his hand. 'Stop it!' I said in a mock stern voice that would have convinced no-one.

'That boy would probably be dead if it wasn't for you, Lily,' he said. 'How on earth did you know what to do?'

I pushed my wet hair behind my ears, 'When he arranged my training, Mr Simmons sent me on a first aid course in case anyone became ill in the Dream Palace. The last thing I ever thought I'd use was what to do if someone was drowning.'

That evening was planned to be special. I was going to introduce Edward to Jean at last. She'd been asking to meet him for ages, but I wanted to keep him all to myself because our time together was so short and precious.

We met again at the Roxy at seven, me in my best dance dress with my hair in loose waves like Frances Dee, and wearing the bright red lipstick Jean had given me. I was so anxious for the two favourite people in my life to get on I was struck dumb with idiotic nerves. I needn't have worried, Jean can talk for England and she soon had Edward laughing as she mock flirted with him. But I soon claimed him back and we danced to some Big Band numbers like *Begin the Begine.* That one gave us a wonderful chance to dance close together, swaying to the rhythm. I was reminded of the first time we met, me hugging his back as we swayed round corners on his motorbike. Then we danced to faster swing numbers like *The A Train* until I got breathless. Jean and her latest lad, Ernie, were having their third drink and tapping their toes to the music, arms linked and lost in each other.

As Edward and I walked to join them, someone walked across our path and blocked our way.

Victor.

His eyes were unfocussed and he reeked of spirits. He stood directly in front of me and tried to grab my arm, 'You're my girl, what're you doing with him?' he said.

A dozen pairs of eyes turned towards us and I could feel a blush moving up from my neck. I looked straight back into his eyes, unsmiling.

'Go away, Victor. I am not your girl.' I held Edward's arm and tried to side step him. Victor moved and stepped in our way. We tried again, he got in our way again.

Edward leaned over and whispered in my ear, 'Want me to deal with him?'

It wouldn't have been a fair fight. Edward was four or five inches taller than Victor and a lot fitter. When we danced I felt how powerful his muscles were. Also, he wasn't drunk.

I looked from Victor to Jean and she understood my meaning without a word passing between us.

'Wait for me,' I said to Edward. Jean and I got one each side of Victor, linked our arms through his and gently but firmly walked him toward the door, talking calmly all the time. He tried to grab me a couple of times but we made a joke of it and he didn't know how to handle us. I think he couldn't make up his mind whether he was in trouble or if two girls had both taken a shine to him.

Jean knew the bouncer. 'Hi, Rob,' she said giving him a wide smile, 'this man is bothering us. Can you get rid of him for us?'

The bouncer knew if girls didn't come to the Roxy, the boys wouldn't come either, so he needed to look after us. Victor tried his 'She's my girl' routine like he used with the policeman, but it fell flat. The bouncer bent his arm behind his back and marched him out. Two minutes later the bouncer was back rubbing his hands. 'You won't see any more of him tonight, Girls. I'll watch out for him.'

Jean and I shook hands like prize fighters at the end of a match. 'Brute force doesn't always win,' she said, flexing her non-existent muscles, 'and I really like your Edward. Can I have 'im if you get fed up with 'im?'

I poked my tongue out at her. 'Hands off!' I said.

'Thanks for offering to deal with Victor.' I said as Edward walked me home later. 'He's so crazy I thought if you were involved he'd have another reason to keep bothering me, and maybe you too.'

He squeezed my arm. 'I know you're a brave girl, but sometimes strength is what's needed. I'm glad it wasn't this time. You and Jean were brilliant.'

I looked up at the stars, wishing all parts of my life were as perfect as right then. A lovely clear night, silky air, and the best man in the world walking arm and arm with me. 'I wish the police would warn him off. He might listen to them, but they won't do anything about it.'

He stopped and pulled me to face him. 'Lily, I'm being serious now. If it gets too much, just tell me and let me deal with it. He'll never bother you again.'

I caught my breath, 'Edward, you're scaring me.'

'Lily, I'm a trained soldier, I've been taught combat. I wouldn't do him any serious harm, but he'd think twice about going near you again.'

When he said goodbye at my door, he kissed me with such passion I moulded myself to his body, or as far as I could considering I'm a lot shorter than him. When we broke away he laughed, 'We'll bring a box next time for you to stand on.'

There was no sign of Victor the next day when we went for our walk and picnic. Edward had an Ordnance Survey map with him and showed me how to read it. He'd picked out a route for us and checked I was happy with it. We walked for three hours, through lush green valleys and pretty villages. We settled by a stream, and the sun, which had been hiding all morning, finally broke through. It sparkled on the water bubbling over stones and the tiny fish that darted between the water plants.

Edward had paid for the Roxy, so I insisted on providing the picnic food. Sausage rolls, chunks of cucumber, sandwiches and chocolate cupcakes. He carried a flask of water. We ate slowly, then lay on the grass, me snuggled up to him with my head on his shoulder, looking up into the leafy canopy above us. He stroked my shoulder and my neck and I felt my insides melt in a very, well, improper way. I looked at him and could see he felt the same.

'Lily,' he said after a while, 'do you think we should meet each other's family? Your mother sounds lovely and I'd like to meet her.'

I thought my heart would stop beating. The thought of meeting Edward's mother properly was terrifying. I just knew she wouldn't think I was good enough for him. What if she persuaded him not to see me any more?

Edward sat up. 'What do you think?' he asked.

I stared into the stream, wondering how to say what I was feeling. 'Edward, well, I'd like you to meet my mum, but let's wait a while until you meet my dad. You know how difficult he can be.'

He nodded agreement, 'I expect we can meet

your mother without him there. What about you meeting my parents? I'm sure they'd love to invite you to dinner.'

Dinner! I'd heard Edward talk about having lunch and dinner. We had dinner and tea in our house, and the thought of knowing which cutlery to use and what to say was daunting.

'But Edward, what if I show you up? What if they don't think I'm good enough?'

He gave a short laugh. 'You couldn't show me up, you don't need to worry about that. And I think my mother would never approve of any girl for me who she hadn't chosen herself. I'm a grown man, a soldier about to go to war. I love her dearly but I don't need her approval. You're perfect as you are. I'd still like you to meet them though.'

I thought for a minute, 'What about your dad? You don't mention him much.'

'He's a real academic, head in the clouds, so busy thinking about ancient history it's hard to get him to notice anything happening now. He even walks along reading a book, oblivious of what's around him. He's kind though. You won't have to worry about him at all.'

We finally agreed that next time he got leave, we'd meet up with his parents in a cafe and just have tea together - not nearly so intimidating.

'Come on,' I said, jumping up and pulling him up

with me, 'let's walk along in the stream and cool ourselves off.'

We peeled off shoes and socks and Edward rolled up his trouser legs. I tried not to laugh, 'Your legs are so hairy,' I said, then worried I'd offended him.

'Men have hairy legs,' he said with a laugh, 'they're just as they should be.' He bent down and splashed me and we got into a bit of a water fight, laughing and squealing all the while. When we'd calmed down, he took my hand and we walked through the bubbling stream, our feet massaged by the smooth stones and the cool water rippling over them.

I threw my arms out wide and looked up to the sun, 'This is such a perfect day. I wish it could go on for ever.'

Edward took me in his arms and hugged me. 'You're the perfect one,' he said.

My feet dragged heavily home that night, with the weekend ending far too soon. It was early evening and the weather had changed, making the wind whip early fallen leaves into tiny whirls. Edward had to return to his barracks ready for duty next day. As I walked into the kitchen Mum was getting in the washing. I helped her carry it and got out the ironing board and iron.

Mum leaned against the sink, 'Come on then, tell

me how it went. I've been thinking about you all day.'

I smiled broader than our street.

'Oh Mum, he's the one, I'm sure of it and guess what. He wants to meet you!'

She blew out a breath, 'Well, he must be serious. He sounds a real gent. But he sounds a bit grand for us, are you sure I'll be up to his standard? I don't want to let you down.'

I understood what she meant because I still struggled with the difference between me and Edward a lot of the time. We used different words for things and sometimes he used long words I didn't even know. When we were out and about he always seemed to know what to do and how to speak to all sorts of different people. It was kind of like he knew he deserved a place in the world and I was still trying to find mine.

I shook out one of dad's hankies and picked up the iron. 'Mum, you'd never let me down. He'll love you, how could he not?'

She thought a minute, 'But what about your dad? Does he want to meet him, too?'

I pulled a face. 'He did ask to meet you both, but I've warned him what Dad's like so we'll meet up with you one day in a cafe. Is that alright? Meeting Dad can wait. Anyway, we can't do anything until we know when Edward will get some more leave.'

Mum reached behind the biscuit barrel on the shelf and pulled out an envelope. 'I forgot, this came for you. Someone must have put it through the door. There was no stamp on it.'

I put the iron down and opened the letter. It was on white plain paper, folded in four. When I saw what it said I dropped it as if it had burned me.

NEVER FORGET I'M WATCHING YOU.

Mum looked at me, 'What's the matter, Lil? You've gone all pale.'

She looked from me and then down at the letter. I tried to snatch it before she could pick it up but wasn't fast enough. As she read it a frown creased her brow.

'I don't understand. Who's watching you? What's this about?' she said.

I sat down heavily on the kitchen chair, my heart racing and my palms sweating. The room seemed to fade away and I could hear a buzzing in my ears.

Mum rushed over to me, 'Put your head between your knees,' she said, 'it'll stop you fainting.'

I followed her advice and after a minute or two got my breathing under control. She sat down beside me. She took one of my hands in hers and gently stroked it.

'Who's sent you this awful thing?'

I could hardly look her in the eye. If I hadn't been stupid enough to be taken in by Victor's charm in the first place, I wouldn't be in this position now. I only had myself to blame.

She shook me gently. 'Come on, tell me.'

I took a deep breath. 'It's got to be Victor. I told you I finished with him, but I haven't told you everything.'

She went very still, 'What haven't you told me?'

'He's being a pest. Sent me a couple of presents I didn't want and never asked for. Followed me a couple of times. Tries to pretend I'm still his girl. That sort of thing.'

She looked confused, 'I don't understand. Why on earth would he do something that odd? Is he nuts?'

I nodded, 'He must be, why else would he behave like that? It's like he's three people, all lovely when I first went out with him, then gradually got nasty, now going between nasty and trying to be extra nice so I'll go out with him again.'

'Hang on a minute,' she said, 'didn't you tell me Bob is his uncle?'

'That's right, he is.'

She nodded firmly, 'Then go and see Bob. Get him to sort Victor out, or get his parents to sort him out. That should do the trick.'

'So did ya?' Jean asked in a break at work next day, her eyes full of mischief, 'You know, Edward. Did you go all the way?'

Sometimes I think Jean could make a living as a spy getting information out of people. She was relentless. 'Go on, you did, didn't you!'

I narrowed my eyes, 'No we didn't and I'm not telling you another thing about my weekend. Now shut up Jean before I thump you.'

She stuck her tongue out at me, 'Spoilsport. Anyway, I've got some news too. I've signed up for a St.John Ambulance First Aid Course,' she said, looking very smug, 'I'll soon know more than you.'

'Brilliant, what made you decide on that? I thought you'd had enough of anything that smacked of school.'

She held her head on one side and looked at me like I was stupid. 'I told you,' she said.

'Told me what?'

'When I came out of 'ospital after my accident, I told you I was thinking of learning to be a nurse. This is the first step. If I think I'll like it I might sign up.'

'Gosh, Jean, you in an army uniform? That'll be a bit different.'

She gave me another *you're so stupid* look. 'I don't 'ave to join the army. The Red Cross and St

John want nurses too. Less lads though, and I always 'ad a soft spot for a man in uniform.'

'You've just got a soft spot for lads!' I laughed.

We left the office and went out into the foyer. One of our tasks was to check everything was in order while the film was on, so the customers got a good impression as they left. We always tried to have at least one person standing by the door smiling and saying 'Good evening' as well.

That evening I had to change the film poster to show what was starting the next day. It was *Jamaica Inn* starring Charles Loughton and Maureen O'Hara. It looked good: intrigue, pirates, beautiful sunny scenery, and crime. The director was Alfred Hitchcock, so it was sure to be good. I couldn't wait to see it and try to spot him in his usual cameo. You'd think working in a picture house would put you off films for life, but that's never happened to me. Like a lot of our customers, I loved losing myself in the stories on the big screen.

Jean and I had just straightened the new poster when the outer door opened. I turned round and there was Victor, a big grin on his face as if nothing unpleasant had ever happened between us. He'd smartened himself up and looked much more like the man I first met.

'Hi, Sweetheart,' he said, coming towards me.

I held up my hand. 'I told you I don't want anything else to do with you,' I said.

He looked at Jean, 'Listen to her, you'd think she didn't love me or something. You tell her, she's lucky a man like me is interested in her. And I've bought her a present.'

Jean stepped towards him, 'You're barmy, you are. She doesn't want your presents and she doesn't want you. Now clear off!' Her voice was beginning to raise.

It's not hard for people at the back of the auditorium to hear conversations in the foyer if they are loud, so I was anxious to keep it quiet. I thought quickly. I could get Victor outside, but it might cause a public scene, or I could take him into the office.

'Jean, Victor, into the office for a minute.' I ordered. Victor smiled in triumph. 'See,' he said to Jean, 'told you she wants to see me.'

I stood just inside the office door and didn't invite either of them to sit. I opened my mouth to speak but Victor got in first, 'I can see you're busy, Sweetheart,' he said, 'so I'll just leave you this present and head off until it's more convenient for you.'

He tried to hand me a small parcel wrapped in brown paper and ribbon. I didn't take it.

'Oh, for goodness sake,' Jean said, turning to him, 'take the 'int, you moron. She doesn't want you or your stupid presents.'

His head whipped round to face her, his eyes wishing her dead, 'Cut the cackle, you stupid tart! This is between me and Lily, nothing to do with you.'

He tried again to hand me the parcel but when I didn't move he put it on the desk and walked out into the foyer. I followed him to make sure he left. Instead of walking directly to the door, he moved the big chair, tilted the poster we'd just put straight and scattered the leaflets displayed on the wall, all the time humming to himself. I waited and watched and finally he left, closing the door with exaggerated care, a little bow and a cheery 'Goodbye Darling, see you soon.'

Jean looked at his departing back. 'Blinking 'eck. He's off his rocker. It really burns me up,' she said. 'You gotta do something to get rid of 'im. Wish I had a gun.'

I felt as if all my energy had been syphoned off, and wanted nothing more than to sit down and get my lungs working properly again, but we had to tidy up first. All the time Jean was muttering, ''im and 'is malarky ..,' 'slap-'appy idiot ...,' 'I'd love to spook 'im ...'

We put the last leaflet away and double checked everything was as it should be.

'Come on Jean,' I said, linking my arm through hers, 'we've got plenty of time for a cuppa before the end of the film. Thank you for helping me with him.'

As I put the kettle on I could hear paper rustling behind me.

'Here Lil, look at this. What a funny thing to give you.'

I turned round and she was holding pretty little pepper and salt pots. They sort of bulged out at the bottom, then got narrower towards the top. Pretty silver flowers ran all the way up the front.

'Why on earth would 'e give you them?' she said, 'does 'e think they're for your bottom drawer or something?'

Remembering what Aunt Mary said about the bracelet I took the pots off her and turned them over. Sure enough, there were little marks underneath. 'These are silver, and unusual too. Must have been expensive.'

Jean snorted. 'There's not a snowball's chance in 'ell 'e paid for these. They're nicked, for sure. Nice though. 'e's got good taste, I'll give 'im that.'

We were interrupted by a tap on the office door. It quickly opened and Ted, our local bobby, stuck his head round the door. 'Cooeee, anyone got the kettle on?' he said, making his way in.

'Sit yourself down,' I said, getting out another cup and warming the pot. 'We could have done with you a few minutes ago.'

He sat heavily on the office chair, his buttocks spilling either side of the seat like each cheek was in a competition to reach the floor first. 'Oh, why's that then?'

The kettle started to whistle and I turned to take the top off. Putting the water in the pot, I said, 'You know the bloke I was with at the bus stop?'

He grinned, 'Oh course I remember. Love's young dream having a bit of a barney.'

I turned round and looked him in the eye, 'He wasn't my dream.'

Jean butted in, 'No, 'e's 'er nightmare. You did 'er wrong not listening to 'er. What're you going to do about it?'

He avoided her eyes and looked like he wished he'd never come in to rest his feet. 'What do you mean? Did I really get it wrong?'

'Yes, you damn well did,' Jean said, her best outraged face much in evidence.

I handed Jean and Ted their teas and sat down with mine, moving the salt and pepper pot out of the way. 'Ted, he won't leave me alone. I only went out with him a few times and now he follows me, he leaves me presents …'

I gestured to the pots.

He glanced at the pots, then his head rose up and he moved them nearer to get a better look. 'Where d'you get these?'

'Don't you listen to a thing?' Jean replied. 'It's 'im, Victor, 'e keeps giving 'er presents. Chocolates, a bracelet, these things.' She waved her arm at the pots.

Ted looked at me, 'A bracelet, you say? You don't happen to have it here, do you?'

I opened the desk drawer and took out the bracelet, 'Yes, I hoped I'd get a chance to give it back.' I handed it to him. 'Here, have it for all I care.'

He looked carefully at the bracelet, then put it next to the salt and pepper pots. He put three spoons of sugar in his tea and sat silently stirring it. That was unusual in itself, Ted could talk for England. He took a sip of the tea.

'It's like this,' he said, 'I've seen pictures of these down at the nick. They're part of a haul that was robbed a few weeks ago.'

Jean's mouth formed a perfect O. 'You're kidding. 'ow come you've got pictures?'

'They come from a big house, Grantham Hall, up on the heath. The insurance company insisted everything valuable was photographed. These here are the first things we've found.'

'Blimey O'Reilly,' said Jean. 'What a cheapskate, giving Lil 'ot stuff. I always said there was something dodgy about 'im.'

Ted put down his cup and saucer and got out his notebook. He turned to me. 'You two sure you're not fingering him because he's being a pest? Making it up like.'

I just put my hands on my hips and looked daggers at him.

He held up his hands in surrender. 'Okay, okay. Don't shoot. Now then, Lily, let's be serious for a minute,' he licked the end of his pencil, 'tell me everything you know about this toe-rag.'

∼

'I don't think he'll be bothering you again,' said Bob, 'he's too scared of what's going to happen in court.'

If only he'd been right.

I'd dropped a note to Bob asking him to meet me. Jean had been saying for ages I should get Bob to frighten off Victor so he'd leave me alone. After all, he was Victor's uncle. Somehow it didn't seem the right thing to do; I wanted to sort it out myself. But all my efforts so far had been unsuccessful and I was getting desperate. I'd received two more presents which I'd taken straight to the police station. Again, they were small things that had been reported stolen. I'd had three cards pushed through the door that were something you'd send a girlfriend. More worrying, I'd had two notes made up of letters cut out of a newspaper that threatened me. One said, 'I'M WATCHING YOU!' And the other said, 'MAKE

THE MOST OF THE DAYS YOU HAVE LEFT ON EARTH.'

I took the first one to the police station, but the copper on duty couldn't even bother to pretend to be interested. I ended up taking it back off him, intending to go back another day when Ted was on duty.

I'd seen a film where the detective solved the crime using fingerprints, so when the second note arrived I was careful not to touch it any more than I had to. I put it in a paper bag and headed back to the cop shop. I groaned when I saw the same policeman on duty. He was reading a newspaper.

'I've had another threatening note,' I said.

He barely looked up.

I tapped the newspaper. 'I want to speak to your boss.'

That got his attention. He stood up straight and put down the paper.

'How can I help you, Miss?'

'I've received a second threatening note. I want to see your boss.' I waved the paper bag with the notes in. He made to take it off me, but I quickly put it behind my back.

'Now, Miss, the Inspector is a very busy man…'

'I'll wait,' I interrupted, giving him a death glare again. He sighed heavily and disappeared through a door behind him. He was back within a couple of minutes.

'The Inspector has asked me to take the details from you.'

I folded my arms and held my ground. 'No. I want to speak to the Inspector and I'm not budging until I do. Go and tell him.'

He put his head on one side, 'Now, Miss, be reasonable. You'll get me in trouble …'

I held up my hand. 'Not my worry. You couldn't be bothered to take me seriously last time I was here. Please get the Inspector.'

I was amazed at myself. Before I'd met Bob and he'd given me the confidence to believe in myself, I wouldn't have argued with anyone in uniform or any professional of any kind. I'd learned a lot from him. Added to which, I was feeling very stressed about the way Victor was carrying on. Every time I stepped outside of home I looked round in case he was lurking somewhere. Every time someone knocked on the door, I jumped. Every time someone walked into the Dream Palace between shows I tensed up.

It had to stop.

'I wish you'd told me about this sooner,' Bob said as we walked through the park. The blue sky of yesterday was gone. Instead an almost relentless layer of grey and white shrouded the world, dazzling when the sunshine broke through but gloomy where it didn't.

'If I'd known I'd have sorted him out. Did the police prove it was Victor sending the notes? I haven't seen anything about it.'

'No, they did a fingerprint test but he'd wiped the paper clean, or wore gloves when he made them. They said they'll look into it, but I can't see how they can prove it was him, or anyone else come to that.'

He rested his hand on my arm, 'I'm so sorry you've had all this worry, Lily. I knew Victor was a troubled lad but I had no idea how bad it was. His mum is so upset. He's had a few clouts round the ear, and I don't blame her.'

We sat on a bench looking at the late summer flowers and Bob produced a bag of jelly babies. 'Bet you've got a favourite colour,' he said.

'Mmm, red and green.' I reached in and greedily took one of each.

'Do you think he'll go to prison?' I said, my mouth half full of sweets.

'It's quite likely. He must have been in the robbery with at least one other person but he's not giving anything away. Keeps protesting his innocence even though he gave you those bits and pieces. The police found more hidden in his bedroom, too.'

Fear made my skin prickle, 'Won't it make him angry with me? He'll know the police learned about him from me. He might want revenge.'

'I know the Inspector dealing with the case and you don't need to worry. Stupid lad that he is, Victor tried to sell some of the stuff in a pawn shop. The police have a good relationship with the shop owner and he looks out for stolen goods for them. He reported Victor just about when you did. There's no way Victor can pin this on you.'

'Won't the police want me to give evidence?' The thought of standing up in court took my breath away.

Bob shook his head, 'They might, if they don't have enough evidence otherwise, but the Inspector said he'll do his best not to involve you. You've suffered enough.'

I nearly slid off the chair with relief, and was unkind enough to hope Victor got a very long sentence.

'Thank goodness, I can't tell you how much of a worry it's been.'

'Well, it's all in the past, so let's talk about other things. I haven't heard from Councillor Tallis yet, but I've spoken to a couple of the Council's Officers. When I put to them your point about evacuation routes they were very willing to listen. We need to check with the army, though they seems to be keeping things close to their chests at the moment. I don't think there's anything else we can do right now, but I'm quietly optimistic.'

'We've had a couple of tanks go up and down our road lately. The kids love it, they ran up and down beside them shouting and waving their flags,' I said.

He nodded, 'Good job the little ones don't know what's probably coming. The tanks are doing manoeuvres. You'll be pleased to know they've been up and down the other side of the wall, too.'

The tanks were a chilling reminder of the war. 'We had some officials round the other day taking all our details for a census. They said they needed them for identity cards and ration books and things.'

He searched through the bag of sweets until he found a black jelly baby. Strange man. 'We had that as well. I read there were sixty five thousand of them going to every house in the country. Finding that number shows how many people are still without work even though the depression is supposed to be over. They want to know what skills we have as well. It makes sense if the war gets going properly.'

18. REFRESHMENTS

Portions of food or drink, perhaps for a snack

'Why don't we invite your mum to tea at the Royal? Would it be a good place for me to meet her?' Edward asked.

I gaped at him. 'What the Royal? The expensive hotel in town that has a doorman and everything? I've never been there and I bet Mum hasn't either.'

He linked his arm through mine, 'Okay, I'll take you there first so you can see what you think. It seems grand, but when you get down to it, it's still a cafe like Lyons Corner House.'

I looked at him in amazement. 'You're joking, aren't you? I bet the waitresses, or do they have waiters in there, look down at anyone like me and Mum.'

He gave a chuckle. 'Know what you need to remember if they do? They're the waiting staff. You're the customer. Without you they wouldn't have a job.'

I took a breath deep enough for diving into a river. Sometimes Edward found it hard to understand how the differences between us affected me. 'Okay, let's go there first. Do I have to dress up? I don't have a tea dress, my life's not like that.'

He squeezed my arm closer to him, 'Just come in whatever you want to wear. You look fabulous in everything.'

We decided to combine my first time at the Royal with meeting Edward's parents. I got him to tell me what they were interested in so I'd have something to talk about with them.

'With my dad, just ancient history,' he said.

'But I don't know the first thing about ancient history.'

'Don't worry, he won't even notice. You can ask him what he's working on at the moment, he'll talk for hours about that.'

Some of my worry evaporated, but there was still his mother. She was the most frightening. Edward reassured me.

'The thing with my mother is, even if she absolutely hates someone, and that won't be you, she's always scrupulously polite. It might be a frosty politeness, but she won't be rude or horrible.'

It was something. 'What's she interested in? I need something to talk to her about.'

He thought for a minute. 'I've been away most of the time for years what with university and the army. I know she likes meeting up with her friends, she likes clothes and she does some voluntary work for the Red Cross. You could ask her about that.'

So it was a double baptism by fire. The Royal and his parents. We sat at a round table for four by the window. The waiter knew his mother by name and made a point of helping her with her chair, leaving Edward to hold mine.

I felt inferior right away. His mother was wearing a blue spotted tea dress with padded shoulders and a flared skirt pulled in with a belt. It was obviously expensive. I looked down at my dress; Mum made it last year and I loved it but there was no comparison. Not only that, his mother must've been for a wash and set that morning, her waves were perfect. My hair had frizzed with the damp as usual and no amount of teasing it in the Ladies got it to look good.

We ordered a wonderful spread and Edward and his parents made small talk until it arrived. As I took a bite of my first sandwich, his mother turned to me, a fixed smile on her face.

'And what do your people do?' she asked.

I almost choked.

It was the question I'd been dreading. I'm not ashamed of what they do, but knew she'd look down on them. There was no point in lying. If Edward and I continued to go out with each other, she'd find out the truth soon enough.

'My dad is a clerk at Simpsons, the factory in town, and my mum's a cleaning lady. She does for two or three ladies in your street.'

I thought her nose would stick to the ceiling.

'Oh, really?' she finally said, 'how interesting.'

She turned to her husband and tapped his arm to get his attention. 'Did you hear that, Rupert? Lily's father is a clerk at Simpsons and her mother is a char. I wonder if she does for any of our neighbours. Such a useful service.'

I could have killed her. 'She won't be doing for them much longer. She's about to start work at the Filling Factory, filling bombs. Vital war work.'

She turned her icy gaze back at me, 'And what do you do?'

I put back my shoulders, and looked her in the eye, 'I'm the assistant manager at the Dream Palace.'

'Oh,' she said, looking most put out, 'I go there sometimes with my friend Veronica. Her daughter Claire and Edward have been friends since they were children.'

Edward leaned across and patted her arm,

'Mother, you know I'm very fond of Claire, but it will never be more than that.'

'But surely, with your background ...' she started.

'Mother, I am touched that you want the best for me, and Claire is a terrific person, but it's Lily that I'm seeing.'

I wanted to kiss him there and then, but I could just imagine her face if I did. Instead I took Edward's advice and asked his father about his work. He hadn't said much until then, apparently daydreaming. He was dressed in grey trousers and a tweed jacket with notebooks poking out of each pocket. He looked every inch the absent minded professor I'd seen in films. 'Well, my dear. Lily, did you say your name was?'

'Yes, Lily,' I replied.

'Lovely name, very pretty flower. And what do you do?'

I pretended I hadn't just told Edward's mother, 'I work at the Dream Palace. I often see Pathe News and I wondered what you've learned about ancient history can teach us about Mr Hitler and this war.'

I didn't tell Edward that I practiced that question. Anyway, it worked. His father took a deep breath and didn't stop talking about the topic for a good five minutes. As we walked out Edward squeezed my hand and whispered, 'You were brilliant!'

It seemed no time at all before I was to go to the Royal again, this time with Mum. Edward came to collect us in a car he'd borrowed from a friend, an Austin 10 he said it was. We so rarely went in cars it was a real treat, especially as we'd spent some time doing our hair and getting ready. Usually, by the time you'd got where you wanted to go by bus or bike, you looked like you needed to start all over again.

We rode to the Royal in style, and I childishly wanted to wave to people like I was a queen. Edward helped us both out with a flourish and gave his key to a doorman to park the car. Another doorman opened the door for us, touching his hat as we walked through. We stood for a minute soaking in the appearance of the entrance hall which looked as it could have come straight out of a stately home. The floor had spotless black and white tiles and there were columns either side of the gold edged door in front of us. To one side was a sweeping curved stairway that led to goodness-knows-where. There was an expensive silence about the place, broken only by the quiet footsteps of immaculately uniformed staff. Even though I'd seen it before when I came with Edward, I stood still drinking in the atmosphere and elegance of it. Last time I'd been too nervous to take much of it in.

Edward walked between us and held out his elbows. 'Ladies, may I escort you to tea?' he said with a grin.

We walked through to the dining room where glasses sparkled on snowy white tablecloths and cutlery reflected the hundreds of glass balls hanging from the chandeliers. Edward held the chair for Mum to sit down while a waiter held mine. I'm guessing Mum felt like me - a fish out of water, yet enjoying the splendid surroundings and the luxury of being waited on.

She picked up the menu, printed on thick, pure white card with gold writing and gasped when she saw the prices.

'See anything you like?' Edward asked.

She hesitated before answering, 'It's very ... can I ...'

'Have whatever you like, it's my treat today,' Edward said. Her smile was all the reward he needed.

After we'd ordered our tea, Mum leaned over to me and whispered, 'Quiet in here, isn't it? Not a bit like all the noise in the Corner House.'

She was right. The waiters put our food and cutlery down on the thick white tablecloths as if scared to make a noise.

'Think we'll get thrown out if we laugh loudly?' she asked.

'Let's try,' Edward said, with a twinkle in his eye, 'I'll tell you a joke.'

I raised my eyes, 'What if it's not funny?'

'You'll just have to pretend it is. Ready?'

We nodded.

'One day Hitler visited a lunatic asylum. Everyone gave the Nazi salute except one person. In his sternest voice, Hitler demanded to know why he hadn't saluted. "I'm a nurse here," replied the man, "I'm not crazy!"'

We chuckled loudly, then got louder just to try it out. A couple of people looked around but didn't seem bothered.

'There,' Edward said, 'we didn't get arrested or thrown out. Now, let's see if I can think of any other jokes.'

~

'He's a very nice young man,' Mum said as we sat down at home after our tea at the Royal. 'His swanky voice takes a bit of getting used to, mind. Yes, you could do an awful lot worse than him. I'd be proud to have him as a son-in-law.'

I laughed, 'I think you're jumping the gun a bit there, Mum. There's been no talk of marriage.'

She took off her best shoes and rubbed her toes. 'That's as maybe, but you've been courting for a while now and people often marry quicker in wartime.'

I stood up and went over the kettle. 'Want another cuppa?'

She undid her skirt. 'Don't know if I've got room after all that food. What was it? Tiny sandwiches cut into triangles, cakes, scones, oh and little pork pies and sausage rolls. I've never seen such a spread at teatime. It's a wonder they're not all very fat.'

I put the kettle on. 'I don't suppose they have tea like that every day, even if they can afford it,' I said, 'and when rationing comes in, who knows what anyone will be able to eat.'

19. ENLISTING

JOIN, VOLUNTEER

Jean and I almost missed the train to London. A sudden shower made us head for cover to avoid spoiling our freshly done hair. By the time it stopped and a watery Autumn sun emerged, we had to run all the way to the station, weighed down by damp clothes and gas masks.

'Think we need to worry about bombing?' Jean said as we got on the train.

'Well, there haven't been many bombs yet, so let's hope they don't start again today,' I said. 'Let's forget about the war and enjoy our day.'

We pushed our way through the crowd getting on the train and managed to squeeze into seats opposite each other. The man next to me smelled of sweat and damp wool, and he smoked a pipe. I nearly choked each time the smelly cloud covered me.

I leaned over to Jean, waving the stink away. 'Where shall we go first?'

'I've been keeping something secret from you. I'm looking at being a nursing auxiliary for the Queen Alexandra's Nursing Service and I want to go into their recruiting office and ask some questions. Would you mind?'

The pipe smoker got off at the next station and Jean came over to sit next to me. We opened a window and did our best to blow away the cloud of pipe smoke he left behind.

'Of course I don't mind. Is this because of that St John Ambulance course you've been doing?' I asked.

'It got me thinking for sure. And I passed the course with flying colours. The teacher said I 'ad a real gift for it. I told 'im I was thinking about being a nurse and 'e said I should. Even offered to write a reference for me.' The sparkle in her eyes showed how much she'd enjoyed herself.

'I haven't told you, but one night a week I volunteer at the First Aid post in town. I get a very fetching tin 'elmet and navy drill overall.' She laughed, 'it does nothing to show off my figure.'

'Wow, Jean, you're amazing. That's fantastic. Not sure I'd be brave enough for all the blood and guts.'

She nodded, 'We only had pretend wounds on the

course, and because we 'aven't really had any bombing, most nights are quiet apart from drunks falling over and people 'aving accidents because of the black-out.'

I was a bit taken aback that she'd done so much more than I realised. Jean had always been a bit flighty, so this was an impressive side of her I'd never seen.

'Is the Queen Alexandra's the same as the QAs?' I asked.

'Yes. I know there's lots of other places we want to go but can we go there first? I've got the address. Trouble is, you can't buy a map now for love nor money. We'll 'ave to ask people 'ow to get there. 'Then we can go to the 'ouses of Parliament, then St. Paul's Cathedral, and I'd love to walk along the Thames a little way. What about you?'

I remembered something I'd seen on Pathe News. 'I'd love to go to the Victoria and Albert Museum if there's time. It looks really special. We won't have time for all that today, we'll just have to see how the time goes. Just having a day in London is a treat.'

The station in London was packed with people rushing here and there. Many were in uniform, carrying kitbags over their shoulders. Couples said tearful goodbyes. There were groups of children being evacuated. Some looked dirt-poor with shoes that were too big and clothes fit for nothing but rags.

PICTURE HOUSE GIRLS

Others seemed to come from comfortably off families and I wondered how the authorities decided who would go to what households. All the children had labels with their names on them, gas masks bouncing against their bottoms; some looked excited at the adventure whilst others sobbed.

The first thing we saw when we left the station was a horse-drawn freight dray, followed by the manure collector. 'I didn't expect to see them,' I said pointing to the dray and wrinkling my nose, 'I thought London would be full of cars. There's not even that many of them.'

'Plenty of trams though,' Jean said. 'But let's go on the Underground. More exciting.'

It was a crisp Autumn day in London with a nip of the changing season in the air. Some trees were still green while others had carpets of gold and russet leaves surrounding them like colourful doilies on a tea tray. Leaves occasionally floated in front of us as if urging us on. As we walked to the underground, we passed an Air Raid Warden wearing his special hat with ARW on it and an arm band. 'I wonder when they'll get uniforms,' Jean mused.

It seemed like everywhere we went we passed men and women in uniform. What with that and Jean's news about the QA's I started to wonder again if I should do more to help the war effort. But what?

Much as I'd have loved working with Jean, nursing didn't seem right for me.

Although the bombing had been much less than the government expected, it was horrible to go past the ruins of people's homes. Exposed staircases looked ready to fall any second and chimneys stood like broken teeth in rotting mouths full of ugly stumps. Here and there, part rooms had somehow escaped the damage; horrible reminders of what had been before.

'Look, Lil,' Jean said, indicating kids playing on the ruins. 'That's got to be dangerous, all those sharp bricks and pipes and goodness knows what.'

'You've got your nurse's head on already.'

'Look, that lad's picked up a picture. Must have been on someone's wall once. I wonder what happened to them.'

～

We were lucky, and the Recruiting Office was only about twenty minutes walk from the station.

'Want me to come in with you?' I asked.

Jean bit her lip, 'I've thought about that, but it might make me look like I'm not grown up enough to do things on my own. Do you mind? There's a cafe over there.' She pointed across the road, 'You could wait there. I don't suppose I'll be long.'

'Of course I don't mind and I'll be glad to have a cup of tea. You go and find out all about it, then come and tell me. You planning on joining up today?'

She looked surprised, 'Gawd, no, I 'aven't made up my mind yet, just want to find out a bit more.'

I left her and went over to the cafe. It was called Fred's *Cafe* and half the people inside looked as old as Fred, the man behind the counter. His eyes were so hooded with droopy skin I was surprised he could see what he was doing. The men mostly wore flat caps and the women had hats, many of them looking home knitted from odds and ends of wool, not always matching. But the tea was good. I looked at the cakes and was tempted but decided to wait until I was with Jean later.

I took my tea and sat down at an empty table near the window so I could see Jean when she came out. There was an Evening Standard on the table and it was full of news of the war.

'Dreadful, ain't it?' an old man from the next table said, pointing to the headlines. 'Glad I'm too old to get called up this time. I 'ope it don't go on too long or my grandson will get dragged in. He's coming up to the right age.'

It was the sort of thing I'd heard a lot of people

saying, and their memories of the Great War were still fresh in their minds. We chatted for a few minutes, then surprisingly quickly Jean came in.

She came and sat next to me. 'How did you get on?' I asked, then remembered the old man. 'Please excuse me, I want to find out my friend's news.'

'You get fifty hours training and then, if you pass, you're a qualified auxiliary. Me, qualified!' She poked her tongue out at me, 'You won't be the only one with qualifications then.'

I put my arm round her shoulder and hugged her. 'It's fantastic. I'm really proud of you. If that's what you want to do, do it.'

The old man leaned across again and looked at Jean, 'You joining up, then?'

She smiled, 'I think I probably will. Nursing Auxiliary with the QA.'

He patted her hand, 'Your mum'll be right proud of you.'

Her shoulders drooped, 'I wish I was sure. She depends on me to 'elp look after the little ones.'

'Have you asked her?' I wanted to know.

She paused for a minute. 'No, not directly. Maybe she will be proud of me, who knows?'

'Jean, do you think you'll want to nurse near home or in London?'

She looked thoughtful. 'A couple of hospitals in London 'ave already been bombed. Did you read about it in the paper? I suppose I'll go wherever they send me and 'ope the bombs don't follow me. They say they haven't had that many yet.'

Next, we went to the Houses of Parliament, and stood gaping at how huge and impressive the building was. People went in and out all the time.

'Think any of them are MPs, making decisions about our future?' Jean muttered. But we didn't see Chamberlain or anyone else we'd seen on Pathe News or in the newspapers.

The rest of our day was a mixture of admiring the sights; and feeling sad about the changes the war was already bringing, even if people were calling it the Phoney War. We walked to the station past buildings protected by sand bags and taped up windows, and curb edges painted with white stripes so they could be seen in the dark. The biggest shock came just outside the station when we were heading for home. A newspaper seller was shouting 'Latest, Latest, read all about it! cinemas and theatres to close!'

With shaking hands I got the money out of my purse and bought the paper. The article said:

With regret the government has today announced that cinemas and theatres will close from next Monday. This step has been taken to protect the population. It is believed the enemy will target buildings where large numbers of people congregate.

'Oh goodness, Jean,' I said, hardly believing my eyes, 'I'm out of a job. What am I going to do?'

∼

I hurried through the door of the Dream Palace as the late afternoon showing was ending. Attendance was poor but I still had to wait for everyone to leave before I could speak to Mr Simmons in private.

He was sitting behind his desk, a whiskey at his elbow, reading the newspaper.

He looked up as I walked in, 'Lily, you look pale. What's the matter?'

'This,' I said, pointing to the paper. 'They're closing the cinemas.'

'Come and sit down,' he said, patting the chair next to the desk. 'You'll be worried about your job, no doubt.'

I nodded, wiping a tear from my cheek.

'Don't you worry, people need a bit of escapism during a war. I'm convinced the government will lift that ban in no time.'

'But what about my job?' I asked, 'should I look for something else?'

'You know we run on a shoestring here, but I can afford to pay you two weeks wages while we wait and see. Can you bear to do that? I know you could walk into one of the factory jobs tomorrow, but I'd hate to lose you.'

I sniffed to stop a sob escaping, 'Do you really think they'll let us re-open?'

'We're not in a high risk area like the big towns. We've got the armaments factory but none of the others are worth the Jerries wasting bombs on. My guess is they'll let cinemas in the smaller towns open but keep some in dangerous areas closed. I can't promise though. What do you think? Can you wait two weeks to see?'

I wiped my nose feeling like a schoolgirl. 'Of course I can, I love it here. But you won't want to pay me to do nothing, will you?'

He nodded, 'Well, we could give this office a good tidy up and even a lick of paint. Then we could plan some events for when we reopen, see if we can get more customers in.'

We didn't get much decorating done. Less than a fortnight later we were allowed to re-open. The outcry from the public forced the government to change its mind. They realised people would need something to keep them cheerful as the war continued. There was protest from the film industry as well because they would lose their business.

The day before we re-opened, Mr Simmons called everyone to a meeting.

'Thank you all for coming. I'm delighted to say we can re-open tomorrow,' he said.

'But what about air raids?' someone asked.

He held up an official looking bit of paper and read, 'On an air raid signal being given, programmes will stop for five minutes, and audiences will be told where the nearest shelter is. Those who wish to leave will do so, and the rest will be able to see the continuation of the films.'

'Hang on,' Frank said, 'that means I don't get a choice. I've got to stay. What if I want to go into the shelter?'

'What about us?' one of the others said, 'do we have to stay too?'

Mr Simmons held up his hand for quiet. 'Those are good points. I'd like to speak to each of you separately to see what you want to do and then we will make a plan.'

The next night we were open for business again.

20. DESSERTION

BETRAYAL, ABANDONMENT

'You sure you're ready to meet my dad?' I asked Edward on his next leave. 'He's a grumpy old sod and I've no idea how he'll be with you. He's been very quiet about it, not a bit like him.'

The morning had started with a light frost, the first of the season, and I could smell a bonfire somewhere nearby. People were wrapped in thick coats and scarves and walked head down into the whistling wind. The trees were nearly bare and the few remaining leaves flew everywhere.

Edward linked his arm through mine. 'Let's see how he is. If he's too difficult we'll make it a short visit.'

'At least Mum will be there, so she'll help if she can. Not that he takes much notice of her.'

I opened the door and called out hello. Mum came from the kitchen looking serious. 'Hi love, hello Edward, lovely to see you again,' she said. 'Let me make you some tea, you must be cold.'

We took off our outdoor clothes and hung them in the hall. 'Dad not in yet?' I called.

'Tell you in a minute. Come and have your tea,' she said, putting the cosy on the teapot. She wasn't herself at all, her back stiff as she put home-made scones on a plate.

'What is it, Mum? What's wrong?' I asked.

She turned to face me and put her hands on the table. 'Your dad's gone.'

'What do you mean, gone? Don't tell me he didn't want to meet Edward.'

She shook her head, 'No, really gone. His clothes, everything, gone. Not even left a note.'

Edward stood up, 'Mrs Baker, this is a difficult time, would you rather I left?'

'No, Lad, sit down again. This is nothing Lily wouldn't tell you about later.'

I felt as if someone had filled my brain with mud, I couldn't take in what she was saying at all. 'You mean ... you mean ... he's left us? Gone to live somewhere else. Where is he?'

She sat down and picked up a scone. 'I expect he's gone to his fancy woman.'

My jaw dropped open, 'You ... you ... know about her?'

She smiled, 'Yes, didn't know you did though. I've known about her for ages. You can always tell.'

'I'm so sorry,' Edward said, 'you must feel shell shocked.'

Her smile grew wider. 'I was for the first half hour after I got home. I kept checking his half of the wardrobe and his drawers as if they'd suddenly get full again. Then the penny really dropped. He's gone. The miserable old bugger has gone, excuse my French. I'll never have to put up with his moans and his fists ever again. It's over. We've got the house, Lily. I went to the phone box on the corner and spoke to the corporation. They won't throw us out. We've won.'

My jaw dropped even further. Any more of this and I'd need it wired back in place. 'But what about money?' I asked.

'I'm earning more now I'm at the factory and there's always plenty of overtime. I've got a little bit put aside I never told him about it. It'll be tight, but I reckon I can manage. If it gets too hard, you and me can share a bedroom and let the other one out to get a bit more in.'

I let out a long whistle, 'Blimey, Mum, that's a turn up for the books. I can't quite take it in.'

'Well, I've had a couple of hours to think about it.

Someone told me she's a lot younger than him. Wonder if she'll want a family.'

I laughed, 'He's a bit old for sleepless nights. Perhaps she'll expect him to change nappies.'

Mum grinned, 'If she manages that, she's a better woman than I ever was. Good luck to her, she'll need it.'

She turned to Edward, 'At least you're spared having to meet him now. With any luck you'll never have to.'

He smiled and put his hand over hers. 'I'm glad you feel that way. If I can do anything to help, please let me know.'

Children's voices outside interrupted us.

'They sound excited,' Mum said. 'Let's go and see what's happening.'

We opened the front door and stepped into the little front garden. The children were running backwards waving and shouting. It wasn't hard to see, or hear, what had got them so worked up. At the far end of the road heading their, and our, way was a tank. The tracks screeched on the road loud enough to make me want to cover my ears. All three of us went and stood on the pavement to watch it go by. A soldier in the tank was standing so his head and upper body were visible. To my amazement, when the tank got level with us the soldier grinned at Edward and saluted. Edward grinned and saluted back. I looked at him then back at the soldier, then back at him. He put his finger to his lips in a 'sshh' gesture and nodded for us to follow the tank.

We grabbed our coats and closed the door, hurrying to catch up. It turned left into the next road and we waited for it to turn left again at the wall.

It didn't turn.

It drove straight through the wall.

The sound of falling bricks competed with the noise of the tank tracks. A huge cloud of brick dust rose in the air blotting out the houses the other side. The children who had run behind the tank turned away, coughing as they inhaled the dust.

'Oh dear, terrible driving,' Edward said, a wicked smile trying to escape, 'manoeuvres went a bit wrong there.'

We rushed to the gap, glad to find no-one was behind it or had been harmed. The tank carried on as if nothing had happened.

I dragged Edward to one side, 'Did you have anything to do with this?' I asked, picking a bit of brick out of my hair.

'I can't tell you military secrets,' he said, with a twinkle in his eye.

I punched his arm, 'Tell me, or I'll. . . I'll …'

'You'll what?' His grin was broad now and I swear I heard a deep chuckle.

I punched his arm again, 'I don't know what, but

I'll think of something. Come on, did you have anything to do with this?'

He pulled me closer, away from the people who were beginning to arrive at the wall, cheering and laughing at the damage.

Edward spoke quietly, 'I can't say I had anything to do with it, but my Commanding Officer did happen to talk about it in the Mess a few nights ago.'

'What did he say?'

'He said the wall was a hindrance to free tank movement and he wouldn't look too closely if it were somehow knocked down. Accidentally, of course.'

I looked at him, wide eyed, 'So you did have something to do with it!'

'I couldn't possibly say that,' he said picking me up and twirling me round, 'Are you pleased?'

I punched him a third time. 'You know I am.' And there and then I pulled him to me and gave him a big kiss.

21. DAZED

BEWILDERED, STUNNED

The bomb blast threw me off my feet and I landed face first on the road, dazed and with no idea of what had just happened. One minute Jean and I were walking away from the Dream Palace towards our bus and the next I was lying on the ground, my clothes pulled up, painful grazes on my forehead and knees, and a loud ringing in my ears.

Feeling like parts of my body could fall off any second, I slowly sat up and looked around me. My skirt was ripped and my clothes were filthy. Jean was across the street and struggling to sit up too; she looked as shaky as I felt. But we were in one piece. Further down the street, probably about a hundred yards, was a different story. I staggered to my feet and helped Jean up. We hugged each other and staggered arm in arm towards the damage.

'Think the Dream Palace is okay?' Jean asked, her voice a whisper.

'I hope so, it should be far enough away,' I replied, hoping I knew what I was talking about. Ahead of us we could see three terraced houses that were completely flattened. Leaning against a neighbouring house that was still standing was one of their bedrooms, the bed half hanging over the edge where the floor had been.

'Oh gawd, those poor people,' Jean said in a whisper. 'Did you hear the air-raid siren?'

'I think so, but there wasn't time to get anywhere.' I'd heard people say that before, but wouldn't have believed how quickly it all happened if I hadn't experienced it myself.

Wiping away tears, Jean pulled my arm, 'Come on, let's see 'ow we can help.'

We staggered and wove our crooked way further towards the damage. On the buildings still standing, windows had been blown out and glass and other debris was everywhere. As we walked glass crunched underfoot and the debris made walking difficult. We could see the sad sight of belongings people once loved: ornaments, books, table-cloths, even a cooker strewn across the road. Small fires had sprung up here and there and we kept well away from them in case there was a gas leak. Walls were pitted with holes where they had been hit with flying objects. As we got closer, we found an old lady lying in the road who looked as if she was sleeping peacefully, apart from her hat bent out of shape. Her shopping was still clutched in her hand. Jean bend down and checked her pulse.

'She's dead,' she said, pulling out a hanky and putting it over the lady's face. 'Come on, let's see to the living first, we can't help her any more.'

A few people staggered out of houses, some looking shell-shocked but unharmed, while others were bleeding and clutching broken bones. Jean took control and told me what to do.

'Gather up them that's not seriously 'urt and take them to sit over there,' she said, pointing to a house that still looked sturdy. 'If no-one's in, just sit them on the door step. Find out who's the most fit and able and put them in charge. They'll 'ave to sit there and wait. I'm going to see to the others. Come over to me as soon as you can.'

I was so relieved she had that knowledge and authority, even if it was just from a few first-aid classes. Very soon we heard the first help arrive. An air raid warden and then an ambulance appeared, soon followed by a fire engine. Quickly the noise of the bomb was replaced by the shouts and banging of everyone doing what they could to help the injured and keep people safe.

A bloke near us shouted, 'Sshh, keep quiet!' He cupped his hand to his ear. After a moment's confusion, we all concentrated, trying to hear whatever he'd heard. Then it came, a feeble cry for help. It was a woman and she seemed to be under the remains of the house where we were standing.

We joined up with five or six other people to dig our way to her, throwing bricks and rubble behind us. All the while Jean shouted encouragement to the woman. It was a terrible job, wondering all the time if we would reach the woman before a ceiling collapsed or a fire started where she was. Our hands were soon bloody messes as we cleared bricks, glass, wood and all sorts of household bits and pieces. We kept coughing and wiping our eyes as brick dust got into everything. Then we lifted an upturned box and a black and white cat jumped out. It blinked in the light, hissed at us and ran away. We all looked at it in disbelief, then laughed with relief that something was alive and unhurt.

Jean looked over at me. 'You look like you're eighty, you've gone grey,' she said. I reached up to touch my hair. It was thick with brick dust. I looked at her, 'Well, you look eighty five,' I replied with a grin.

The air raid warden came to check how things were going several times.

'You look done in,' I said, seeing his drawn face, smeared with dirt and tear trails.

'Did a twelve hour shift at the factory and now a six hour shift. I saw you two cover the old lady up the road. She lived opposite me when I was a lad, lovely old girl. Horrible to go like that. Hope she didn't feel anything.'

I stopped digging for a moment to touch his arm, 'I'm so sorry, that's really sad, but thank goodness you can help other people.'

He came up several times more and got us to stop digging while he listened for anything that might suggest the wall standing nearby might collapse on top of us.

'You can't do no good if you're dead,' he said.

We held our breath while he checked. I glanced around from time to time and saw ambulance men helping the injured. Then they carried off two figures on stretchers; sheets covering their bodies and heads. Firemen unrolled their hoses and shouted instructions to each other. Across the street another group was doing what we were doing, trying to dig someone out of a house. Three or four people just stood around, too shocked to do anything useful. From further up the street I saw a VAD lady appear and she gathered them up and walked them away. She'd already taken the group I'd left sitting on a doorstep earlier. The second group followed her away like zombies, not seeing anything around them. I spotted a little lad in a coat that must have belonged to his big brother. He was barefoot. He couldn't have been more than four or five but he was walking on the collapsed building, picking his way across the bricks as if looking for something.

My attention was soon turned back to the task in hand.

'Dunno about you lot, but I'm getting close to being all done in,' said one of the other people digging with us - a man aged about 60. I was feeling just the same and wished some other people were free to help. Then we heard it. The woman cried for help again, but this time she sounded closer. And a baby was crying.

'Bloody hell, there's a baby in there!' said the older man and we all found the energy to pick up speed again. My heart beat faster with every second that passed. Would we be in time to save the mother and baby or would one or both of them die while we worked? How on earth did the people who do this sort of work all the time cope with it, I asked myself. The agony of being too late and the person dying while they worked must seem worse than finding them dead in the first place.

It took another fifteen minutes, then we saw a

sort of tunnel through all the bricks and wood lying everywhere. Shining a torch we could just see the woman's face. You could hardly make out her features for all the brick dust. Stress showed in every line, and her forehead was streaked with blood.

'Take my baby first,' she said, holding him up. He was crying loudly and it was a wonderful sound. It wasn't too difficult to get him out and I passed him to Jean. Walking away, she cuddled him close, and started rocking him and singing a lullaby.

'Right, then,' I said, 'let's get this baby's mother out.' Luck was with us and we managed to make the hole bigger without any serious collapses. Another ten minutes and Jean was reluctantly handing the baby back to his mum, who couldn't stop crying. She kissed the baby over and over again. 'Thank you, thank you,' she kept saying, and stopped kissing the baby long enough to kiss each of us.

The warden saw what had happened and came over again. 'You lot've done a great job. Now get yourselves over there, someone's brewing up some tea. Make sure you have plenty of sugar in it.'

Jean and I went over to the tea station and all but collapsed on the ground. Someone handed us some jam sandwiches and hot, sweet tea but our hands shook so much we had trouble drinking it without spilling the lot.

After a couple of minutes, I leant on Jean's shoulder, 'We did well, Jean, especially you.'

She looked thoughtful, 'Tell you what, this lot's finally made up my mind. I'm joining up with the QAs tomorrow.'

Her determination made me think. The cinema was important for morale while things were so horrible, but I was fit and healthy and the work I was doing could be done by someone older or less fit. It was time for me to be doing something more important to help the war work. I'd been mulling it over for ages, now was the time to commit myself. Or so I thought.

The next day something happened that delayed my joining up. Mr Simmons at the Dream Palace fell and broke his leg, poor man. I took the bus and went to visit him in hospital. He looked very pale and shaky, not at all his usual self. It was strange to see him in striped pyjamas instead of his usual scruffy suit, but he managed a brave smile when I sat next to him and handed him a book wrapped in brown paper.

'What's this then? he said tearing the paper off. 'Well I never, a book. I'm not much of a reader, but I'm going to get plenty of time to change that while this thing heals,' he slapped his plaster cast. He read the title, it was *Cold Comfort Farm* by Stella Gibbons. 'This is a funny one, isn't it?' he said, 'just what I could do with. Thanks Lily, don't know what I'd do without you.'

I gave a guilty smile. I'd been planning to tell him next day that I was joining the Auxiliary Territorial Service, but there was no way I could leave him and the Dream Palace in the lurch.

'You will stand in for me, won't you?' he went on, 'you know what needs to be done and I'll be stuck here or at home if you need any advice.'

He saw me hesitate. 'There's a good pay rise in it for you until I get back,' he said, trying to persuade me. So it was settled, and life returned to normal but without his regular appearances. I wrote to Edward every three days, and he wrote at least twice a week, and managed to get one weekend pass. Now that I'd decided to join up, I couldn't help feeling impatient and took more interest in what was happening in the war. It was surprising that after a small amount of initial bombing, there wasn't any more. But with all the precautions we saw everywhere, we couldn't forget we were at war. The people in Poland and some other countries couldn't forget it either, and we knew it was coming our way.

In the end I joined up a whole three and a half months after I'd first decided to. Mum was pleased, although she worried that something would happen to me if I was sent somewhere dangerous.

22. ENGAGEMENT

BETROTHAL, COMMITMENT

As a child the smell of a railway station always excited me. The clouds of smoke, smelling of oil and coal; the chug-chugging of the train wheels; and even the little black bits that stuck to your skin and sometimes made you choke, meant we were going somewhere and having a change from the everyday.

Train journeys were rare. Apart from my holiday with Jean and her aunt, we had only ever had two or three holidays, and they were to stay with my gran. Mum and Dad had no money for anything else, but we didn't think about it much because everyone else was the same.

This day the station was packed. There were throngs of men in uniform with kitbags slung over their shoulders and their wives and children clinging to them, crying or trying to be brave. I suppose a few were secretly relieved. There were trains every few minutes and loudspeaker announcements no-one could understand. Porters hurried here and there, pushing trolleys loaded with cases while dodging people's ankles. Conductors waved flags and blew their whistles. Posters warned, *Careless talk costs lives*, *Carry your gas mask everywhere*, and *Children are safer in the country*.

The film posters for *Gone with the Wind* and *The Wizard of Oz* tugged at my heart. I wondered if I'd ever work at the Dream Palace again. Would it even still be there, or be bombed out of existence by that awful Mr. Hitler? But I'd always be grateful for my time there and finding I was up to the job of assistant manager. Not to mention seeing a lot of great pictures for free. And bossing Jean around.

I'd already said goodbye to Mum at home.

'You look after yourself and write often,' she had said as we sat at the kitchen table. 'You know I'll be worried about you all the time.'

'I won't be fighting the Germans, you know. They don't let women do that.'

Her face crumpled and she struggled to hold back tears. 'What if this war isn't over by Christmas like they all say? Who knows where they'll send you?'

'You know I might not be able to tell you where I am?'

She nodded, head hung down.

I gave her a hug. 'There's always letters - and leave. I'll come back every time.'

'Don't be daft,' she said with a watery smile, 'you'll be wanting to see that nice Edward sometimes. Make the most of it. Who knows what the future has in store?'

'You sure you're all right for money? I'll be sending you some every week.'

She stirred her tea, 'It's tight, I can't say otherwise, and if you can spare a bit now and then I'd be very grateful. Not every week, mind, you need some to spend on yourself.'

'You going to stay at the munitions factory?'

'Yeah, the money's better than charring and I've got some good mates there,' she said, pouring tea from the brown china pot she'd used for as long as I could remember. 'And I might have a very special friend, too.'

It took a minute for the penny to drop. 'You… you've got yourself a boyfriend?'

'Sort of. He works with me and makes every excuse to stop and chat. He's asked me to go out with him. I haven't agreed yet, but I think I will soon. Would you mind?'

'Mind? I'd be thrilled,' I said, hugging her again. 'Good for you. I just hope he's the perfect one for you. You deserve someone kind and generous to look after you.'

Mum looked thoughtful for a minute. 'You know, I was thinking. Lily, the wall started all this for you.'

'Yes, and my hand volunteering me to help on the committee, without me knowing it was doing it.' I grinned and pretended to slap the hand, 'Naughty hand!'

'I've never said it as such, Lily, but I'm real proud of you. Look how far you've come. Passing all those exams, getting a good job, meeting a decent bloke. And now, being brave enough to join up.'

'It's only what lots of people are doing, Mum, and some are going to do much more dangerous things than me.'

'I suppose, but that doesn't take away from all you've done. Oh, I meant to ask you what happened to, what was his name, that nuisance bloke you had trouble getting rid of?'

I couldn't help but smile, 'Victor. He's inside. Got six months for robbery. Pity they couldn't add on some more for bothering girls.'

'I wonder if he'll get called up as soon as he's out?'

'I think he's a year too old ..,' I said.

'They're sure to extend the conscription age soon. I won't mind if he gets sent somewhere dangerous.'

'Me, neither.'

'Now tell me again how it is you're meeting Edward at the station.'

'He's on his way to somewhere he's been posted, he can't say where, but he's getting an earlier train than he needs so he can get off and spend a bit of time with me.' I smiled at the thought of seeing him very soon.

'And you'll be there anyway because you're going to your training camp.'

I crossed my fingers. 'If all the trains are on time, we'll have about an hour together and we'll both be in uniform for the first time.'

She smiled, 'You'll make a very handsome couple, too.'

Mum packed me up some sandwiches and scones and we hugged at the door for so long I thought my time with Edward would be halved. We'd agreed we'd say goodbye at home. But she watched and waved to me all the way to the corner of the next road. I stopped and turned round, blowing her a big kiss, then I hitched up by kitbag again and strode towards the station and my new life.

I was scared and excited in equal measures to be joining the forces. I knew I'd be learning a lot of new things, meeting a lot of new people and leaving behind people I loved. I'd miss Mum and Jean so much, but also Bob and Mr Simmons and Rose as well as other friends.

Edward's train was fifteen minutes late. As I waited, each train that wasn't his was a torture ripping my heart in two.

A woman saw my tears of frustration and patted my arm, 'Looking for someone special, Love? Could be a long wait. The trains are all over the place.'

I moved from one foot to the other the whole time, watching couples part, the men waving out of the windows until they were hidden by smoke or too far away to be seen. When they'd gone, their mothers, or girlfriends or wives and children dragged themselves over to the exit to start life without them. It wasn't all men in uniform though, there were some WAACs and ATS women and I felt proud to be one of them.

Then the train whistle blew yet again, and another train slowed to a halt. Craning my neck, I saw Edward lean out of a window to open the door. Next second, I was running down the platform into his arms. He looked so dashing in his uniform I thought I could fall in love with him all over again. I saw several women nearby stare at him. I was getting used to the fact that his looks were always going to get noticed. The best thing was, he didn't seem to realise it.

He hugged me so hard I couldn't breathe, then kept hold of my hand and took a step back. 'My goodness, Lily,' he said, 'you look wonderful in uniform. I'll be worried every day someone will steal you away from me. Come on, let's go to the cafe and make the most of our time.'

The cafe was packed and filled with chatter, cigarette smoke and cooking smells. We squeezed ourselves and our kitbags into a tiny corner table and ordered tea and London buns.

'I suppose it's no good asking where you're going?' I said.

He took my hand and kissed it. 'Can't tell you, I'm afraid, but I wish you were going with me.'

'So do I.' I kissed his hand back, wishing we were in a more private place. Since the war started, things were a bit more relaxed. Before we wouldn't even have kissed like that in public.

'We never have long enough together. When do you start training?' he asked.

'We get allocated our sleeping quarters tonight and start early tomorrow. I wish I knew what work I was going to do, but I'm going to try for being a driver.'

He shook his head, 'I almost wish you hadn't joined up. Perhaps you'd have stayed at home and been safe and free to meet me when I get leave.'

'I can't do nothing, not now things have got so serious.'

We were interrupted by a family on the next table

gathering their stuff and leaving. The table was immediately taken by a couple, two bored children and a small dog that decided we were worth sniffing.

Patting it absentmindedly, Edward bent down and searched through one of his bags. 'There's something I've been trying to pluck up courage to ask you,' he said.

I smiled and kissed his cheek, 'You know I'll wait for you. No other soldier looks nearly as good as you in uniform. Got to be a reason why I'd stay with a toff like you!'

'Well, it's kind of to do with that ...'

He stood up and to my surprise dropped to one knee, almost flattening the dog who yelped and ran to hide under a table.

Edward held my hand and looked into my eyes. 'Lily, will you marry me? I can't think of anyone else I'd like to spend my life with.'

Well, people had noticed what he was doing and there was a sudden silence, no-one said a word. It was like everyone was holding their breath and waiting for my answer.

'But Edward,' I said, 'I'm going to war too, and I want to go. I've already signed up and everything. They might not let me if I'm married.'

'Go on, Girl, say yes!' some bright spark shouted.

Edward gave him a big grin. 'Yes, go on, say 'yes'. We can get married when this war is over. I'll wait for you. We'll wait for each other.' He opened a velvet box. Inside was a sparkling engagement ring, with a diamond bigger than I'd ever seen in my life.

'It was my grandmother's and I know she'd love you to have it.'

I looked at the ring, my mind in a whirl. I found I'd lost my voice.

'Come on, Love, make up your mind, we've got a train to catch,' someone shouted.

Edward was holding the ring and my left hand. I looked from the ring to his lovely face. My heart sang and, taking a deep breath, I smiled and he put the ring on my finger.

I had to swallow hard before I could speak. 'Yes. Yes! I'd love to marry you.'

The whole room erupted with cheers and congratulations. Edward leaned over and kissed me, right there in front of everyone.

'I'm never going to be a little stay at home, do nothing wife, you know,' I said, 'even after this war is over. I've got a mind of my own and I'm going to use it.'

He rubbed his thumb over the ring, grinned and got back into his chair.

'That's one of the things I love about you, Lily. I'd be bored to death with a meek little wife. You'll never be that.'

The cheers died down, and the noise changed as a

handful of tables full of people made to leave. Several people came over to shake our hands and wish us well.

I looked at the treacherous cafe clock and my heart sank.

I made to pick up my bags. 'My train's due in ten minutes, Edward. Come and see me off.'

We walked to the train hand in hand, wanting every minute to last an hour. Our goodbye kiss seemed over in a second. All too soon I was one of the people waving out of the window, eyes smarting in the smoke, until I could see Edward no more. Who knew what the future might hold? Separation, wars, new roles, so many changes ahead.

One thing I felt sure about. Our feelings for each other would stay as true as ever.

THE END
of The Picture House Girls, but not the end of Lily's story. Below you'll find the beginning of her next adventure in **The Telephone Girls**

Leaning from the train window, I waved goodbye to Edward, the man I'd been engaged to for less than an hour. The smoke from the engine made my eyes water and I blinked away the little black specks that flew everywhere. I stood for a minute, even after he was lost from sight, wishing he was still with me and reluctant to start my new life without him. Brushing a tear from my eye, I picked up my case and struggled along the corridor, full of conflicting emotions. I wanted to be with Edward, but I'd joined the Auxiliary Territorial Army because I wanted to do my bit for Blighty. Marriage would have to wait. We had our whole lives ahead of us.

'But what if he's killed?' a wicked voice inside my head taunted.

'He won't be!' I said out loud, and got a funny look from a woman next to me.

I pushed my way past dozens of soldiers standing in the corridors, several times tripping over their kitbags. Each time, one of them helped me right myself with a cheeky comment or a wink; their cheerfulness lifting my mood. But none of them looked as good in uniform as my fiancee. I'd never called anyone that before, and it felt very special.

With aching feet, I walked the whole length of the train, but there were no free seats anywhere.

'Come and sit by yere,' a voice said, just as I was fit to collapse. The girl was about my age and sitting on a case. She greeted me with a smile.

'Room for a couple of little 'uns like us in this corridor,' she said. I had to smile back. Even sitting down, it was obvious she wasn't little. Slim, yes, but a good bit taller than my five foot three inches. She shuffled along, making a bit more room for me to join her. I put down my small case and leaned against it, keeping my handbag on my knee.

'I'm Bronwyn, from Swansea,' she said, holding out her hand, 'bet you'd never guess from my accent!'

I shook her hand, 'I'm Lily, from Oxford. Before you ask, no, I'm not a clever clogs from the university. I bet you can tell that from my accent.'

'No, you don't sound like a nob.' she said, grinning, 'Where're you going? I'm off to Aldershot to start ATS training.'

My jaw dropped, 'You're never! I am, too. We'll be training together then. I'm terrified - never been away from home before. I'm so glad to meet you. At least I'll know one person now.'

The train stopped with a sudden lurch that threw us against each other. We looked up, but no-one was taking any notice. 'We'll probably be hours late,' Bronwyn said, 'timetables have gone haywire since this war started.'

'Do you think we'll be in trouble? Can they put us on a charge because we're late?'

She laughed, 'Well, they'd have everyone on a charge if that was the case, like. Mind you, we're not properly part of the army yet, so I don't know how that works out. No, they must be used to people being late. Anyway, they're meeting us at the station, aren't they?'

'There's so much I don't know. Got any idea what you'd like to do once we've done our basic training?' I asked, 'Not that I think we get much choice.'

'Oui.' she said, winking, 'je veux être un téléphoniste. I want to be a telephonist.'

'You what? Is that French you're speaking?'

'Oui. I speak three languages. English, French and a little bit of Welsh.' She ticked them off her long fingers.

'How'd you do that then? I can only speak English and not always very well at that.'

She ran her fingertips over her light brown cheeks, 'See this lovely colour? See this crinkly hair I can never do anything with? I owe them all to my ma. She's from Martinique.'

I tried to remember my geography lessons from school, but came up blank, 'Where's Martinique?'

'It's in the West Indies, a little island with lots of mountains. The French colonised us, so we speak French as well as the native language. I never learned that though, ma thought it was better if we stuck to French and English.'

'But you're not very dark. Is your dad Welsh?'

She pulled a face, 'Is. Was. He never hung around long. Like a lot of blokes around Swansea, he probably had a wife in every port. He sailed off into the sunset when I was three and we never heard another thing about him. Good riddance to bad rubbish, I say.'

I thought we had that in common; rubbish fathers. Mine was horrible and bad tempered, probably because of what he suffered in the first war. My mum had to put up with a lot. But he'd left her not long ago for another woman, and my mum was free of his nastiness at last.

'So why do you need to speak French to be a telephonist, then?' I asked.

'You don't if you stay here, but if you do they might send you to France. Maybe even Paris. I've never been further than Cardiff before today.' She got a faraway gaze in her eye, 'Just imagine, Paris! I got a book out of the library and it's tidy, it is.'

I began to think I'd need a translator. 'Tidy? How'd you mean?'

She laughed and slapped her hand, 'I forget not everyone speaks like we do in Swansea. Have to watch that. Tidy means it's really nice. Eiffel Tower, lovely buildings, French food, though I'm used to that because ma cooks it. Well, her version of.'

I went into a daydream. I'd never been further than London. I remembered learning about Paris at school and looking at the pictures, wishing I was there. I started to dream about a honeymoon in Paris. That'd beat Weston-Super-Mare which was all most people round our way managed, if that. I knew Edward's family were a lot better off than ours, but didn't know if he could afford Paris. I wondered if I'd be able to save something from my ATS pay. We were to get eleven shillings a week and I wanted to send some to my mum regularly. At least our board and lodgings wouldn't cost anything. Paris…

***

Do Lily and Bronwyn go to Paris?

What adventures face their life in the army?

Get your copy of *The Telephone Girls* from Amazon today to follow their stories! Available in large print in most countries.

OTHER BOOKS BY PATRICIA MCBRIDE

Lily Baker Series:

The Telephone Girls

The ARP Girls

The Deptford Girls

Standalone Books:

Winner Takes All

Murder, mystery and Magic

Non Fiction:

How to be Assertive

Time Management for the Office

The Assertive Social Worker

The EI Advantage (with Susan Maitland)

CVs and Applications

Excel at Interviews

Study Skills for Success

ACKNOWLEDGMENTS

As always I would like to thank the many people who helped me with this book. My husband Rick for helping me with plot ideas, my friend Fran Johnston (Smith) for ideas and masses of general support, and Maggie Scott for brilliant proof-reading.

Thanks also to my kind readers who offered opinions, spotted any last typos and were invaluable:
- Dreena Collins
- Margaret Smith
- Samantha Sherratt
- Jacqui Kemp

Printed in Great Britain
by Amazon